PAINT THE STORM

Book 1 – Golden State Trilogy

A Christian Contemporary Novel

Dawn V. Cahill

Paint The Storm

Cover design by Dineen Miller
Edited by Steve Mathisen, Odd Sock Proofreading and Copyediting
Formatting by Rik, Wild Seas Formatting
(http://WildSeasFormatting.com)

ISBN-10: 0-9974521-3-7
ISBN-13: 978-0-9974521-3-6

"Arise, cry out in the night: in the beginning of the watches pour out thine heart like water before the face of the Lord: lift up thy hands toward him for the life of thy young children." Lamentations 2:19

To my beautiful sisters, who believed in me. Without your encouragement, this story would not have been written.

Chapter One

Meg swept ruby red acrylic across the canvas, forming a span over gray-blue water. Streaks of raspberry pink infused the Golden Gate Bridge with a romantic glow. More paint splattered onto her smock, which always looked like it had just emerged from Paintball Central. Barry might laugh at her smock, but he'd love the finished product on her easel.

Her phone chimed just as she added a dab of silver-gray to the fog rolling over the Bay.

Linzee's picture graced the screen.

"Hey, you."

"Hey, Mom."

Instead of dull brown rock, vibrant kelly green formed the lookout spot at Point Bonita, complete with blinding white lighthouse.

"What time is Uncle Brad's Fourth of July shindig?" Linzee said.

"Noonish." More ruby red stretched to the sky. Those famous towers, supporting the weight of the structure on their graceful shoulders. Not everyone could paint and talk on the phone at the same time. But, like most moms, she could multi-task with the best of them.

"Good," said Linzee. "I'm going to bring Nena."

Meg paused, her red-tipped brush suspended above the canvas.

"You and the family will finally get to meet my significant other."

"Why can't you just call her your friend?" The words blurted out before she could stop them.

She could almost see Linzee bristling on the other end.

"Do you call Barry your 'friend'? I'm not going to hide our relationship just because you're a homophobe."

A flood of frustration came over her. She dropped the paintbrush to the easel tray. "Linzee! You know that's not true."

"You are, Mom. Remember what you said when I asked your opinion on gay marriage?"

"I was simply being honest. Just because I believe homosexuality is wrong doesn't make me a homophobe." She bit her lip and pulled air deep into her lungs, then opened the studio door and paced the hallway. "Look, Linzee, I'm tired of arguing about this. If you don't like my opinions, don't ask for them."

"I'm exposing your hypocrisy. You say you're a Christian, but you make Nena feel like an outcast. She thinks you hate her."

"How can I hate her? I don't even know her."

"That's because you keep making excuses not to meet her. How do you think that makes her feel?"

"It's not that I don't want to meet her . . ." She let her voice trail away as her pacing feet carried her first to her bedroom, then back to the studio.

Gulping, she floundered for the right words. "When you moved back after college, I was hoping we could spend more time together. Just you and me, without your friend…"

"Girlfriend."

"We haven't gotten together and talked in ages."

"There's a reason for that. You're a hypocrite and I don't like your attitude." Linzee's clipped tones came through loud and clear. "Anyway, I'm done. I need to go. Bye."

The phone went silent.

***

Her daughter's words rang through Meg's mind all night. *Homophobe. Hypocrite.* By the time her alarm rang at six a.m., she wasn't positive she'd slept at all.

Bleary-eyed, she took a quick shower and downed a cup of coffee. Fighting back tears, she pondered her heart—heavy with helpless regret. Linzee wanted Meg to accept her lifestyle. Yet Linzee wasn't willing to respect Meg's convictions.

Standing inside her closet, she scanned an array of work skirts and blazers, wishing she could stay home. But the anticipation of seeing Barry after work lifted her spirits a notch. He'd offer sympathy and a listening ear, maybe some words of wisdom, and finish with a comforting hug and tender kiss.

Finally on her way, she merged onto the 101 and poured her heart out to God. Her broken heart couldn't handle any more reminders of how far Linzee had strayed from God. And Nena was the biggest reminder of all.

She'd nearly reached the Golden Gate Bridge when she realized that, in her frantic rush, she'd forgotten her cell phone.

Stifling an oath, she got off at Sausalito. She had to have her cell phone. Even if it meant she'd be late for work.

Sighing, she retraced her route back home, then found her phone and saw a text from Barry reminding her he'd see her tonight. The thoughtful, unnecessary gesture brought a smile to her face. How could she forget? She keyed a reply, *Yes! Looking forward to it!*

After she'd grabbed another cup of coffee to go and sent her boss an apologetic text, she hopped into her car and headed back to the city.

Half an hour later, her high heels clacked on the sidewalk as she rounded the corner onto Post Street, only to be distracted by noise from Union Square, where bodies and signs packed the area and police swarmed.

Meg stopped next to a man in a suit and asked, "What's going on over there?"

He replied without looking at her, "They're celebrating the legalization of same-sex marriage."

"Look." The spectator next to Mr. Suit pointed. "There are those Haight Street Church picketers."

The first man cursed. "Hope they get thrown in jail."

The protesters' signs read, "God Hates Gays" and "Gays Will Burn." The local media had dubbed the group "The Hate Church on Haight Street."

Over the din, the speaker at a podium shouted, "San Francisco, we're witnessing the dawn of a new era—marriage equality for all!" His words bounced off surrounding buildings.

Through a megaphone, a second voice rose. "You're going to Hell!"

The speaker responded, "Doesn't God hate haters, friends?"

The crowd chanted, "God hates haters, God hates haters…"

"God hates fags!" megaphone man yelled.

Meg cringed, wanting to wrest his megaphone away and smash him upside the head with it. How dare he claim God hated her daughter?

"Haters!" shouted the speaker. "Love wins!"

"Love wins!" the crowd joined in. "Love wins!"

Meg could only imagine Linzee yelling in triumph.

Glancing at the time, she elbowed her way to Noelle Marquette's glass doors and rode a mirrored elevator to the sixth floor Merchandising Department, where she nearly collided with Craig from Receiving.

"Megan St. John." He sang her name as he accompanied her to her desk. "You've got mail." He dropped a parcel on top of her mile-high inbox and pranced away.

Meg plopped into her chair, turning to Julie, her cubicle mate. "The day has barely begun, but I can already tell it's going to be a stressful one."

Julie leaned toward Meg. "Are you seeing Barry tonight?"

"I am. It's been three long days since our last date."

"The downside of a long-distance relationship."

"We live sixty miles apart. More like semi-long-distance."

"Meeting in Redwood City?"

"Of course, he likes me to meet him halfway." If only she could close her eyes and wake up at five o'clock. The prospect of a relaxing evening with Barry, still hours away, left her jumpy with impatience. "At least we don't get tired of each other."

"The upside of a semi-long-distance relationship."

As she clutched the computer mouse, a photo flashed across her screen, reminding her of happier times. She and Linzee leaned their heads together, flashing smiles white as daisies. Playful glints shone from identical green eyes, and freckles dotted both faces. Linzee's hair, partly covered by a tasseled cap, hinted at sunshine and yellow roses. Meg's own coloring suggested wheat fields and Golden Retrievers.

Julie cleared her throat. "What's bugging you?"

"Why do you think something's bugging me?"

"Whenever you thump your mouse on the desk, something has you riled."

She stared at the cheerful photo. "It's Linzee. Ever since she moved back last month . . . we haven't been getting along."

"Why did she move back?"

"She graduated from UCLA and starts a new job in September. In the meantime, she's working two part-time jobs. She and her partner are renting this tiny apartment that's costing them an arm and a leg."

"Her partner?"

She swiveled slowly to face Julie. "Linzee's gay."

"She is?" Julie's eyes widened. "I had no idea."

"Please don't repeat this to anyone." She hoped she wouldn't regret confiding in Julie. "She came out in high school. I kept hoping she'd grow out of it. Just a phase, you know. Then she met Nena at UCLA, and now she claims she's in love." She flinched at the pain slicing across her insides. "I'm just having a hard time wrapping my brain around it." *And my heart.*

Julie's mouth twitched. Dismay filled her face. "I hear you."

Meg jostled the mouse, and the bittersweet photo disappeared. "You know that Proverb, 'Train up a child in the way he should go, and when he is old he will not depart from it'?" Lifting the mouse, she let it drop with a *thwunk.* "Well, she departed."

***

Linzee pulled little Jack onto her lap and opened the storybook. Jack chortled and bounced on her knee. "Hip Hip Hippo!" Eight tiny children made a circle on the floor. Across the room, the director of Little Tykes Preschool, sweaty hair frizzing around her face, gave Linzee a smile and the okay sign.

Nuzzling Jack's hair, Linzee read, "'No, son,' said Hip Hip's momma. 'You can't play with Rine Rine Rhino anymore.' 'Why not, Momma?'"

Uttering the words on autopilot, she saw her own mother's stricken face superimposed over the childish pictures. "'Rine Rine makes you do bad things, like run through Mrs. Bun Bun's garden and knock over her hutch.'"

She could still hear Mom's judgmental retort last night when she told her she was bringing Nena to meet the family. *Why can't you just call her your friend?*

"'Hip Hip went to find Rob Rob Robin. He looked in the pig sty, but Rob Rob wasn't there.'" She forced a smile, her gaze circling the tots. "Kids, where do you think Rob Rob is?"

"In his nest?" a little girl ventured.

Jack squirmed off her knee and plopped onto the floor. "In a twee!"

"No fair, Jack, you already know the story. 'Hip Hip looked in the doghouse, but Rob Rob wasn't there either.

6

Finally, he found his friend in a tree by the river.' And you know what? I bet Hip Hip was so happy to see him, he jumped up and down for joy."

The kids giggled, and she couldn't help smiling at the mental picture of a barrel-bodied hippo hopping around on stubby little legs.

But another memory intruded and chased away the smile—the bitter words she'd flung at Mom. *I don't like your attitude.* The mother she both loved and resented couldn't even look at her anymore without silent rebuke in her eyes.

She exhaled. "'Good morning, Hip Hip,' said Rob Rob. 'Will you let me ride on your back when you swim across the river?' 'Yes, I will,' said Hip Hip. 'Will you carry me on your back when you fly to the sun?'"

A bird carrying a hippo on its back sounded about as likely as Mom endorsing same-sex relationships.

Stuffing the memory deep inside where she wouldn't have to see it anymore, she turned the last page. "'Hop on,' said Rob Rob. 'You've got my back.'"

Chapter Two

When the office clock hit five, Meg wasted no time heading to her romantic rendezvous. But road hogs clogged the southbound 101 for as far ahead as she could see. She'd be late, and Barry hated lateness. A throbbing headache was pounding away at the base of her skull, keeping in time with the bass guitar pulsing from the stereo.

The black Saab ahead shuddered to a stop. She slammed on the brake with a jerk, her blood pressure spiking at the near miss.

If she were driving a flying car, she could lift off and soar over all these motorized tin fortresses. She'd be Marty McFly in his flying, time-traveling DeLorean.

She smiled for the first time since leaving work, buoyed by thoughts of a world full of gravity-defying cars. Road rage could be eradicated. But she suspected that, in time, road rage would turn to sky rage.

"This is KRQA, your Bay Area Christian music station." The radio DJ jolted her back to the present. "And here is Jeremy Camp with Overcome." The song was hers and Barry's favorite, and she cranked the volume. She hoped it portended good fortune for the rest of the evening. A wind gust swept her hair into her eyes, and she flung it back. Barry liked the windswept look on her, and he sure would get it tonight.

She needed Dr. Barrett Dworkin tonight. Wise, practical Professor of Music B. C. Dworkin. Smart, serious Barry "Sweetcheeks" Dworkin.

When the Redwood City exit finally appeared, she

snaked her car to the right, catching a glimpse of a middle-finger salute from the driver she cut in front of. "Sorry, mister." After cutting off two more drivers, she yelled an apology to the red-faced young man behind her as she aimed her metallic blue Mustang toward Caffe Amore.

Although she and Barry had not yet mentioned the love word, some of their recent conversations had included words like future, and marriage. She often reminded herself, love was a simple matter of time, and not to be rushed.

But a nice, long goodnight kiss would be a great way to end the evening.

A smile lingered on her lips as she walked through the door, the rich scent of espresso chasing away her headache. But her smile faded when she saw grim-faced Barry waiting for her in their usual corner booth. Maybe she could sweet-talk him into a better mood.

He stood and watched her approach.

Hoping to wipe the frown off his face, she widened her smile and threw her arms around him. "Oh, it's so good to see you. Thank you for this, Barry. I really needed it." He patted her back, but offered no kiss, and no "I've missed you." On pulling back, she saw only his you're-late-again face.

"I'm glad you made it, Meg." She wilted at his long-suffering tone. She needed to work on her punctuality.

Settling into the booth across from him, she ordered a latte, her appetite having vanished on the 101. He ordered coffee and his usual tuna sandwich as she related the day's events. Tonight he sported a pained, rumpled look, making him look even more like Tommy Lee Jones. If his foot injury from last weekend had flared up again, it would explain his gloomy mood.

After the waiter had brought their orders, she grabbed the nutmeg and cinnamon shakers and sprinkled her drink with abandon.

Barry watched her. "That's kind of a lot, isn't it?"

9

She ignored him. This wouldn't be the first time he'd criticized her love for spices. Swirling a sip of latte around on her tongue, she savored the kick of spice-laden caffeine. "I brought you something."

"And I brought *you* something." He held out his hand. "You first."

She picked up her phone and scrolled, then handed it to him. "I wanted to show you what the painting looks like."

He squinted at the screen. "Nice. But the bridge is a little on the pink side. Did you intend that?"

"Is it too pink? I was going for a romantic look. International Orange just wasn't doing it for me."

"No, it's pretty. And I see you made the brown cliffs very green."

"Art is one of the few areas of life in which you can make your own rules."

"Not so for music." Barry set the phone down, reached into a paper bag, and pulled out a thick book. *All About Classic Cars*. "I got this for your son yesterday."

She grasped the hefty book, and it forced her hand to the table. "Thank you. Richie will love this."

"Here's the photo CD of your daughter's graduation." He held out a wrapped disc. Meg took it and squeezed his hand, but he'd turned his attention away from her and onto his sandwich.

"Speaking of Linzee, Barry —"

He lifted his head, sandwich halfway to his mouth.

"You're going with me to my family's Fourth of July barbecue, right?"

"My day is wide open."

"I'm glad. I'm going to meet Linzee's friend for the first time. She actually thinks I hate her." She sucked in another sip of latte. It felt so good to unburden herself. "Linzee and I had a heated conversation last night."

Barry swallowed and frowned. "Another one?"

Meg squeezed her cup, sending spurts of brown liquid

over the rim and down the side. "She—" her voice cracked. "She called me a homophobe and a hypocrite." Seizing a napkin, she wiped her fingers, then dabbed the dampness from her eye.

He picked up a napkin and patted his mouth. "In the minds of the gay community, anyone who isn't on board with their lifestyle is a homophobe."

"I know. I hate that label."

She searched his face, but Barry avoided her gaze, his way of telling her he was ready for a change of subject. She adjusted her skirt and crossed her legs. "Why are you sitting way over there?" She tilted her head. "Come sit over here next to me like you usually do." She patted the seat beside her.

His smile didn't quite reach his eyes. "No thanks, I want to look at you."

She flinched at the odd remark. Barry's already unpredictable sense of humor seemed to have gone AWOL tonight. In the five months they'd been dating, he'd rarely laughed or smiled. If she laughed at something on the radio or TV, sometimes he would look at her as if she were a naughty child. If she shared an amusing incident, he might offer a lopsided grin.

Like Forrest Gump with his box of chocolates, she never knew what she was going to get.

She needed to loosen him up. "Do you want to hear something funny?" Reaching for the nutmeg shaker, she sprinkled her latte again. "One of my co-workers got a birthday card today from her husband, but she wouldn't let anyone see it. Then, when her back was turned, one of the guys picked it up and read it to the rest of us."

Barry's face finally relaxed in a tiny grin.

"It said, 'Roses are red, Wives are hot, Especially the wife this hubby's got.' You should have seen her face." She laughed and waited for his reaction, wondering what he would pull out of his box of chocolates this time.

Although he smiled, his eyes held a stony expression.
"You didn't like that?" He might as well have slapped her. "I can tell you aren't amused."

"No, it was cute. I've had a lot on my mind lately, what with classes and all."

Puzzled, she sat back, searching his face again for some clue as to what he was thinking. "You seem tired tonight. Is everything okay?"

Instead of replying, Barry reached for her hand. His pause stretched for several seconds while he caressed her fingers.

When he lifted his head, a weary shroud seemed to settle over him. "To be honest, I've been thinking about the conversation we had about Caroline."

"Caroline?" She thrust her chin up. "The opera singer who brought 'music to your soul?'" With her free hand, she formed air quotes. "The one who inspired you to write the best music of your career?"

"Compared to that relationship, Meg, ours lacks music."

Her jaw dropped. "Barry, you've been telling me for months I have the qualities you want in a woman. How would you feel if I told you our relationship lacks art?"

He shrugged. "'A painter paints pictures on canvas. But musicians paint their pictures on silence.' Leopold Stokowski." Barry pulled his hand back, oblivious to the fact that his words had just slashed her paintings to ribbons.

She reeled, stunned into silence.

But Barry wasn't finished. "I've been so confused lately about you and me. Remember the romance novel I checked out from the library?"

"Yes."

"I was hoping it held the answers I was looking for."

"What answers?"

"The answers to what's missing in our relationship." His calm, factual manner belied the hardness of his eyes.

"I still can't believe you did that." She wanted to roll her eyes. "The love experts say love is a choice—"

"Anyway, I read it and realized *something* was missing between us." He nearly spit the words, then recapped the story of the two fictional characters and the romance that had developed between them. "That wasn't happening between you and me. *Something* is missing, Meg. And it has caused me to rethink the importance of shared passions in a relationship."

With a burst of clarity, she knew what he had come here to say. His mixed messages, his dismal mood, the diminishing phone calls—the pieces of the jigsaw puzzle fell into place. Frozen, she listened with growing dread.

"What I'm trying to say is— it made me realize I'm not falling in love with you."

The invisible blow flung her back against the seat. His voice reverberated through the fog in her head. "This is the end for you and me."

Heart pounding, she groped for her purse, hoping to make a swift getaway. He'd played her for a fool. Lured her all the way down here with a promise of coffee and a meal.

"You are a beautiful and talented woman." His gaze, hard as green marbles, never left her face. "And I know you had high hopes for us. I know you had loving feelings—"

"Barry." She'd never seen this sanctimonious side of Dr. D. "I chose to open my heart to you because I trusted you." She stood and scrunched her lips together. She couldn't let him see how much he'd hurt her. "I can't believe you made me drive all this way so you could dump me."

"I wanted to tell you in person."

"I know you thought you were doing the right thing." Her face flamed. "But you could have told me this over the phone."

She reached for her purse to head to the exit, but he wasn't finished. "Don't you think you deserved better than a phone call?"

Pulling her purse to her chest, she clung to it like a

protective shield. "If doing this face to face was so important to you, Barry, you could have driven to San Rafael." She turned and hurried to the exit, her heart pounding in time with her heels.

"Here." She jerked to a stop at the sound of his voice behind her. "You left the book and the disc."

She spun around and nearly collided with his outstretched arm. "I don't want your guilt offerings." She just wanted to go home.

His mouth compressed into a solid line. She made herself meet his chilly expression with her own. "Buh-bye, Dr. Dwork." Without waiting for his reaction, she rushed to her car, fumbling with the remote in her haste to leave. With her car alarm howling and panic threatening, she punched at the remote until the noise stopped. Wrestling the door open, she enclosed herself inside her Mustang and exhaled.

Craggy brown hills zoomed by as she retraced her route on the 101. Shock kept her blessedly numb until she reached the city, where she gave in to the urge to kick herself. Deep down, she'd wondered if Barry's dwindling phone calls meant he had leaving, not loving, on his mind. But she'd ignored the red flags and convinced herself he was too much of a gentleman to do exactly what he'd done tonight.

She fingered the tiny cross around her neck that Barry had given her last month for her forty-third birthday. "Wow, Lord. You say all things work together for good. So, what was that all about?"

She glanced down at the paisley skirt she'd chosen that morning with such anticipation. She'd selected a drop-dead red blouse to wow Barry with. But he'd been unfazed. Here she was, back on the market again.

She wouldn't be on the market in the first place if husband number one hadn't traded her in for a newer model.

Wispy fog danced around her car as she approached the Golden Gate Bridge. The orange sun dipped lower into the

Pacific. A dense wall of fog, as thick as the tears she wiped away, accompanied her across the bridge and into Marin County.

In her driveway, she texted a message to her brother. *Hi Brad, Barry and I won't make it to your BBQ after all. Sorry. Hope you all have a great time.* Someday she'd be ready to share the demeaning account of the breakup with her family. But not today.

As she entered her front door, she breathed in the stillness, letting it seep through her pores and invade the crevices of her spirit. Even after twenty-two years, her flat-roofed, earth-toned Mediterranean home still had that effect on her. Its wide windows looked out onto family-friendly Reno Drive. A lone willow graced the barren front yard.

She wandered past her painting studio, through the kitchen and past the courtyard where a lonely old swing set sat rusty and unused. In the distance, majestic hills formed a jagged silhouette against the darkening sky. As a child, she had gazed at those same hills from her home on the other side of town. When she'd squint her eyes just so, she could make out the bulk of a gigantic brontosaurus crouching on the horizon. Then she would open her eyes wide, and the brontosaurus would revert back to tree-covered hills. Even now, when she visited her parents at the old homestead, she would sometimes go into her childhood bedroom to see if she could still see that brontosaurus.

Smiling at the memory, she made her way to the Jacuzzi, gripped with a need to soak away her dreadful evening with Barry.

***

Meg painted with furious strokes, moving her mouth in sync with the brush. "I may not know an oboe from a bassoon, Barry, but I bet you don't know oil from acrylic. Or charcoal from graphite."

Black swirls, gloomy blues, and murky browns exploded on the canvas as she wiped out the romantic

15

tableau underneath. "Oh, and God?" Her voice, swollen with unshed tears, stretched as taut as a rubber band approaching its breaking point. "Am I expected to meet Linzee's same-sex partner and pretend I'm happy for her?" She twisted the bristles into the surface so hard, the handle nearly snapped in two. "My beautiful, graceful daughter is in love with a woman, God. Why? Why would Linzee want to be with a woman instead of a man? I don't get it. I don't understand."

Swallowing hard, she stepped back and studied the canvas, widening her eyes in surprise at the glowing tornado she'd created. She tilted her head to the side. From this angle, it could pass for a lethal whirlpool, gathering momentum as it prepared to suck up everything in its path.

Shuddering, she expelled the rest of her pent-up emotions and flopped on the red velvet chaise. Shadow, her aging German shepherd, lay dozing on the floor. She kneaded his fur and stared at the artwork dotting the stark white walls.

She remembered how eager she'd been to show Barry this room, her private space, filled with framed and mounted pieces of her soul. A watercolor she'd named "Dancing Poppies" had intrigued him, and she could almost hear the wheels spinning in his head as he'd studied it. She'd nibbled her fingers, all nerves, wondering what his intense scrutiny meant.

Then he chuckled. "I see what you did here. You joined their leaves together like hands. You made them look like they're actually dancing." He turned to her, admiration shining from his eyes. "You want my honest opinion?" he'd said. "You're quite talented."

"Thanks." She'd smiled, relishing the warmth inside her.

"Dear God." A groan wrenched from her throat at the memory. "This has been *the* worst day ever. My daughter is angry with me. My boyfriend dumped me just when I needed him most." A tear escaped and trickled down her cheek. "God, I need your peace right now. I need to feel your presence."

She stayed motionless, eyes shut, mouth puckered, her heart sending silent prayers heavenward. At last, the peace of God began to fill her. His presence flooded her, enveloped her, loved on her.

Swiping away the wetness with the back of her hand, she whispered her favorite Psalm. "Thou wilt show me the path of life: in thy presence is fulness of joy; at thy right hand there are pleasures forevermore."

Chapter Three

A morning sunbeam streamed into Latte Love Shack, heralding the new day. Linzee, sitting inside the beam, licked the foam off the top of her hazelnut latte. Directly across the wooden table from her best friend-slash-soul mate, Nena.

"Kudos to us." Nena lifted her cup. Her sharp brown eyes glowed.

Linzee held her cup aloft. "So, what's this majorly important question you're dying to ask?"

Nena flashed the boyish grin that softened her tough veneer. "Ain't it time we make it official and tie the knot?"

"Whoop, whoop!" Linzee exclaimed with her fist in the air. All their hard work—the rallies, the demands for justice—had paid off. Today's celebration was only the beginning. "Let's do it." She felt her smile stretch from ear to ear and held up her palm for a high-five. "I want Reverend Suzette to marry us."

"That would be cool, but Suzette ain't gonna be back from vacation 'til September." Nena frowned. "You really want to wait that long?"

"Suzette would be hurt if we asked anyone else."

A barista bearing a tray of drinks approached. She leaned a hip against their table, displaying a scorpion tattoo from her elbow halfway up her arm.

Linzee grinned. "Hey, Drucie."

Drucie shifted her tray and grinned back. "Dude, what up with that ginormous smile?" Her voice came out rough as a cheese grater. "You look like Big Mouth."

Linzee laughed. "We're taking the plunge. Tying the knot."

"Yo. Get down with your bad self." She studied Linzee with eyes the color of cast-iron. "We oughta throw you a reception."

"Awesome."

Light glinted off Drucie's tiny eyebrow rings as she moved to the neighboring booth. Soon the coffee shop manager approached their table and offered his congratulations. His white teeth gleamed inside a broad smile. "Keep us posted on the date, will you?"

Everybody was happy for them. Everybody except Mom.

As her heart free-fell, she sought Nena's eyes. "What am I going to say to my mom?" she whispered. "She is not going to like this."

"Yeah, I'm sorry about your mom." Nena's jaw hardened. "Bummer for us she's such a homophobe."

"A mega-homophobe."

"I guess I'll call her Megaphobe, then."

Linzee snorted, then burst into giggles. "You're hilarious."

"I don't mean to diss her, but she's got to get her head out of the last century."

Her giggles faded. "I wouldn't count on that."

"Let's get it over with." Nena pointed at Linzee's phone. "Send her a text, tell her we're comin' over tonight with some news."

Linzee shook her head. "No, let's just drop by unannounced. She's been putting off this meeting for far too long, and I'm not giving her any more chances to say no."

***

Meg closed her eyes for a moment and savored the heavenly aroma of cinnamon and nutmeg she'd just sprinkled over freshly sliced apples. Opening her oven door, she prepared to pop the apple crisp inside. Then the doorbell rang.

Sighing, she shoved the pan into the preheated oven and hurried to the door.

Linzee stood there, the porch light wrapping her in a halo, accentuating the hardness in her eyes. So she probably hadn't come to apologize.

"Linzee!" Meg stepped forward anyway, her arms outstretched. Until she saw Linzee's companion. The woman's beady eyes stared back at her. A shock of jagged black hair framed Nena's face and tattoos snaked down her arms.

A jolt hit her, and she froze. Recovering quickly, she invited them in. Linzee made introductions in a frosty voice, but Meg was too shaken to do more than give Nena a stiff nod.

Meg dropped to the green suede sofa, clutching the cushion's edge. Linzee, her hand in Nena's, sat pigeon-toed on the floral loveseat across from Meg, wearing skinny jeans and her favorite red ankle boots. The angelic waves of her hair floated around her head.

The silence stretched at least ten seconds before Linzee spoke, her tone as determined as her eyes. "Mom, Nena and I have decided to get married."

Meg gripped a couch pillow to her chest while an earthquake shuddered through her. "Married?" She heard her own sharp intake of breath.

"Married." Linzee tsked. "Haven't you been keeping up with the news? Now all adults have the right to marry, not just straight ones."

Her lips trembled as she struggled to reply. "Marriage has always been between a man and a woman."

"Not anymore, Ms. St. John." Nena's froggy voice grated on her nerves.

"Call me Meg."

"Meg. Times have changed. We finally got a legal right

to marry."

Her nose tickled with unshed tears. "You've always had a legal right to marry, as long as it's to someone of the opposite sex."

Linzee rolled her eyes. "That's no right at all if I can't marry the person I love."

"You know I can't give you my blessing for this, Linzee."

"Why am I not surprised, Mom?"

She was about to reply when Richie burst through the door, home from his job at an auto body shop. "Do I smell apple crisp?" The door thudded closed behind him.

Meg dug her fingers into her palms. In her desire to shelter her son from the unpleasant realities of life, she'd neglected to tell Richie of his sister's sexual orientation. What a mistake, she realized too late. With Linzee off to college for the last several years, brother and sister had grown apart. No doubt it never even occurred to him to question her sexual preference.

What a way to find out now.

"Hey, Linz." Richie glanced at them once, then twice. "Who's this?"

"Richie, this is my fiancée, Nena Vasquez." Pride seeped into Linzee's voice. "Nena, this is my little brother Richie."

"Fiancée?" Richie's mouth hung open, then shut.

"Yeah, we're getting married." Linzee smirked at him. "Aren't you going to say congratulations?"

"C-congratulations." Richie stumbled over the word. "Is this, like, a joke or something?"

"No joke, Rich. Didn't they teach you about same-sex marriage at that Christian school of yours?"

"Well, yeah." Richie looked a little dazed. "I know about same-sex marriage." He swiveled to Meg, then to Linzee again. "You mean, you're one of *them*?"

"Surprise." Linzee laughed.

Richie looked to Meg for confirmation, and when she gave a somber nod, he twisted his lips. "Gross!" Doubling over, he pretended to gag. Linzee stared at him, her lip curled.

"Richie, that was not necessary." Meg gestured toward the armchair. "Sit down. Let's talk about this."

Richie settled his long body in the La-Z-boy and glared at his sister. "What about relatives? Should we let them marry each other too?"

Linzee cast him a disgusted look. "You're a sicko."

"Whatever floats your boat." Nena's cackling laugh mocked him.

Richie's voice grew louder. "Isn't it discrimination that relatives can't marry each other? Even if they looooove each other?"

Linzee narrowed her eyes at him. Nena raised her brow and smirked. "For the sake of consistency, we ought to let relatives marry, too."

Richie slapped his leg. "Will you marry me, dear sister?" He threw his head back, shaking with mirth.

"Oh, shut your mouth and grow up, Richie." Linzee stood. "Nena, let's go."

"Wait." Meg beckoned her to stay. Linzee stopped and gave her an impatient look. "Don't let your brother scare you away," Meg pleaded.

"Are you serious? He's being absurd." Linzee stalked to the door like a soldier on a mission, then turned to scowl at Meg. "Marry my brother? Yeah, right!"

The door slammed. "Marry your girlfriend?" Richie mimicked in falsetto. "Yeah, right."

Meg, gripped by an uncharacteristic urge to slap her son, settled for glaring at him. "Thanks for chasing her away."

He got up and followed the apple-crisp aroma to the kitchen. "You're welcome."

She shot to her feet and tailed him. "Don't even think of

running away. What got into you?"

Richie planted himself in front of her, staring down his nose. "How long have you known she's gay?"

She wrested her gaze away, remorse eating at her. "Look, I'm sorry I didn't tell you. I know I should have. But—"

"Yeah, you should have." Richie brushed past her and stormed into the living room. "Thanks for making me look like a clueless dweeb." He didn't wait for her reply but headed to the TV room.

"Richie—" But a sitcom laugh track drowned out the words she'd been about to say.

Chapter Four

Meg followed Laura Flynn to a cool arbor beneath a weeping willow, far enough from the noise of the church picnic to talk without shouting. Gripping a cup of weak coffee in one hand, she unfolded a lawn chair with the other, relishing the stillness. From here, the distant shouts from the softball game and screams of children playing lent pleasant background noises to the peaceful setting.

The youth pastor's wife eased herself into the lawn chair and stretched out her legs. Her pregnant abdomen bulged as if she'd swallowed a soccer ball. Meg peered at Laura's baby bump. "How's the little one?"

Laura grimaced and placed her hand on the bulge. "Baby's rambunctious. See?" Her hand jerked as the soccer ball bounced around.

Meg tilted her head. "I miss those days."

"You do? I hope I'll feel that way someday."

"Trust me, you will." She sought Laura's eyes. "Are you ready for my big news?"

"I'm dying to hear your big news."

"It's about Linzee." A tear ran down her cheek as she poured out her story, finishing with, "I remember how I felt the day Linzee told me she loved women. That was bad enough. Now, with her talking about marriage, I've lost hope that it's just a phase." She sniffed and sipped her lukewarm coffee. Puckering her mouth, she upended the cup and watched the brown puddle flow, then slowly soak into the grass.

Concern shone from Laura's eyes. "Does Linzee's dad

know about this?"

Meg wiped the tear away. "Phillippe left us and moved back to Canada seven years ago."

"Your poor kids."

"Unbeknown to me, he'd been corresponding with a woman in Vancouver." She frowned at the memory. "I never once suspected my passionate French-Canadian charmer had a cheatin' heart."

"I didn't know he was from Canada."

"He was born near Montreal, raised in Vancouver by his mom and step-dad."

"Then, how did you two meet?"

"We met at an art show when I was in college, and he was working for Intel." A memory intruded, bringing with it a reluctant grin to her face. "Later, he told me he had no interest in admiring blobs of paint on canvas, but he'd seen me from afar, and, well, the rest is history."

Laura sighed. "I can't imagine how difficult it must have been when he took off like that."

She hung her head. "I wish I'd married a strong Christian man like you did. I made a bad choice. And I paid dearly for it."

"I'm sorry."

Meg shrugged, unable to reply.

"Do you and Phillippe communicate at all these days?"

"Once a month, I get his check. Other than that, no." She felt her mouth twist. "He and that woman divorced after five years and two kids, and now he's living with another woman."

Laura shook her head. "What a prince of a guy. Can I pray for you, Meg?" Laura reached for her hand, and peace flooded her as Laura lifted her and Linzee in prayer.

When Laura had finished, she squeezed Meg's hand. "By the way, would you be interested in a Christian support group for parents of gay children?"

A ray of hope pierced her heart. "I didn't know there

was such a group. I need all the support I can get."

"Have you ever heard of FOGY?"

She chuckled. "As in Old Fogy?"

Laura smiled. "No, FOGY stands for Families of Gay Youth. They meet once a week to encourage and pray for each other. The Smithsons from our church attend the group. Their son is gay."

"I'd love to meet them."

"I don't think they're here today, but I can introduce you tomorrow at church. Then you won't have to feel so alone."

***

Outside Linzee's apartment, the evening sun cast long shadows, turning the pygmy palm into a gigantic caricature splayed across the parking lot. A screechy violin from the teenager next door clashed with the rock music playing in the apartment on the other side. A typical Saturday evening at Corte Madera Apartments. Linzee upped the volume on the boring CNN broadcast to drown out the dissonance. Easier to tune out droning newscasters than the squawks and blaring stereos from her neighbors.

She rejoined Nena on their cheap rummage-sale sofa, returned her attention to the Facebook app on her smartphone, and saw a waiting message.

"Nena, who's Edward Levens?"

"Say what?"

"I got a message from someone named Edward Levens." She held out the phone. "Look. The profile photo is Johnny Depp as Edward Scissorhands."

She opened the message and read, *Linzee U r a disgusting dyke.*

Recoiling, she threw the phone down. "Yikes! Check it out, Nena."

Nena leaned over to read the post, then cursed. "Just some homophobe trying to scare you."

She pressed delete, but as soon as she clicked on her

26

game app, a text message popped up from an unknown number.

U don't deserve to b here.

She gasped and showed Nena the message.

Another text came in seconds after the last one. *Do us all a favor and kill urself, dyke.*

With shaking fingers, she started to reply, but Nena put her hand out. "Don't send it, Ruca. You're playin' right into his hands."

"Who is this creeper, Edward Levens?"

"Never heard of him. It probably ain't even his real name."

"But it's obviously someone who knows me." She eyed the phone warily. "Do we know anyone named Edward who's homophobic?"

"Remember them anti-gay bozos at UCLA? He could be one of them."

"Why would he have my number?"

Nena pointed at the phone. "Your profile, Querida. You've got to tighten up your privacy settings."

"What if he comes after you next?"

Nena cursed again. "Anybody who messes with me will be sorry."

Despite her anxiety, she felt a smile break free. "You're such a toughie."

Chapter Five

Meg waited in First Baptist Church's parking lot for Ray and Deb Smithson to arrive, rubbing her clammy hands on her Capri pants and nibbling her fingers. She'd lowered the convertible's top, but the gentle breeze couldn't cancel out the eighty-plus temperatures still lingering. Now rivulets of sweat crawled down her belly like teardrops.

She leaned against the headrest, studying the ancient, stately brick church she'd visited one time in her life. Set in the heart of downtown San Rafael, its tall white steeple pierced the blue sky, and its freshly watered, clean-cut green lawn contrasted with the steel and concrete structures surrounding it. Built in 1905 and well-preserved, it was listed on the state's Historic Registry of Buildings.

The Smithson's car pulled up, and her new friend Deb greeted her with an enthusiastic hello and hug. She and Ron led Meg inside to a cool basement fellowship hall, where several people were gathered in a circle — a family of four, a lone man on each side of them, and two couples. Deb waved and smiled, comfortably at home here, unlike herself.

One of the men greeted them cheerfully. "Here come the Smithson's. And a guest to boot." He stood and offered Meg his hand and a smile. Warm brown eyes welcomed her from behind wire-rimmed glasses. "Hi, I'm Jon, and they tell me I'm the leader of this group."

She smiled, her tension dissipating. "Hi, I'm Meg."

"Please, have a seat." Jon's genuine, open-book manner put her at ease. As they found chairs, Jon handed her a couple of flyers. "Deb, did you tell her we have initiation rites for rookies?" He winked at Deb, then smiled at Meg. "I'm kidding."

He sat and looked around the group. "Since we have two guests tonight, why don't we go around the circle and introduce ourselves. Tell the rest of us what brought you here to FOGY. The nutshell version, please, not the thesis."

Laughter rang out, and someone said, "No worries, Camille isn't here tonight." For a surreal moment, Meg felt as though she'd been transported to a movie scene of Alcoholics Anonymous.

What am I doing here?

The clean-cut man to Jon's right began. "Hi, I'm Dean, this is my wife Esther, and our two kids. We're here because our twenty-year-old son is gay. We've been attending these meetings for about a year now. The support we get here is so encouraging."

A grim-faced man to the right of them said, "I'm Mike, and this is my first time here."

"Welcome, Mike," said a few voices around the circle.

Mike gestured toward the family man. "I know Dean from work. I'm here because I have a daughter who's gay." His round face grew pale. "My wife blamed me for it and left two years ago."

He turned to a blond woman in glasses to his right. The woman smiled, showing even white teeth. "Hi, we're Jim and Kathy." Her hands gestured as she talked. "We have a fifteen-year-old foster son who believes he's gay. We sought the Lord, and He led us here."

Deb's mouth trembled when her turn came. "Our son Preston is a senior in high school. He's in a relationship with a twenty-four-year-old man, still considers himself a Christian, and doesn't believe the Bible teaches homosexuality is a sin. He claims God made him that way. He's stopped attending church because he feels judged." Deb turned to Meg and laid a warm hand on her shoulder. "And this is our new friend Meg. She goes to our church."

"Hi, all." She waved. "I have a gay daughter. Her gayness has torn us apart. We used to be so close. But now every time we talk, it turns ugly. Worst of all, she's now engaged to her girlfriend." To her alarm, tears burned her eyes, and she clamped her mouth shut.

"I'm so sorry." The petite African American woman on her right patted her hand, eyes shiny with compassion. "How hard for you. I'm Trish, and this is my husband, Jerome. We have a grandson who's gay."

"Glad to meet you both." She managed a brief smile. "Glad to meet all of you."

"And I'm Jon." The leader had a self-assured, yet approachable, air about him. "I got asked to start up this group because the Napa Valley group was overflowing, and we saw a need in this area. I've been involved with FOGY almost since its founding." He cleared his throat with dramatic emphasis. "So you could say I'm an old FOGY."

She heard chuckles and someone piped up, "We've heard that one before."

Jon's wide grin gave his face a boyish look. Then his grin vanished, and he studied his twiddling thumbs. "Even though neither of my two sons are gay, I do have a gay brother, and an ex-wife who left me for another woman."

Ouch.

He lifted his head, scanning their faces. "For you newcomers, I want to briefly touch on who we are and what we're about. We're all about love, meaning loving our gay family members with Christ-like love, in hopes they'll be drawn to God's love. Ray, do you want to read our mission statement?"

"Sure." Ray held up the pamphlet. "'Our Mission: Showing Christ's love, compassion and grace to our gay loved ones.'"

"Thanks, Ray. Anybody want to read 'What We Believe'?"

"Sure." Deb raised her hand. Meg leaned over and

followed along. "'We believe God loves gays, and that He desires to save them through His grace. We believe God is their judge, not us. We believe Christ calls us to love them as He does.'"

Jon finished with, "The organization started in a Southern Cal church by a group of parents who had gay sons or daughters. The concept caught fire, and now there are groups in almost every state. Most of you know I will be stepping down from leadership at the end of August, and Dean and Esther here will be taking over the reins."

He sat back. "Does anybody have anything to share about their week? Any opportunities to emulate Jesus?"

"Anyone know where Camille is?" one of the women asked.

"Not me."

"Hey, it means we'll be out of here earlier than usual." More chuckles but Meg could tell the teasing was good-natured. She hoped this Camille woman was a good sport.

"I have a question," she blurted, and ten faces turned to look at her. Her heart raced with nerves.

Jon nodded at her. "Go ahead."

She scooted forward on her chair. "My daughter believes people are either born gay, or they are not. I'm curious what the ministry's stance is on that."

"Dean, do you want to take that one on?" Jon said.

"Sure." Dean draped his arm across his wife's shoulders. "FOGY doesn't take a stance on that issue. That's not what we're about."

Esther added, "We're not here to push an agenda. We don't know if a gay gene exists. But we do know all of us were born with a sin gene."

"There have been studies on that issue," Jon told her. "Come see me after the meeting and I'll get you the websites."

During prayer time, Meg knelt beside her chair, hands folded, head lifted heavenward. The prayers were fervent, desperate, and tears flowed freely.

A prayer burst from her mouth. "Father, set my Linzee free. Do whatever you have to do, in Jesus' name."

Jon closed with a heartfelt plea. "Father God, we love you. We feel your presence with us tonight—"

By the time Jon uttered the final Amen, she felt depleted but cleansed. The Lord had reached down His hands and given her a massage—a spiritual, deep-tissue massage. She wanted to stay on her knees and bask in the Lord's presence. But the room began to fill with conversation as the others headed toward the refreshment table.

She stuck close to Deb during the post-meeting visiting time until a vibration from her pocket interrupted their small talk. "Excuse me." She turned away and found a text from Linzee. *Mom call me tonite pls.*

Linzee rarely texted her unless she had bad news. Meg patted Deb on the back and mouthed a thank you as she clutched her phone and pulled up Linzee's number.

She waited until she reached the privacy of her car. "Linzee, what's going on?"

"Mom, something strange is happening." Tension stretched Linzee's voice thin. "I've been getting hate messages for a couple of days. It's freaking us out."

"Hate messages?" She stared blankly at the darkened church building. "From who?"

"Someone named Edward or Eddie, but we don't know who he is."

"Can't you trace the phone number?"

"No, it's unidentified. We were wondering if it's, like, anyone you know? Like, someone at your church who hates gays?"

As stunned as if Linzee had slapped her, Meg managed to reply, "You think this person might be someone *I* know?"

Nena had to have put such a poisonous thought in her daughter's head.

"It doesn't hurt to ask."

"No, Linzee, I don't know anyone who would send hate messages." Her tone sent a sharp rebuke. "I don't attend Haight Church."

Linzee's voice rose. "He's been telling me I should kill myself."

A recent news story flashed through Meg's mind, and she gripped the wheel. A gay college student had committed suicide after claiming two bullies had targeted him. The victim's family was suing for half a million dollars.

"Please don't be like that poor kid in Oakland."

"I'm not going to kill myself, Mom. I'd never give him that satisfaction." Meg massaged her neck as Linzee paused. "But for the sake of argument, let's say I did. Would you sue him for harassment?"

"You bet I would." She heard the question behind the question—do you still care about me that much? Half a million dollars worth? "Please call the police. And change your number."

"Of course."

She gripped the steering wheel tighter. Linzee sounded almost like her old self, like the daughter she once shared style tips with, who used to ask her advice on everything from school work to career paths.

Emotions she hadn't felt for months were surging through her.

"I love you, Linzee."

A pause answered her. "Love you back," Linzee finally whispered, reluctance in every syllable.

Chapter Six

Meg glanced around the office. Murmuring phone conversations from her Buyer's Guild teammates assured her nobody needed her at the moment. Time to check her personal email. She opened her browser, but instead of the usual names in her inbox, a new name jumped off the screen.

Sent by: SausalitoJon
To: cinnameg9; mike_in_IT
Subject: Info for you.

She smiled as she read Jon's message. How nice to get an email from a man again, even a strictly platonic one.

Meg and Mike, It was good to have both of you join our small but mighty team last night, and I hope it was edifying for you. As promised, here are some links. In Him, Jon Paulson.

Mr. Jon Paulson. A sturdy, trustworthy name. Sir Jon Q. Paulson. The Honorable J.Q. Paulson, Esquire. A suit, briefcase, and Rolex kind of name. But she had a feeling Mr. Jon Paulson was not a suit-and-briefcase kind of man.

From: cinnameg9
To: SausalitoJon
Hi Jon – It was edifying, and I am looking forward to more. What a great concept for a support group. You guys made me feel welcome. Thank you for the links. Meg.

Jon replied almost immediately.

Meg – Super. Glad you liked us. You wouldn't believe how many people walk through the door one time, express interest, and are never seen again. It can get frustrating. The folks you met last night are pretty much the core team for our group.

I also have some brochures, etc, that you might find informative. One of them lists statistics on things like the increase in same-sex households across the US, which might surprise you.

Will you be at the next meeting? Or maybe I could get them to you sometime this week. Jon.

Meg bit into her sandwich and re-read Jon's email. Tapping her foot, she set the sandwich down and composed her reply.

Jon, I don't know if I will be at the meeting Monday night. May I get them over the weekend?

Jon replied before she finished her lunch, and they arranged to meet at Latte Love Shack Saturday morning.

***

Linzee chanted the lyrics to "Poker Face" as she stepped out of the shower and wrapped herself in her deep purple robe. Dancing into her bedroom, she two-stepped over to her dresser and picked up her phone. A new message from an unknown number awaited her, and she gasped.

"No!" She flung the hot-pink phone as if it were tainted with nuclear waste. It landed with a soft thud on the bed. How did Eddie get her new number? Tremors jittered up her legs. Her breath came fast and furious. She needed Nena, but Nena had left for work.

Who was Eddie, and why did he want her dead?

Chapter Seven

Meg pulled open a wooden door flanked by two squat palms and inhaled the pleasing aroma of spiced teas mixed with pungent coffees. Handwritten words on a chalkboard greeted her inside the door. WELCOME TO LATTE LOVE SHACK, it said. This was no Starbucks. This was Far East meets West Coast.

Once inside, the temperature dropped at least ten degrees. She hoped the chill wouldn't permeate her lightweight sundress.

Jon, waiting at a window table, stood and waved as she approached. "Hello, Meg. Here's the literature I promised you." He pointed to a stack of brochures on the table as she slid onto a bench across from him. Jon's navy-blue tee proclaimed the message, JESUS SAVES.

"This is my son, Tanner." He sat and gestured at the silent middle-school-aged boy beside him. "He was hungry, so we went ahead and ordered something. Mike might drop by later."

Jon, one long leg draped over the other, sat as stiff as the partition behind him as if he were making it clear this was ministry business, not a date. For a moment, she regretted having chosen this place. She concentrated on the décor — dark wooden beams crisscrossed the ceiling. Ficus trees formed canopies over thin-legged wooden tables. On two walls, someone had painted murals of California landscapes.

Jon's dry voice broke the silence. "Look, Tanner. Do you think the person who painted those murals used to get in trouble as a kid for drawing on walls?"

The boy glanced at a mural of Yosemite's Half Dome and shrugged. Meg placed her hands in her lap, kneading her fingers to keep from nibbling on them. "I used to draw on walls with Magic Markers, which did not go over well with my parents."

"Same here. My parents took away my coloring privileges for a week. I was devastated."

Hoping to break the ice, she cast him a teasing smile. "And now you're scarred for life."

A grin broke over his face. "That does explain a lot."

A square-foot slab of wood jutted from the surface of the table. She pushed on it, and it slid to the side, exposing a shiny black box. "What's this?"

"It's their computerized ordering system." Jon slid an identical panel in front of him. "You put in your order, and voila, here it comes."

"Impressive." The table had four embedded touch screens, one at each seat.

Jon nodded. "Very cutting-edge."

"Yeah, that's cool." Tanner spoke a complete sentence for the first time.

"I can see why my daughter raves about this place." When she tapped the screen, it sprang to glowing green life, and she made a selection from the menu. "Doesn't a green tea smoothie sound good?"

"Green tea is good for the heart. And the noggin." He tapped his head.

She couldn't hold back a laugh at his comical expression. "I could use some help for my noggin."

"That makes two of us."

A barista, displaying spikes of burgundy hair poking up every which way, approached the table. "Welcome to Latte Love Shack." She set a stack of napkins down. "Is this your first time here?"

Meg nodded, wondering how much weight the hardware on the young woman's face added to her boyish frame. Her name badge identified her as DRUCIE.

"Any questions about the ordering system?"

Jon shook his head. "No, we're good."

"Okay, back in a few."

"She looks familiar." Meg watched the barista saunter to the next table. "But I can't recall where I know her from."

She glanced at the pamphlets in her hands. One asked the question, "Why are American Christians losing the culture war?"Another contained graphs and statistics. "Wow. Same-sex households in the US increased fifty-one percent in *ten years*." She flipped to the next page, eager to delve deeper. "San Francisco is still numero uno among US cities in percentage of LGBT citizens. No surprise there."

The barista returned with a tray of food and drinks. "One green tea smoothie. One venti Mexican Mocha with half-and-half. One brunch sandwich with bacon, one hot chocolate. Enjoy."

"You nailed it." Jon offered the girl a thumbs-up. "One big tip for Drucie, coming right up."

Drucie gave a reluctant laugh. "It's why they pay me the big bucks." She drew back her shoulders, all business now. "Are you interested in subscribing to our weekly specials? You can save up to fifteen percent. Just follow the instructions on your order screen."

"Thanks." Tapping the screen, Meg input her information, then sucked in a straw full of smoothie. "This tastes amazing. The best smoothie I've ever had."

Jon, smacking his lips after his first taste, nodded. "Mine's good too. Shockingly good."

"They must have a special ingredient."

Jon met her smile with a serious expression. "Did you get a chance to look at the rest of the links I sent?"

She stole a glance at Tanner, who happily munched his sandwich, a pair of ear buds blocking out the conversations around him.

"I've read a couple." She kept her voice low, even

though the closest table sat several feet away, unoccupied. "I liked the one about the identical twin studies. If a gay gene did exist, then if one twin were gay, the other one should be too."

"Good stuff, huh?" Jon's eyes lit up. "But you don't ever hear about it. There is a definite agenda out there, but the good news is, we have the power of God on our side. I have to keep reminding myself and the group we aren't fighting against flesh and blood, but against the principalities and powers of this age."

Goose bumps crawled up her arms.

"Good material to tell your daughter about next time she claims she was born gay."

The goose bumps subsided, and she swigged her drink.

"Do you have other kids besides Linzee?"

"I have a son who's about to start his senior year of high school." She relaxed against the whitewashed wall. "He attends the Christian academy."

"No public school for him, huh?"

She fingered a frond of ficus leaves and shook her head. "In Linzee's junior year at public school, her health teacher gave them an exercise to determine their sexual orientation." She took a deep breath and eased it out. "The questions were inappropriate, but by the time I found out about it, it was too late to object. Linzee claimed the test confirmed she was gay."

"I know the test you're talking about. I served on the board of our local school district and fought for years with the other board members over it." His jaw clenched. "Even though it was highly inappropriate, they said it was needed because bullying and suicide were on an upswing. I finally gave up and resigned."

"Their loss. School boards need more members like you."

Nearby, someone cleared his throat. Mike, the other newcomer from Monday night, hovered next to the table, clutching a large cup.

"Mike. Have a seat." Jon gestured to the empty place next to Meg. Mike sat and offered her a mumbled hi, and Jon handed him some brochures. Tanner, his ears still plugged, bobbed his head to the music.

"Mike, this is my son Tanner."

Mike stuck out a hand for the teenager to shake. "Sorry I'm late. I had to run some errands."

"Not a problem," said Jon. "You're heading to work after this?"

"Yeah. One to nine."

"Where do you work?" she asked.

"The same place as Dean Woods. Have you heard of Oversite? The internet security startup in San Rafael?"

"I've heard of it."

"That's us."

Jon thrust his thumb up. "A happening place, so I've heard."

Mike smiled and nodded. "We try."

"One hundred percent growth in one year. Pretty impressive."

Mike took a sip from his cup. Tanner's fingers tapped out a rhythm on the table. Jon sipped his mocha. "Right before you got here, Mike, we were talking about my battles with the school board."

Mike glanced at the brochures in his hand, then back at Jon. "What kinds of battles?"

"The same sort of battles I've had with my brother." Jon lowered his voice. "The one who's involved in the gay-rights movement. Last year, out of curiosity, I went to one of their rallies. It was crazy."

"Crazy how?" she asked, thinking of the rally in Union Square.

"The leader's diatribe was full of four-letter words directed at organized religion and Christians. He held up a Bible and subjected it to all kinds of abuse, the kind of stuff they won't show you on TV."

"Sounds like a rally I saw on TV. Same-sex couples kissing and cuddling, chanting slogans like 'Equality for All.'"

"When I asked Curtis, my brother, why they singled out Christians, he said, 'Because you religious people have oppressed us for years.'"

She held out the booklet in her hand. "This writer says Christians are losing the culture war."

"That we are. One reason is that the other side is screaming louder than we are."

She ran her finger around the booklet's rim. "I think another reason is because of groups like Haight Street Church."

"You have a point." Jon nodded. "In the minds of the gay-rights crowd, they represent Christianity."

"I saw them in action last week." She shared the events of the Union Square rally. Jon's eyes narrowed. Mike listened and nursed his coffee, but so far had not contributed to the conversation.

"Unbelievable." Jon shook his head again. "I've been wondering lately if God is calling our group to undo some of the damage that church has done. What do you think about protesting the protesters?"

She sat up. "You mean, making our own signs?"

Jon flashed a smile. "Exactly."

"What sort of signs did you have in mind?" Mike asked.

"'God loves gays.' 'Jesus died for gays.' That type of thing."

She wanted to applaud. "What an awesome idea."

"I like it," Mike added, raising his palm in a high-five.

"But . . ." She leaned forward, her tone tight with intensity. "I wish we could find a kind, compassionate way to protest what the gay-rights people say about us. Not even Jesus would tolerate the things they say and do at those rallies." Her eyes sought Jon's. "How *should* a Christian be

Jesus to people who vandalize God's word?"

His gaze beamed approval at her. "Great question. I believe Jesus would have been outraged if he'd been there. But here's the thing about Jesus." Jon steepled his hands and rested his elbows on the table. "No matter how angry he got, it was never from hostility. He never hated his opponents."

***

Linzee stood frozen in the parking lot and stared at her car. What a fitting end to the week, her hands-down worst ever.

"Nena, you have to come see this," she shouted, desperation knifing every syllable. "Nena!"

Not that she'd never had bad weeks in her lifetime. The time her dad left and moved to Canada had to be near the top of her all-time worst list.

"Nena!"

If that wasn't bad enough, two years later, she was poised to make history as her school's first openly gay Homecoming Queen. Instead, she'd lost to Natasha Volski by ten lousy votes. To think a place in history awaited her, only to see it fizzle—what a hard blow.

But compared to this week, those events ranked about as bad as getting stranded at the mall without a wallet.

Linzee didn't know who Edward Levens was, or why he hated her with such mystifying intensity. Her heart jolted whenever UNKNOWN showed up on her phone, or Levens_Ed appeared in her email inbox. She feared leaving her apartment and the suspense of not knowing his identity was nearly killing her.

Yesterday, Nena replied to one of Eddie's emails, telling him to leave Linzee alone or she would call the police. But Eddie flaunted his anonymity, just like the movie villain who hid behind his website, cybercasting his murders for all to see, mocking the FBI for their inability to find him.

"They won't find me," Eddie boasted. "And neither will

you."

None of her college friends remembered anyone by the name of Edward Levens. An internet search had turned up nothing.

It did no good to change her number. She'd already changed it twice. Somehow, he'd traced her phone number each time.

At Nena's suggestion, she had purchased a prepaid drugstore phone to use in case of emergency. This time, she told no one her new number, and Nena promised to check her old phone for messages. She opened a new email account, and only Nena accessed her old account, the one Eddie kept sending messages to, telling her she needed to kill herself.

Until today, he hadn't harmed her or anything of hers.

But, there sat her car. Someone had viciously slashed all four tires.

Only now did she realize that Eddie would, in fact, stoop to physical damage . . . or more. A chill ran down her spine as the reality engulfed her.

Chapter Eight

"**M**om, can you drive me to game night?" Richie stood in the studio door, the pleading expression he used on her virtually unchanged since his toddler days. "My car is making weird noises, and I shouldn't be driving it."

Meg, her paintbrush poised over the canvas, made sure Richie heard her irritated sigh. Lately, whenever she wanted to spend some quality time painting, something interrupted her.

She hoped to complete two more paintings by next weekend. Her booth at Saturday's Arts and Crafts show was reserved and paid for, but she wouldn't have a lot to show if she didn't spend a chunk of time this week in her studio. Her side business of selling her paintings wasn't exactly lucrative yet. In fact, she needed to sell at least two of her top-of-the-line pieces at each event just to break even.

"Do you think you could get a ride home?" She tossed the words at Richie as she looked down at Shadow, then back at her easel. A rudimentary outline of a crouching, playful Shadow, tail in mid-wag, smiled at her from the canvas.

"Maybe." Richie sounded doubtful. "I promised my friend Dustin I'd pick him up."

She hated leaving her painting unfinished while in the middle of inspiration. But it was important Richie participate in as many church activities as possible. She regretted her annoyed reaction.

They climbed into her Mustang and headed toward the boulevard. Despite the sponge-painted clouds overhead, heat waves poured down on them. She raised the convertible top and cranked the air conditioner.

Richie navigated her to a neighborhood of upscale stucco homes. "That one, Mom." She pulled over to the sidewalk, and Richie strode up the walk, returning with his friend.

Dustin, a soft-spoken Asian boy about the same age as Richie, gave off an air of utmost politeness. He climbed into the passenger seat and held out his hand. "Hi, I'm Dustin Z."

"Glad to meet you, Dustin. I'm Meg. What's the Z stand for?"

"It's my last name." He pulled the seatbelt around himself as the car rolled down the street. "It's Chinese, spelled X-I. Like the Roman numeral for eleven."

From the back seat, Richie chimed in. "Your parents should have named you Kevin."

Dustin shifted, eying Richie. "Why?"

"You'd be Kevin Eleven."

His hoots of laughter joined Meg's snickers. "You are too funny." When the hilarity subsided, she glanced at Dustin, whose smile had barely widened. "Are you doing anything fun this summer, Dustin?"

"Mostly working. I work at a coffee shop in Mill Valley."

She braked at a red light. "I visited a coffee shop in Mill Valley this morning called Latte Love Shack."

"That's it." His voice rose from soft to mild. "The place where I work."

"Small world." She chuckled. "It's my daughter's favorite hangout. How long have you been working there?"

"About a month."

"Do you know Linzee?" She gave a brief description as she accelerated through the intersection.

Dustin offered a small smile. "I know her."

Behind her, Richie scoffed. "My gay sister. Marrying a

girl. Yuck."

Dustin nodded, his face unreadable. "She's friends with another lady who works there named Drucie. She's gay, too."

Meg perked up at the name. "I met Drucie this morning. I thought she was nice."

As she pulled into the parking lot of Church on the Rock, it came to her why Drucie had looked familiar. "She and Linzee were friends in high school. But I don't think she had purple hair then."

Instead of replying, the boys unbuckled their seatbelts, clanging metal, and flung open the car doors like ten-year-olds on a sugar high.

"Thanks, Mom."

"Thank you, Ma'am."

She watched them join the throng flowing into the gymnasium. "Kevin Eleven. Holy cannoli." She leaned her head on the headrest. Laughter bubbled over and spilled out.

She stayed in the lot and shook with intermittent giggles, watching kids drift in and out of the building while her engine idled. Loud voices floated over the heat waves.

Call Linzee, came an inaudible, yet unmistakable, voice.

She jumped, her giggles forgotten. "Wh—what?"

Call Linzee.

"God, is that You?"

Call Linzee.

She shut off the engine and called Linzee.

Her daughter answered on the fourth ring. "Yeah, Mom?" The words rushed out of her.

"Is this a good time to talk?"

"Good as any, I guess."

"Any plans for tonight?"

"Not much. We're doing a movie night." A suspicious pause followed. "Uh, why?"

"We haven't talked for a while. Wondering what's new

with you."

Another tense pause vibrated in her ear. "I don't think you really want to know what's new, Mom."

"What do you mean?"

"I mean, I've had better days."

She sat up. "What made it so bad?"

"Promise you won't freak out?"

She tensed. Alarms went off in her head. "I won't freak out." At least, not outwardly.

"Thanks." Linzee's drawn-out hesitation made Meg wonder if she had changed her mind.

Finally, Linzee spoke. "This morning, I found all four of my car tires slashed."

"Oh, dear God." Her head hit the headrest, sending throbs of pain through her skull.

"Mom?" Linzee's decibel level surged. "You said you wouldn't freak."

"Sorry. But how could a mom not freak out over that?"

Linzee tsked. "Anyway, my insurance will pay for anything over five hundred dollars."

"That's a lot of money."

"Nena will help."

She kneaded the achy spot on the back of her skull. "Do you think it was related to the harassment?"

"We're assuming so."

"What's the guy's name again?"

"Um, Edward Levens. Why?"

"I take it you told the police about him?"

"Of course. And showed them his messages."

"Did you notice if any other cars were vandalized?"

"Nope. Just mine."

A rush of air exploded from Meg's lungs.

"It's pretty obvious I was targeted, Mom."

"Do you mind if I say a prayer for you?"

Linzee sighed. "Whatev."

She squeezed her eyes shut and closed her mind and

ears to the noise around her, concentrating only on God's presence. "Dear Lord, I pray you will cover Linzee with your powerful hand. I ask you will render harmless whoever is harassing her, Father." Linzee stayed silent on the other end.

"Father, please continue to keep her safe from all enemies, and help us find the culprit. In Christ's mighty name, amen."

"Amen," Linzee echoed.

The Lord's presence filled the car and her heart. "I love you, Linzee."

"Love you back. I need to go, Mom."

"Okay. Take care of yourself." She disconnected the call, started the engine and turned toward home. One of her knuckled fists gripped the wheel, the other punched the radio dial. Christian rock music blared, taking a bit of the edge off her anxiety.

Once home, she rushed to her studio where the unfinished portrait of Shadow waited. Snatching a brush, she jabbed at the paint, her sighs piercing the silence.

"Who do you think you are, Mr. Levens?" she muttered as she smeared paint on the canvas. "What did my daughter ever do to you?"

Shadow's shape and color emerged out of the strokes. She glanced affectionately at her sleeping dog, his soft snores whiffling through the room, then turned back to the easel, dabbing, smearing, and swiping.

As the image clarified, her breathing relaxed. Her strokes slowed. She set the brush down and stepped back, head tilted.

Gray and orange clouds roiled on the canvas. Shadow crouched, poised for attack. Her beloved German shepherd glared at her from the easel, his teeth bared in a snarl. His eyes glittered with yellow light.

Linzee's red-booted legs floated in the fog behind him.

She stared at the painting and shivered, then tottered,

robot-like, to her bedroom closet, where she found her white sweater and threw it around her shoulders. She returned to the easel and stared some more.

"Go get 'im, Shadow," she whispered. "Sic that Edward Levens." She knelt and patted the dog's head, wishing, for a moment, Shadow truly could chase away the dangers that threatened her daughter.

Chapter Nine

Meg rushed into the FOGY meeting five minutes late, trying to slow her breathing. She hated being late. Tension stretched her facial muscles, making a mockery of her attempt at nonchalance.

"Good to see you, Meg." Jon beamed his now-familiar smile.

Taking a seat next to Deb, she received her friend's welcoming hug. Deb whispered into her ear. "Are you okay? You look stressed out."

Meg forced a smile and shook her head. A deep need to confide her fears for Linzee was building up steam in her heart, but Jon had the floor so she merely replied, "I'm fine."

Jon, all business now, called them to order. "Looks like we're all here. I'll open with prayer."

After he finished with a fervent amen, she peeked around the circle of faces. Across from her sat an unfamiliar, fifty-something woman with a mass of hair rivaling Carrot Top's. The woman leaned forward, her blue eyes inquiring.

Jon gestured at the red-headed woman. "Camille, would you like to go first?"

The woman shrugged. "I had an okay week."

"Camille," Jon said, "why don't you give a quick background on your daughter since we have a couple of new people."

"Hi, new peeps." Camille moved her eyeglasses from the top of her head to her nose, amplifying her sharp eyes. "Anyhoo, my daughter is gay and wants to marry her girlfriend." Camille paused for the empathetic murmurs. "I have to be honest. At first, I couldn't stand the woman. I thought she was foul-mouthed and obnoxious, and I didn't see how Hilary could stand to be with her." Meg had to admire Camille's brutal honesty.

"This group has been helpful, 'cause otherwise, I wouldn't have had a clue how to be Jesus to that bag."

Meg stifled a giggle, and Camille regarded her with a glint in her eye.

"But there's more." Camille flung one leg over the other at a forty-five degree angle. "For my barbecue on July Fourth, I planned to invite Hilary, but not her partner. Then I thought, that's not what Jesus would do. That's what Camille would do. Jesus would invite them both. So I did." The applause from the others brought a shy, pleased look to her face.

"Then I had to deal with their PDA. They were holding hands and snuggling, so I pulled Hilary aside and asked if they would please save the PDA until they got home. She rolled her eyes at me, and I said, 'Hot Patootie, girl, it's simply common courtesy to keep that stuff private.'" Camille waited for the chuckles to subside. "She said, 'Mom, you wouldn't say that if I was with a man,' and I said, 'Yeah, I would.' But it ended well. Hilary gave me a hug when they left."

Camille came up for air, heaving a deep breath.

"I also found out Carmen, her partner, isn't so bad. I invited them for Sunday dinner yesterday and got a chance to get to know her a little better. She even made me laugh a couple of times. It's like God was telling me Carmen's not my enemy. Hilary would still be gay, even without Carmen in the picture. So thank you all for your prayers and encouragement. Maybe there's hope for me yet." Applause rang out again, and Meg gave her a thumbs-up across the circle.

Nena's not my enemy.

"Anyone else want to share?" Jon said, eying Meg.

"How about you, Meg? Anything new with your daughter?"

She hesitated, her need to confide wrestling with her fear of saying too much.

Deb reached over and squeezed her hand. "Nothing you say is going to leave this room."

Reassured, she gripped her knees and plunged in. "Thank you. It's been a rough week. Linzee is being harassed by some homophobe. Then on Saturday, she found her tires slashed."

At the exclamations of dismay all around, combined with the memories of the tense months between her and Linzee, her throat tightened, and she clamped down on a sob. Someone murmured soothing words in her ears. She swallowed hard. "Sorry about that. Anyway, she and Nena assume her harasser did the despicable deed. The police interviewed people in their apartment complex, but nobody saw anything."

"I'm sorry, sweetie," said Trish. "We will pray for you both."

"About that word homophobe—" The words tumbled from her mouth. "I wish the term could be outlawed. It implies that if we disapprove of homosexuality, we see it as a threat."

"I hate it too." Camille gave a vigorous nod. "You know what else grinds my gears? Hilary's high school counselor told her if someone thinks her being gay is repulsive, it probably means the person struggles with same-sex attraction themselves."

Several heads nodded. Camille pantomimed as she talked. "Next time I saw the woman, I put my hand on her shoulder and said, 'You may not know this about me, but I think roadkill is gross. Do you think that means deep down I really want to take that dead animal home and stick it on the barbecue?'"

Giggles and snorts resounded. "You tell 'em!" someone shouted.

"Thanks for the laugh, Camille." Jon, still chuckling, moved along the circle. "Mike? Do you have anything to share?"

Mike shook his head. "I just want to listen tonight."

Sharing time continued for another half an hour, the prayer time as heartfelt and desperate as last week's. John closed with his standard speech. "Remember what is shared in the group stays in the group."

Meg shifted, about to make a beeline for the refreshment table, when Jon's voice stopped her. "Before you go, I have a couple of announcements."

She settled back into her chair.

"Don't forget the potluck at Dean and Esther's on Saturday." He nodded toward Dean. "Then on Sunday morning the gay-rights group SMERFA will be picketing Haight Street church. I thought we could get a group together and do some picketing ourselves."

Jon had their undivided attention. "Who's with me?"

Meg raised her hand, along with Mike and Camille.

"What's SMERFA stand for?" someone asked.

"Sex and Marriage: Equal Rights For All," said Jon. "Let's meet here eight a.m. to carpool."

Afterward, Meg, clutching a potluck flyer, found herself alongside Camille and Mike at the refreshment table. Camille laid a hand on her shoulder. "Girl, I feel for you."

The words brought a lump to her throat, and blocked her reply. Camille peppered her with speculations about Linzee's slashed-tire episode. She nodded along, more than willing to let someone else do the talking.

Mike cleared his throat. "Has she tried to trace the number?"

"Yes, but the number isn't traceable. She's changed her number twice, but that didn't stop him."

Mike set his plate on a nearby chair. "I might be able to help trace it. I work in IT." He fumbled in his shirt pocket and removed a business card. "Here. Text or email me when you have some free time, and I'll see what I can do."

***

Meg lay on her bed and texted her daughter. *Linzee, I know someone who might be able to help you trace Eddie. Mind if I enlist his assistance?*

She half expected Linzee to retort, "Why are you all up in my business?" Instead, she replied, *Maybe. Tell me more.*

Next, she texted Mike, who suggested they meet at the mall across from his office the following evening. Linzee agreed to the plan, then concluded with, *Just fyi that Nena will be with me.*

Meg nibbled her fingers.

Nena's not my enemy. Not my enemy.

How would Jesus handle someone like Nena? Jesus had never dealt with same-sex issues.

The answer, when it came, wasn't accompanied by flashing lights or sirens, but with a tiny flame of certainty in the depths of her heart.

Neither do I condemn you. Go and sin no more.

She suspected Linzee and Nena would be receptive to the first part of the message, but not the second.

Neither do I condemn you.

She could live with that. She sent her reply. *OK. Love you, baby girl.*

An old term of endearment she hadn't used for years.

***

Linzee's gaze remained glued to her smartphone. "Please, Eddie. Please text me."

The irony of her daughter's plea nearly made Meg laugh. She and Mike, Linzee, and Nena had gathered around a table in the mall's center court. An untouched basket of fries lay next to Mike's open laptop, the tracking software loaded. They had exactly one hour to get this done. As long as Eddie texted Linzee within Mike's dinner hour, the program would do its thing.

Nena snorted. "Never thought I'd hear you say that."

The girls' appetites clearly hadn't suffered from nerves. They'd gobbled down a small mountain of chicken strips and had nearly finished off their twenty-ounce smoothies.

Meg hoped God didn't mind she was taking pains to ignore Nena. The woman still rubbed her the wrong way, and, judging by the animosity in Nena's eyes, the feeling was mutual. If God wanted her to put up with Nena, He needed to change her heart. Both of their hearts.

Linzee sighed, a deep, pent-up sound that echoed in Meg's heart. "What'll we do if he doesn't? I have better things to do than sit in front of my phone for an hour."

"Baby Girl, I've been praying all day that we'd get some answers tonight." Meg's workday had dragged as she launched arrow prayers to God. Hope would bloom, giving way to doubt, then hope again, round and round, like a couple of boxers circling the ring.

Linzee rolled her eyes. "Well, in that case, tell God to make Eddie text me in the next five minutes."

Meg didn't miss the edge of sarcasm. Instead of replying, she reached across her daughter's shoulders and squeezed, then concentrated on finishing her berry-topped frozen yogurt, the only food her dry mouth could handle right now. "That's some pretty sophisticated software, Mike."

He nodded. "I used to work for the county sheriff and still have access to some of their resources."

Mike admitted the usual means of tracing a number wouldn't work in this case. "Most likely, he's using a disposable phone which he paid cash for."

"So, now what?" She peered at Linzee's phone, their only connection to her unseen adversary.

"The program can narrow down the location of the sending phone when her phone receives an incoming message."

Linzee's taut face relaxed a few degrees. "How does it

work?"

"I enter your number. When a text comes in, we'll be able to tell where the sender's approximate location is."

"I suppose he could be in China, for all we know." Meg shivered, feeling like she'd landed in a CSI episode.

Nena thumbed back over Linzee's incoming texts for the day. "Eddie sent two texts so far," she announced. "But I ain't repeating 'em."

Nor did Meg want to hear them. As they waited, the echoing voices and noises of the food court coalesced into a single roar, filling her head like an ocean.

By six forty-five, all the food had been consumed. Linzee's phone hadn't received a single text, except for the test message Meg had sent. The software noted the location of the sender as San Rafael. "Good, it's working," Mike said.

He tapped his fingers on the table and checked his watch. "We're just about out of time."

The phone dinged. Meg jumped. Four heads almost collided above the hot-pink phone.

Eddie.

Mike squinted at the laptop screen. "Mill Valley, California."

They exhaled nearly in unison. "Can you tell where in Mill Valley?" Linzee's voice trembled. "Like, could he be in my apartment complex?"

Mike moved the laptop so she could see the map laid out on the screen. "Show me where your building is."

Linzee's finger made circles above the screen, then zoomed in. "There."

He cleared his throat. "That building is within the parameters. But this tower covers about a five-mile radius." He moved his finger around the map.

Meg moved closer. "Linzee, where do you spend most of your time?"

"Latte Love Shack, Long's Drugs, Whole Foods. The library." Linzee pointed to the four spots as she spoke, all of which fell within the five-mile radius. Her face sagged. "He could be anywhere."

Mike peered at the screen. "What about your work? Where's it located?"

"Both of my jobs are in Larkspur. I work at a daycare two days a week, and an urgent care clinic on weekends."

"Find out if any of your coworkers live in Mill Valley." Mike logged off and closed his laptop. "I need to get back to work now. If there's anything more I can do, please holler."

Meg laid her hand on his arm. "Thank you, Mike."

Linzee nodded. "Yeah, thanks."

"Not a problem." He turned and hurried toward the exit. Linzee made a face and flung her Nike-clad foot at a chair leg. Meg gathered Linzee close, breathing in her daughter's sweet jasmine scent, and caught Nena's eye. To her surprise, an unexpected feeling stole over her—a surge of empathy for the young woman whose distraught face no doubt mirrored her own.

Chapter Ten

Meg, praying for the new day ahead, had barely started her engine when her chiming phone interrupted her communion with the Lord. A text from Mike flashed on her screen.

Meg – Mike Bachman here. I thought of something else that might help track down Cyber Bully. Call me before 1 pm or between 6 & 7 pm.

Her heart leaped, wondering what new trick Mike had up his sleeve. She would call him on her morning break. Mike Bachman, she typed, adding his name to her contacts. Such an ordinary name for a man of extraordinary brains. Mr. Michael Q. Bachman. The renowned Dr. M. Spockman, University of CyberSpace.

With a renewed sense of purpose, she backed out of her driveway, her hopes as high as the Golden Gate spires.

***

"Dude, what up with you?" Drucie's steely gaze drilled into Linzee. "You look like somebody died."

"Can you sit down?" Linzee patted the chair beside her.

"Nope, not 'til my shift ends," she rasped. "Be back here at two."

At the appointed time Linzee parked herself at a table near the patio. Drucie slipped her green work apron over her head and leaned against the counter, deep in discussion with Dustin, the barista reporting for duty. Noticing Dustin's gaze on her, Linzee blinked, wondering if they were talking about her. His mouth curved in a thin smile, and she quickly looked away.

Outside on the patio, Drucie plopped her elbows on the table. Under the afternoon sun, the tats on her arms and hands stood out against her white skin. "My dude. Who died?"

"Nobody." Linzee leaned forward, her hands clasped beneath her chin. "Somebody's been sending me hate messages, and then my tires were slashed last weekend."

"Whoa. What kind of hate messages?"

"Telling me to kill myself kind of hate messages."

"Dude." Drucie bolted upright.

"Which is why I look like somebody died. Somebody obviously wants *me* dead."

"That sucks." Drucie's trendy black shades mirrored Linzee's white face. "Any clue who it is?"

"He goes by Edward Levens, but we think it's a fake name. We know he's local."

"How do you know he's local?" Drucie squirmed around on the bench as she grasped one foot then the other, bringing them together in the lotus position.

Linzee recapped the events of the previous evening. "The tracing software showed he was here in Mill Valley. He could even live in my apartment complex." She tugged one side of her hair, tilting her head to the right. "I changed my number twice, and the guy was still able to track me. But I can't figure out how. Can you think of anything?"

"Don't ask me. I'm a technological ignoramus." Drucie gave up on the lotus position and extended one leg in the heron pose. "Can I see the phone?"

"Why? I don't use it anymore. Only a little disposable one for emergencies."

"I just want to see what kind of dude would do that. Do you mind?"

"Well, okay. It's out in my car. We can go out there if you want."

In her car, now sporting four brand-new tires, she dug through the glove box for the smartphone. "Be warned, he's a mega-homophobe. An uber-homophobe. Mr. Homophobe Universe."

Drucie, scrolling through the messages, puckered her face. "Is your girlfriend getting these too?"

"Not so far."

From the nearby boulevard, a car honked. Drucie held up the phone. "Do you want my take on it?"

"Of course."

"It sounds like bad karma to me. Do you know anyone who has a grudge against you?"

Linzee's jaw dropped as long-ago memories surfaced. In Drucie's high school world, life boiled down to two things: "good karma" and "bad karma".

"I don't think so." She white-knuckled the steering wheel. "I've always tried to be a kind, good person. I was raised to follow the golden rule. If I did something to hurt this Eddie person, I wish he'd tell me so I could apologize."

"Doesn't sound like he's looking for an apology."

"But I would never intentionally hurt anyone."

Instead of replying, Drucie kept scrolling. Linzee leaned her forehead against the steering wheel and gazed at her knees.

"Wowza." Drucie handed back the phone, her voice like fingers scraping on a blackboard. "That's some hard-core stuff. If you ever need to talk, you know where to find me."

Linzee tried for a grin. "Thanks."

"No problemo." Drucie yanked the door handle. "Take care of yourself."

As her friend strode away, Linzee sighed, heavy with the knowledge that somewhere along the road of life, she had made a dangerous enemy.

She couldn't think of any hurtful deed she'd committed. Nor to whom. As she sat contemplating, her mind swept back over the twenty-three years of her life.

Then it dawned on her. At least two guys might have reason to harbor a grudge against her.

In eighth grade, the year she realized she didn't like boys the way other girls did, she had a run-in with Alex, the class bully. Linzee and most of her middle school classmates hated Alex. He loved to taunt anyone and everyone. To say he had a chip on his shoulder didn't come close to describing his high-decibel hostility.

She remembered the day when Ms. Pearce asked Alex to come to the front and point out Scandinavia on the map. Alex refused, and she heard herself blurt, "I'll bet it's because he doesn't know where Scandinavia is." She watched Alex's surprised face turn red with fury. "I'll bet you don't even know how to spell Scandinavia, do you, Alex?" The entire class roared, but she found, to her horror, it only made Alex turn on her. He had badgered her for a week.

But after Alex taunted a mentally-challenged classmate, she decided it was time to teach that gangster a lesson. She and her friend Briana, built like a female sumo wrestler, ambushed him after school and left him lying on the dirt in a screaming heap. But he never told anyone who had beaten him up. She thought she understood why. To an eighth grade boy, getting beat up by a couple of girls was humiliating enough. Everyone knowing about it would be the end of world.

She and Briana decided to keep it quiet. If Alex ever acted up again, the threat of exposure would be their ace in the hole.

Afterward, each time she caught sight of him, he glared at her with caged ferocity. The bullying declined but didn't stop. And he never committed any more dirty deeds in her presence.

Alex had reason to wish her dead. Could he be her tormenter? But he had dropped out of high school and had been off her radar for years.

But then there was Blake, her classmate at UCLA. He surely had cause to wish her harm. She let her mind drift back two years into the past, to her junior year at college. She recalled a dark spring night and the momentous events that rocked the campus as if an earthquake had swept through it.

***

A muffled scream made Linzee lurch to a stop and nearly trip over her feet. She grabbed Nena's arm and pulled her to a stop. "Ssshh. Did you hear that?" Darkness hung over everything like an opaque veil. She wasn't sure which direction the scream came from.

She hoped the rapist hadn't struck again. In the past two weeks, four female students had been assaulted on or near campus. Since the attacks happened after dark and the perp always wore a ski mask, none of the women had been able to identify him. No one knew if he was affiliated with the university, or if he lived in the community. Campus security, newspapers, and social media were all on high alert.

The perp followed the same modus operandi each time. After an intense struggle, he would overpower the woman, then tie her hands behind her back. Each of the women claimed he seemed to enjoy prolonging the process as if her terror were gasoline on the fire of his gratification.

This confirmed beyond a doubt Linzee's belief that most men were slimy creepers.

She and Nena had been studying with friends and were returning to their apartment—a pair of blissful fools strolling through a dangerous stretch of town as if it were Disneyland. Creeping closer to a nearby deserted building, she and Nena peered around the corner. Somewhere, a light bulb cast a faint beam, and they could make out shadows undulating behind a row of Dumpsters.

They tiptoed toward the movement and heard another strangled cry, as though someone had a hand clamped over her mouth.

"Got your flashlight ready?" Nena whispered. Linzee clutched the smartphone inside her pocket, prepared to activate the flashlight.

They listened without breathing for several seconds on the off chance they had heard an amorous couple back there. Linzee couldn't imagine who might want to get passionate amidst an array of corroded garbage receptacles, but this was LA. Nothing was out of the question.

As the whimpers and curses grew louder, Nena mouthed, "You call campus security. I'll grab him."

"Wait for me, then we'll get him together."

Linzee moved away to make a whispered call, then returned to the Dumpsters, blinking until her eyes adjusted to the dark. Then, with a nod at Nena, they charged at the shadows and pounced. Together, they grabbed fistfuls of fabric attached to someone's body and yanked.

A startled bellow sliced through the night. The lanky attacker, thrown off-balance, flailed his arms. Nena threw a karate kick at his kneecap, and one at his groin. He bellowed louder amid a flurry of flying limbs, curses, and grunts.

They slammed the perp face-first against the wood fence with all their weight, and Linzee anchored herself between Nena and the Dumpster, pinning him against the fence.

The victim's silhouette made a dim outline on the ground, and her gasping sobs undulated like a frightened child's. "Why don't you wait over there?" Linzee said. The woman rolled over, eased to her feet, and limped to a wall. The perp struggled and shouted four-letter words while they waited for police to arrive.

"Shut up." Nena hissed at him. "You're not going anywhere, scumbag."

Two uniformed officers ran around the corner, guns drawn. "Over here," she called.

One cop grabbed the perp's arms, the other handcuffed him, frisked him for weapons, and pulled off his stocking cap.

Linzee shone her flashlight into the rapist's face, then cursed. "Blake Mannson?"

***

Glowing sunbeams beat down onto Latte Love Shack's gravel parking lot and into Linzee's car. The incident had shocked the university. Blake Mannson, a casual friend of hers, had been a fellow Community Health major. He and Linzee worked together on team projects, sipped coffee together. The epitome of a non-descript, all-American guy, he'd shown no hint of a dark side. But instead of graduating, Blake was convicted of rape, added to the state register of sex offenders, and sent to prison.

Blake had every reason to seek revenge. But, if Blake was her tormenter, why wouldn't he target Nena as well?

With sudden resolve, she started her engine and sprayed gravel while exiting the parking lot, anxious to get home and Google Blake Mannson.

Chapter Eleven

Clacking computer keys from the next cubicle mingled with hushed, professional phone voices of the buying team. Meg released her computer mouse and glanced once again at the clock.

"What?" Julie said. "You keep sighing."

With a jerk, she forced her thoughts away from her upcoming phone call to Mike and back to the pricey Stella McCartney sheath dresses scrolling across her screen. "Francine has only ten Stellas left. They're selling like hotcakes. Her shipment, which was supposed to absolutely, positively be here yesterday, won't leave the dock until three today."

"Those rich housewives will just run over to Sak's for their Stellas."

"That's the problem. Sylvana will be furious if we lose any more business to Sak's." And if Meg couldn't find a way to resolve this crisis, at least two eager candidates waited in the wings to replace her as Lead Buyer.

With one eye on the clock, Meg made another phone call to the shipper, doing her best to comply with her boss's instructions to "light a fire under them." Not something that came naturally to her, but something she had to do to keep her job.

After extracting a promise from the shipper to overnight the goods, she hustled to the lunch room and pulled up Mike's number. He answered on the second ring.

"Hi Mike, it's Meg. I'm calling about your text from yesterday."

"Right." His breathing filled the silence. "I was thinking of some ways we could track our friend Eddie. I have a password breaker program, and we might be able to hack into his Facebook profile or his email account for identifying information."

"You're so awesome." Hope brightened her spirits. "What do I need to do?"

"Meet me at the mall again tonight, same time. Tell your daughter to bring her laptop and phone."

As she ended the call, raised voices floated into the room. "I think they deserve life in prison." Francine and Rhonda, Manager and Assistant Manager of the Women's Apparel Department, marched in, wearing identical expressions of scorn.

"Who deserves life in prison?" Meg asked.

Francine pulled out a chair. "Those idiot bullies in Oakland. The judge found them not guilty today."

She felt her heart rate accelerate, knowing a heated discussion would ensue. "Their lives are already ruined."

"Good," said Rhonda. "They brought it on themselves."

"How so?"

Rhonda's nostrils flared. "They pushed that poor guy to suicide."

"They claimed to be innocent."

"Of course, they did."

She sat on her hands to still their trembling. "Don't you think it's better to let a guilty person off the hook than to ruin an innocent person?"

Francine dropped her elbows to the table, sending vibrations through Meg's clenched teeth. "Innocent?" The word seemed to hiss from Francine's narrowed eyes. "Why would the kid have ID'd them if they were innocent?"

Sylvana chose that moment to swish into the room and eye them curiously. Meg gave her a smile and lowered her voice while Sylvana occupied herself at the soda machine.

She mustered a calm tone. "Even if they did harass him,

or call him names, they did not kill the kid. They didn't force him to do anything. It was *his* choice. A terribly tragic one."

Francine and Rhonda stared at her for a moment. "You're such a bleeding heart, Meg," said Francine.

"Why do you always give the benefit of the doubt to bad guys, Meg?" said Rhonda.

"Don't you have a gay daughter?" Francine added, her tone low and strident. "What if it were her that got bullied and driven to suicide? Bet you wouldn't be so sympathetic then, would you?"

Meg shot to her feet, face flaming. She knew she shouldn't have confided in Julie. "Why do you always judge before knowing all the facts, Francine? What if it were your son or daughter accused of driving someone to suicide?" She planted her feet and glared at her co-workers. "Because of people like you, there's too much judgment in this world and not enough grace."

She hurried out the door and down the hall, refusing to look anyone in the eye. Once she reached the ladies' room, she allowed the tears to run free.

Anchored against the countertop, her breathing slowed as she examined her dampened eyes and the dark brown smudges pooled underneath.

She had been so quick to jump to the alleged bullies' defense, and not the suicidal kid's. What was her gut trying to tell her?

Pictures from TV newscasts pummeled her mind. The two young men with their stunned faces. Their baffled stutters when asked why they'd bullied the victim. The "homophobe" label slapped on them.

The taller one and his uncanny resemblance to Richie.

She grabbed the thread of thought and held it under a mental microscope until a memory emerged. A memory of Richie spewing "Gross!" when Linzee announced her engagement to Nena. His mocking laughter and contemptuous sneer.

Her mind continued to travel to an inescapable conclusion. Yet, she couldn't fathom her own son could be capable of Eddie's vicious behavior.

She blinked away the wetness in her eyes. The restroom door opened, and in walked Francine and Rhonda. Ignoring them, she hurried out, wondering if she was heading for a meltdown.

She jumped when her desk phone rang. *Sylvana Marcelli*, read the display.

"Meg, may I see you a moment?"

Approaching Sylvana's office, she hesitated, fearing her outspokenness in the break room had offended her boss. Sylvana's bland expression revealed nothing as she motioned Meg inside, where she sat, studying a desert painting on the opposite wall while her heart did flips.

Sylvana, still model-thin at fifty, gazed at Meg from an impeccable face. "I just want you to know that what you said in the break room was admirable." She plucked a piece of lint off her blouse with a crimson lacquered fingernail. "I agree that there's too much judgment in the world and not enough grace."

Meg felt her face relax into a smile. "Thank you, Sylvana. You've made my day."

***

The State of California's sex offender database proved easy enough for a two-year-old with one eye closed to use. Not that a two-year-old should ever need to use it.

"Blake Mannson, where are you?" Linzee singsonged. Within seconds, the screen noted Blake's current location as El Sobrante, California. His status: on parole. His release date: May, a mere two months ago.

Linzee, fairly certain El Sobrante was somewhere nearby, pulled up a map of California. She found the town on the other side of the bay, just a short drive from the Richmond-San Rafael Bridge.

Blake could reach the bridge in a few minutes, drive across the bay, and be at her doorstep in no time.

She shivered and tugged her hair, wondering if the rippling anxiety would ever subside. If Blake *was* the tire-slasher, how had he found her? The UCLA Alumni database? With unsteady hands, she pulled up the website. It listed her current address as Westwood, a few blocks from UCLA. She shook her head, frustrated at yet another dead end.

Next, she opened Facebook and typed Blake's name into the search box. Several profiles popped up. She checked each one, but most of them were set to private. A Blake Mannson on the east coast appeared to be about forty — obviously not her old friend. The last one she looked at also had private settings, but she sucked in a breath when she saw the photo — a UCLA Bruin.

She heard the front door open and noticed it was already three o'clock. Nena, home from work, walked through the door.

"*Hola.*" Nena dropped her bag on the bed. "What's up?" She peered over Linzee's shoulder. "Why are you lookin' at Blake Mannson's profile?"

"I think he might be Eddie."

"Blake? Eddie? How come?"

"I talked to Drucie today. She — "

"Y'mean Drucie, the weirdo?" Nena's tone sharpened, and she let out a harsh chuckle. "Even her name's weird."

Linzee snickered. "Her mother named her after an old seventies song. Drucilla Penelope Ward."

"She always be like, Dude this, and Dude that."

Linzee nodded, squelching a smile. "Yeah, I know. In high school, she was always Karma this, and Karma that. She's a little weird, but she's still good people." Her smile faded. "Like I was saying, today I told her about Eddie. I showed her his texts, and you know what she said? She thought it might be someone who has a grudge against me.

After I thought about it, I go, hey, what about Blake Mannson?"

After Linzee filled her in on what she'd discovered, Nena made an O with her mouth. "Y'mean, Drucie doesn't think Eddie hates you 'cause he's a homophobe?" She sounded almost dismayed.

"Exactly. I've been assuming the messages were homophobic."

"Well, snap." Nena borrowed Linzee's favorite expression. "We gotta tell that cop who has your case we got ourselves a suspect."

"For sure, love." Linzee looked around the room. "But before I forget, could you check my phone for messages?"

Nena retrieved the phone from Linzee's bag. "You got one from your mom. 'Linzee, I hope you're still looking at your messages. Can you meet Mike and me at the mall again tonight? Bring your phone and laptop. He has some more tricks up his sleeve.'"

"Tell her we'll be there."

Chapter Twelve

Meg crossed her fingers as Mike's computer screen booted up. He maneuvered the laptop closer to Linzee and Nena. "Technically, what I'm about to do is illegal."

She glanced around the secluded corner of the mall, hoping nobody had overheard. But the nearest person sat across a space the width of a basketball court, next to the theater, his nose buried in his tablet.

Nena didn't once look her way, which was fine by Meg. They seemed to have reached an uneasy truce, an unspoken agreement, and that was good enough for now.

Linzee, who no longer looked like she hadn't slept for days, had updated Meg on Blake Mannson. Relieved, Meg latched onto the revelation. If Blake were indeed the culprit, she could abandon her silly fears over Richie.

Mike sat still as a stone. "Before I go any further," he looked her in the eye, "I need your word that if we get an ID tonight on our friend, the Dastardly Mr. Levens, you won't involve me if you go to the police."

Linzee snorted. "He's a dastard, all right."

Meg spurted with laughter, wondering if *dastard* was a real word. "I didn't realize the risk you're taking, Mike. We won't give you away."

Mike gave a little shrug. "If my daughter were in a bind, I would want someone to risk their hide to help her."

Nena puckered her mouth. "How come you got an illegal program?"

Mike's lips twitched. "I can use it legitimately when I do contract work. Clients have a way of forgetting passwords.

Happens more often than you would think."

He set to work loading the password breaker. "Just a side note. Normally, it takes less than a minute for this to work, unless the password includes a symbol. Then it's nearly impossible. So let's hope our man used an easy one."

First, Mike had Linzee open up an email from Eddie. "I need to find the IP address for his computer. Then I can hack into it hopefully, break the password, and dig around for anything useful. Like name or address."

Meg tapped her foot, never lifting her eyes from the screen as Mike opened a browser and attempted to log on to Eddie's account. "LevensEd," he muttered as he typed. "Bingo."

She leaned closer.

"The password is L-I-N-Z-E-E."

"Eeew, I am *creeped out.*" Linzee clutched her middle as if she were gagging. Meg stared at the screen, distaste curdling her stomach. Nena looked slightly sick.

Mike drilled down into the account until he found the account holder name and service address. Linzee and Nena's faces lit up, their mouths gaping.

"He's got Edward Levens as the name. The address is on Grand Avenue in downtown San Rafael." Mike opened a new tab and loaded a map site.

"San Rafael?" Linzee sounded disappointed. "I was hoping it would say El Sobrante."

A map of San Rafael was laid out on the screen. "The address on Grand is a FedEx office." Mike drummed his fingers. "Smart guy. He knows how to cover his tracks."

In her mind's eye, Meg pictured a black-clad, hooded young man slink into the downtown FedEx store with a skateboard in his hand. "Do you think he works there?"

"Not likely. He probably walked in off the street and used one of the public computers."

"Is there a way we could get an ID from FedEx?"

"Probably not unless you get a subpoena, and then they

might be able to release video footage if the time and day could be nailed down."

She nibbled her fingers. "We can get the time and day off the email, but what are the chances we could get a subpoena?"

"Not good, unless you can prove a crime was committed."

Linzee stood with hands on hips. "Okay, so we're looking for someone who's clever and devious. Can we look at his emails?"

Mike clicked on the inbox. Nothing but spam, roughly twenty altogether. "Looks like he only uses this account to harass you."

"What's in the sent box?"

About ten sent emails, all to Linzee, including one from earlier that day.

Linzee wrinkled her nose. "I don't even want to know what it says."

"This ain't tellin' us nothin' except he's obsessed."

"He's a sicko." Linzee grabbed her midsection as if she were about to hurl. "A mutation. A degeneration."

"Still could be Blake, y'know."

"Who's Blake?" Mike asked.

Linzee brought Mike up to date, then guided him to Blake's Facebook page. Mike tried various combinations for the logon name, hitting pay dirt after several attempts.

Within seconds, he chuckled. "Holy spit. That was too easy. The password isn't LINZEE this time. It's B-R-U-I-N-S."

Linzee and Nena chortled. Blake had used the UCLA mascot as his password.

Meg leaned in further. "Do you see anything in there that looks suspicious?"

They looked around Blake's profile for several minutes. It appeared to be a seldom-used account. Photos of Blake's days at UCLA dominated his wall. Linzee exclaimed each time she recognized a name in his friends list.

"Can we look at his messages?"

Mike opened Blake's message box. They read each one from the last couple of months—messages regarding his job search, his nosy neighbors, his judgmental parents, and his parole officer. Remorse at having lost two years of his life. But none expressing vengeance toward Linzee.

"Snap." Linzee snapped her fingers. "Another dead end. Can we look for the Edward Levens profile while we're here?"

"I want to go back to Eddie's email account." Mike tapped the screen. "One of the emails in the inbox rang a bell. We can come back to this."

He clicked on the email account tab and pointed to one of the early emails. "Linzee, did you ever get a text from Anonymous at this website?"

"Yeah, a couple, but not recently."

"He opened an anonymous texting account. That site tracks IP addresses on its account holders. The site administrators use them to track exactly this type of situation. If someone is using this site to bully, the originating computer can be traced."

Linzee and Nena exchanged toothy smiles, and Mike found the anonymous texting website. The silence pulsed with hope. They heard nothing but Mike's congested breathing and the percussion of computer keys clacking out a rhythm.

"I'm going to take a wild guess and say his username is his email, password Linzee."

The IP address popped up in red. Linzee sucked in a breath.

Mike clicked on an icon which took him to a remote desktop. Three sets of eyes watched, unblinking, as he keyed in the IP address.

A new screen flashed up, superimposed over the old. WELCOME TO MARIN COUNTY LIBRARY.

"The library?" Nena croaked.

Linzee stomped her foot. "He's just too smart."

Nena scowled at the laptop. "Don't that beat all."

Linzee sighed, a deep, discouraged sigh that resonated in Meg's spirit. "Can we look at the Edward Scissorhands Facebook page now?" She opened her Facebook message box, scrolling back over the past couple of weeks.

"I know it should be right in here." Linzee's nose nearly touched the screen. "Nena, what day was it when we saw the Edward Scissorhands profile?"

"I don't remember. Couple of weeks ago, maybe?"

"I'm not finding it." Linzee made a face along with a little whimper. "Does it mean he deleted the profile, Mike?"

"That's my educated guess." His jaw sagged. "I have to admit, I'm not used to so many dead ends. When I worked with the sheriff's office, my specialty was using technology to outsmart bad guys." A shadow crossed his face. "But if I think of anything else, I'll let you know."

He closed his laptop and packed up. Disappointed, Meg embraced Linzee and held her tightly for several seconds. When she released her, she searched her daughter's downcast face. Linzee puckered her mouth, the way she did as a little girl when she was holding back tears. "Thanks for trying, Mom."

"I'm praying for you, Linz." Meg patted her shoulder. "God's watching your back."

"Okay, Mom. I know you mean well and all that."

Linzee and Nena departed into the main section of the mall, and Meg stared after them, reluctant to give up so easily. She didn't want to accept that Mike's magic hat may have run out of rabbits.

"I can't believe this, Mike." She stared into the depths of the shopping center. "There's got to be a way to find this guy. He's terrorizing my daughter."

"He can't be found if he doesn't want to be found." Mike stood. "Technology can be a useful tool, but dangerous

75

too. Smart bad guys can use it to hide if they know what they're doing. And this guy does."

"But—"

"You have to wait for him to slip up. Eventually, he will. Even the smart ones do. In law enforcement, cops know perps eventually get cocky and careless, and that's when they nab them."

"I really appreciate what you're doing."

"Not a problem." Tiny lines deepened around his eyes. "Like I said, I'd want someone to do the same for my daughter if I were in your shoes." He slid his laptop case off the table. "Are you going to the Woods' potluck Saturday?"

Meg, baffled, tilted her head. "The Woods?"

"Yeah, Dean and Esther Woods from Monday group."

"Oh. Right." She nodded. "This Saturday I'm showing my paintings at the Arts and Crafts show in Tiburon. I'll be there until six, but I might drop by afterward."

"I was going to offer to pick you up if you were going. I have the day off."

"Oh."

"But we could do lunch on Sunday, after the Haight Church event."

She lifted her lips in a polite smile. "Sorry, I'll be going to my dad's birthday party."

Mike's eyes narrowed slightly—his rendering of a smile—then the impassive face he usually wore slipped back into place. "Some other time then. Can I walk you to your car?"

***

Linzee sniffed back tears and found Nena's hand. "Okay, who's the alien that's taken over my mother's body?" The feel of Mom's embrace still remained on her skin, like a blanket fresh out of the dryer. Mom's eyes, lit with love, no longer dark with condemnation, lingered in her mind.

Nena snorted. "Maybe she finally decided to be cool about you and me."

"I doubt that." She shrugged. "It's a conundrum. Anyway, what did you think of what went down back there?"

"I think Blake ain't gonna put anything incriminating on his Facebook page. That is if he's smart."

Linzee glanced over at the food court, suddenly hungry. "I don't remember him being uber-bright. I don't think he was super knowledgeable about technology either. In a way, he doesn't fit the profile."

"Unless he's in cahoots with someone."

They looked at each other, open-mouthed. They hadn't yet considered that possibility.

***

The whoops of alpha males in competition greeted Meg at home. Peeking into the family room, she saw Richie, Dustin, and Jake yelling at the big-screen TV, game controllers in hand. Two high school girls, skinny to the point of frail, sat on the floral futon and cheered. She recognized one of them as Kassidy, Richie's new girlfriend.

"You guys want anything?"

"No, we're good." Richie lunged at the screen. "Mmmmph. Noooo."

Jake cackled. Kassidy groaned.

Meg folded her arms and watched her son indulge in good, clean fun. There was nothing in the least Eddie-like in his behavior. His two friends were nice young men from decent families. Dustin and his family had been attending Church on the Rock for a few months, and last Sunday she'd chatted with Mr. and Mrs. Xi for the first time.

Jake and Richie had been good friends ever since Jake's family moved next door three years ago. Although weren't Christians, their level of kind regard for their neighbors could put some Christians to shame. Jake tagged along with Richie to youth group, and she hoped that, sooner or later, he would come to know the Lord.

Unfolding her arms, she made a beeline for the Jacuzzi, consumed with an urge to soak away the gut-wrenching events of the day.

Easing into the scented water, she replayed her conversation with Mike. Not since Barry had a man expressed a desire for her company. Still, she hesitated. He reminded her too much of Barry. Serious and brooding. One of those people who kept to a preplanned schedule with the same precision as the computers he studied all day. Yet he had done so much for her and Linzee. What could it hurt to spend time with him?

But she didn't need another Barry. She needed humor and good cheer, traits Barry had lacked.

She needed a man after God's own heart.

"Lord." Her wail sounded pathetic to her ears. "Is there a King David out there for me?"

But even though she turned her ear to heaven, the Lord stayed silent.

Chapter Thirteen

A refreshing breeze swept over the Tiburon art and crafts fair and rippled Meg's hair. She glanced out at the water and the humps of brown hills in the distance, grateful she'd chosen a lightweight peasant skirt this morning. She adjusted the chunky beads draped around her neck and straightened the scarf around her hair.

"Thanks a bunch, Richie, I appreciate you sticking around." She and Richie finished unpacking the bubble-sheathed paintings and hanging them around the booth moments before the first visitors arrived.

"Not a problem." She knew his bored sigh meant he was only in it for the wad of cash she'd promised him. No doubt he'd spend most of the day with his nose buried in his iPhone.

She pasted a gracious smile on her face and allowed herself to enjoy a few moments of serenity before the browsers invaded her booth.

By noon, she had sold five of her smaller paintings. She and Richie dug out the lunch she'd packed.

She was two bites into her sandwich when a familiar voice greeted her. Whirling around mid-bite, she saw Mike standing outside the booth, next to a hard-faced teenage girl who bore a strong resemblance to him.

She swallowed and gaped, unable to hide her astonishment. "Mike."

"Hey." Mike looked around. "Wanted to drop by and see what this was about." He pointed a thumb at the scowling girl. "This is my daughter Sheyla."

She recovered her poise and smiled. "Nice to meet you, Sheyla, I'm Meg." She dropped her sack lunch on the chair. "It's good to see a familiar face."

Mike and Sheyla walked around the booth and examined each picture. "I like this one." He tapped the piece she'd dubbed Tornado in Z Minor, her post-breakup painting.

She rubbed her forehead. "That one is three hundred, which includes the cost of framing and matting."

"I like it too," said Sheyla. "Will you buy it for me, Dad?"

Mike, an unreadable expression on his face, whispered something in Sheyla's ear. Meg caught the word "spendy." Sheyla shrugged and whispered back.

An idea came to Meg. "I have a smaller, unframed print a lot like Tornado." She thumbed through a stack of canvases. "Here it is. Why don't you take it? This one's on me." Mike deserved a freebie for all he'd done to help her.

"Thanks, ma'am." Sheyla's grin matched her father's. "This will look great in my bedroom."

Mike knelt next to her as she finished her energy bar. "Is your daughter getting any more messages from her nemesis?"

She leaned closer, grateful he kept his voice low. "I don't know. I haven't heard from her since Thursday. She told me to text Nena if I need to reach her."

She keyed a message to Nena. *Is Linzee is still getting messages from Eddie?*

"What an irony, right? Nena's my liaison to my own daughter. This must be God working in His mysterious way."

Soon a reply arrived. *Not since yesterday.*

She showed the text to Mike, who said, "It's interesting that Eddie was able to track her number each time she changed it. I'm thinking he had access to a database somewhere. Who's her carrier?"

"Silicon Wireless."

"And the phone she's using now is a prepaid?" He frowned in thought. "Not on her Silicon service?"

"Correct."

"He could've hacked into the Silicon database, but he'd have to have some sophisticated knowledge to pull it off. Not sure if he's at that level."

"Remember that movie in which the stalker was someone who worked for his victim's wireless carrier?"

Mike searched her face, brow lowered. "You're saying Eddie could be someone who works for Silicon?"

For a moment, bells rang in her head, as though she had chosen the correct answer on a game show. Holding her breath, she texted Nena again. *Do either of you know someone who works for Silicon Wireless?*

"Silicon has probably twenty stores in the area." She tapped her foot, not daring to lift her eyes from the phone. "It would be difficult to narrow it down."

Nena replied in less than a minute. *Don't think so. I'll ask her.*

As she fought back disappointment, Richie planted himself in front of her. "Mom, someone wants to buy your tornado painting." Next to him stood a well-groomed sixtyish couple.

She stood, offered her hand and a smile. The woman gave her a cool-handed shake. "We think it will look fabulous in our Palm Springs pool house. The color scheme is perfect." As were her teeth.

"I'm glad you appreciate it."

The man pulled a wallet from his pocket and handed her some bills.

"Thanks." She clutched the cash and watched Richie bubble-wrap Tornado in Z Minor, along with the pieces of her heart contained in it. A pang of sorrow needled her, and she turned away.

Mike spoke in her ear. "Let me know what you find

out." He turned toward the exit. "See you tonight at the potluck?"

"Maybe. Thanks for dropping by."

Mike and Sheyla disappeared into the crowd. Richie hoisted the painting and carried it to the customers' car. She stuffed the cash in her bag, taking small comfort in the stiff, fresh stack of bills.

***

Nena scowled at Meg's text and threw the phone down. Linzee's mom wasn't as uncool as she used to be, but that didn't mean she wanted the woman texting her all the time.

She lounged back on the sofa and stared at a baseball game on TV. In the bottom of the seventh, the Oakland A's were kicking the Seattle Mariners' rears 10 to 1.

A heavy-set woman strode past the living room window. The woman's two small children tugged on her hands, their mouths twisted in pouty whines. Rolling her eyes, Nena thanked the stars above she and Linzee would never end up like that *mama gordita.*

A smartphone commercial interrupted the game, reminding her of Linzee's phone hidden away in a bedroom drawer. She hadn't checked it for new messages since Linzee left for work this morning.

A new text awaited from an unknown number. *Die, lesbo*

She glared at the phone. "Maldito!" Holding the phone high, she pretended to fling it, wishing she could throw *el telefono perverso* against the wall and shatter it to smithereens.

On second thought, she wished she could throw *el Eddie perverso* against the wall, shatter *him* to smithereens.

The last time she felt like throwing someone happened seven years ago, after her stepbrother Santiago violated her for the final time. She remembered how, as a child growing up in the *barrio* of East L.A., she'd admired and looked up to her fine, handsome older brother. How she'd mispronounced his name Saint Eggo. How his affectionate gestures morphed into something ugly as the years rolled on.

How he'd turned her off to men for life, with no going back.

She dropped the phone and stomped back to the sofa, where harsh memories assaulted her, and mingled with the text's mocking words.

***

Meg absently smiled at everyone who passed her booth, and all the while Mike's words replayed through her mind like a warped CD.

You're saying Eddie could be someone who works for Silicon?

Endless possibilities stretched before her along an infinite highway, and her shoulders sagged. The thought of narrowing down hundreds of suspects to just one person overwhelmed her.

"Dad?" Richie's voice behind her interrupted her thoughts.

She whirled, heart leaping, then saw he was talking on his phone. Her heart rate decelerated. Keeping one ear cocked to the conversation, she nodded at a couple who'd entered her booth.

Richie beamed like the Cheshire cat. "Next week, huh?" He glanced at her and turned away.

What was next week? She searched her mind for any upcoming events she may have forgotten.

Richie lowered his voice. "I don't think so. You want me to tell her?

"Yeah, yeah. I'll see you then." Richie ended the call and turned to face her. "Guess what, Mom." His grin widened. "Dad's moving back to town."

An invisible hand squeezed the breath from her lungs. "Your father? He's moving here? To the Bay Area?"

"Well, duh."

"But why?"

"He and that woman split. He wants to start fresh."

"Oh, dear Lord."

"Intel's transferring him to Santa Clara."

"Whew." She doubled over, hand on heart. "Thank the Lord he won't be right next door." Looking him full in the face, she said, "How long have you known this?"

"Couple of weeks."

"And you didn't tell me?" Accusation laced her tone.

"Uh—did you want to know?"

She stared at Richie, at his cropped blond hair, football-player physique, well-chiseled features—Phillippe's clone.

"Well, duh, son."

Maybe she fretted for nothing. Most likely, she and Phillippe would not ever have to cross paths. She prayed it would be so.

***

Richie's eyes betrayed his awe over the amount of money Meg handed him. "Thanks, Mom." He shifted in the passenger seat and stuffed the bills in his pocket. "Who the heck was that girl?"

Meg steered north onto the 131. "What girl?"

"That girl built like a linebacker."

"Richie. That was so not nice."

"But it's true, Mom. Maybe my team could use her."

Laughter flew from her lips, and she clapped her hand over her mouth. "You must mean Mike's daughter. He's a new friend who's been helping me find Linzee's stalker."

"Serious?" From the corner of her eye, she saw him gaping. "Linzee has a stalker?"

"Someone named Edward Levens has been flooding her with vicious text messages." Her grip tightened on the steering wheel. "Know anyone by that name?"

"Heck, no. Is it because she's a pervert?"

"Richard Eric!"

"Well, she is. Come on, Mom. You know it."

"Do not use that word."

"Pervert, pervert."

Meg's hands shook. "Have you been sending hate messages to your sister?"

"You accusing me of something?"

"You've done nothing but mock her since she announced her engagement."

She could feel his glare on her, as fierce as the sun's glare on her car. "You mean since I found out she's a fag? Which you never bothered to tell me?"

"Like you never bothered to tell me your father was moving back to town?" Heart racing, she punched the radio dial to drown out his angry retort.

Chapter Fourteen

"Here comes Meg," someone hollered. She grinned, recognizing Camille's voice, and ventured into Dean and Esther's backyard, determined to put her daughter's troubles out of her mind and enjoy herself. She scanned the green expanse where a few young children ran about, and roughly twelve adults mingled. Jon's son Tanner and another boy shot hoops next to the garage.

Esther, clad in a white polo shirt and matching shorts which set off her tanned legs, approached Meg and greeted her with a hug. "So glad you're here! Most of us have eaten already, but go ahead and help yourself."

Camille and her broad white smile neared as Meg filled her plate. Camille's skirt, paired with a yellow blouse, could pass for a tropical garden. Meg could almost smell the plumeria scent floating from the fabric.

"Meg, I want you to meet my boyfriend, Bill." Camille stepped aside, revealing a gray-ponytailed man with a friendly, open face. He stuck out a meaty hand as Camille made introductions.

"Nice to meet ya." His smile showed teeth the approximate color of light beer.

Camille surveyed Meg. "Got a man in your life, Meg?"

A throb of resistance went off inside her. She was tired of people asking about her love life.

"No, not right now." She tried for nonchalance. "I'm between relationships."

Camille laughed. "I like your attitude." Sobering, she added, "Do you know why it's so hard for women over forty to find a man?"

"Tell me."

"Because so many men over forty are busy chasing women half their age. Unlike my Bill." Camille almost cooed at the man beside her. "Thank the Lord you don't like 'em young, Snookums."

Bill's laugh sounded like a gravel pit. "Who wants Kool-Aid when you can have fine wine, Sugar Pie?"

Meg tried to stifle a snort, but it spurted out anyway. Camille smirked at her. "Don't mind our sweet-talking, honey." She ran her hand over Bill's elbow. "We've been together five years now. You'd think we would've stopped by now."

"It's why she won't marry me." Bill and Camille exchanged fond grins. "She figures that's the best way to kill a romance."

"He's kidding." Camille back-slapped his arm. "We're probably going to get married next year."

"My third, her fourth." Bill's dry tone belied his affectionate expression. "We decided to save the best for last."

Meg laughed. "Congratulations." The scent of grilled meat wafted toward her, and her stomach growled in response. "Let's go sit down."

Jon, clutching two plates, passed them and nodded a greeting. They found seats in a circle of chairs and exchanged hellos with the others. Next to Meg sat an unfamiliar brunette.

"Hi," said the dark-haired woman. The rest of her sentence was drowned out by a basketball pounding the backboard.

Meg leaned toward her. "Sorry, I didn't catch your name."

"Quincy." Her voice was soft as a child's.

"Hi, Quincy, I'm Meg."

"Nice meeting you. Not to be rude, but Jon was sitting

there."

"He was? Sorry."

She stood and looked around; then Jon reappeared in front of her. "Hey, Meg. Glad you're here. You met Quincy already?"

"I met her when I stole your chair."

Jon wore a black tee with large white letters. "People-hugging God worshiper," it said.

"That's an awesome shirt, Jon," she said. "We have too many tree-hugging earth worshipers around here."

He grinned, still facing her. "It's a pretty old shirt. I've had it for years."

She chuckled. "You must be one of those men who never throws anything away."

"You got me pegged. You know us single guys. If it still fits, why throw it away?"

"That's what wives are for," said Ray.

Once the snickers died down, Meg found a seat next to Camille, who said, "Jon has a whole collection of gospel-preachin' shirts. He likes to wear his faith on his sleeve."

Jon, a small smile tugging at his mouth, sat next to Quincy and handed her a plate of chocolate cake. "Whatever you say, Camille." Jon lifted his burger and caught a dribble of ketchup on his tongue. "It's definitely a door-opener."

Meg settled back in her chair. "I bet it gets people's attention."

"It does. I've gotten some good conversations out of it. But sometimes I get flak, too."

"I don't think I'd be brave enough to wear a shirt like that."

Quincy nudged Jon and whispered something. Meg watched, trying not to be obvious. She hadn't known Jon was dating anyone, but with his easy-going manner and friendly ways, he could likely land any woman he chose.

She concentrated on finishing her burger, grilled with exactly the right amount of barbecue sauce. She lifted a forkful of potato salad to her mouth—cold and firm, crunchy with celery, not too much mustard. Just the way she liked it.

Mike moved to the empty seat next to her and spoke in an undertone. "Did you talk to your daughter?"

So much for her temporary respite from Linzee's issues. Annoyance flashed through her like a lightning bolt. "Yes, but let's not talk about it right now."

He nodded, and they finished their meal over small talk.

As the group fellowshipped over the next hour, the dusk deepened and painted the sky indigo blue. More than once she caught Mike glancing her way. Each time she turned away and joined in the laughter and chitchat. No doubt he wanted the scoop on Linzee. No way would she interrupt her fun to give him an update.

By the time the dusk had given way to a star-spangled night sky, Linzee's troubles seemed as far away as last night's dreams. Jon and Quincy stood, said their goodbyes, and then walked across the yard side-by-side. The two basketball players trailed after them. Someone touched her shoulder, and she whirled around.

Mike stood there, his eyes lit with a rare curiosity. "So what did your daughter say?"

Sighing, she resigned herself to the inevitable. She'd give him the news he wanted, then head home.

She moved to a secluded stretch of lawn where the grass tickled her bare feet. With Mike planted beside her, she faced him. "Linzee isn't sure if anyone she knows works for her mobile carrier," she said, "but she'll start checking her friends' profiles. She and Nena think Blake could be in cahoots with someone."

After a long, dense silence, he said, "I can see how someone working for Silicon could be in on this with him." Another pause. "And it wouldn't have to be someone she knew."

Meg wilted at the words. So many possibilities, so many unknowns, pressed down on her. She didn't know if she still had the energy to keep digging through this haystack for that elusive needle. "But remember? We saw nothing on his Facebook page about Linzee. I'm just not convinced it's him."

She couldn't voice her fears that Eddie could be her own son. Suddenly angry at Mike for forcing her back to reality, she said goodbye and drove home.

***

Linzee's eyelids popped open. In the dim room, awareness came slowly. She glanced at the clock. Not yet six a.m. Still groggy, she heard a scraping sound outside her window.

Fully awake, she leapt from her bed, half-dreading what she might find, and peeked between the drapes.

Red streaks marred the hood of her Ford like angry lightning bolts.

"Snap!" she shouted, kicking the wall and wishing it was Eddie. "Nena!" she shrieked. "You're not gonna believe what Eddie did this time."

Nena mumbled in reply.

She grabbed a jacket and burst out the front door, where the smell of fresh spray paint assaulted her. With her hand over her nose, she examined the damage in the dawn light.

When a hand grabbed her shoulder from behind, she lurched forward. Then an arm clamped around her waist and squeezed the breath out of her. Adrenaline rushed her veins. She stomped her attacker's foot and threw her elbow high, making contact with something harder than mere flesh. With a muffled moan, the person released her. Spinning around, she saw a blur of white and black twisting away from her. She dropped to the ground and tried to grab the person's legs, but he was already racing toward the corner of the building as if he were an Olympic sprinter.

"Hey, what's goin' on?" Nena, still in pajamas, appeared and reached out a hand.

Linzee pulled herself upright. "I came this close to catching Eddie." She held her fingers inches apart. "But I was too off-balance." A painful twinge in her right knee left her gasping.

"Eddie was here?" When she saw Linzee's car, she cursed. "That scumbag. You hurt?"

"I bashed my knee when I tried to catch him." Gasping with sobs, she limped to the doorway. Eddie had picked a good time to drop by. Nobody ever moved about at this time on a Sunday morning.

"Did you get a good look at him?"

"No, he was covered in black and wearing a 'Scream' mask." She sniffed. "He was smaller than I expected."

"It must've been Blake's partner in crime, man. Better call the cops."

"We know we're looking for a track star." She hobbled through the door. "I've never seen anyone run so fast except at the Olympics."

"Guess this means we'll miss the SMERFA rally this morning."

"You go on ahead. Don't worry about me."

"No way, ruca. He might come back."

"My whole day has been ruined. Thanks to El Creepo." She plopped on the sofa, knee elevated, and swiped her tears. "El Pervert. El Freako—"

"Yeah, I get it."

She snatched Nena's phone off the end table. "I'm calling Officer Klein right now to tell him they need to put surveillance on Blake Mannson."

Chapter Fifteen

Meg, her stomach churning, dropped to her knees beside her bed. "God, I've never done anything like this before." She swallowed hard. "Let us be channels of your love and peace." Her toes pounded a rhythm. "Even if the SMERFA folks defile Your Word."

She glanced at her clock radio. "Oh, no, I'm going to be late." She bounded to her feet and hurried to her car, praying all the way to the church, and pulled into the lot with seconds to spare.

Jon, Mike, and Camille relaxed against a black Jeep Liberty. They waved and gestured, appearing untroubled as they watched her approach.

"How can you guys be so calm at a time like this?" She attempted a teasing tone. "I'm as jittery as a first date."

Jon smiled. "Sorry if we scared you." He wore a tie-dyed shirt with a white peace symbol flanked by the words, "Jesus, Prince of Peace."

Camille reached for her shoulder. "Stick with me, girlfriend. You'll be fine."

Her trembling hands grabbed a tuft of her hair and secured it with a scrunchie, then the four of them climbed into the Jeep. "Is anyone else coming?"

"Ray and Deb will meet us there." Camille, in back next to Meg, eyed Meg's tank top and shorts. "You look cute today. Pretty in pink."

Meg rolled her eyes. "I'm too old for cute."

"You're never too old for cute." Camille smirked. "Someday you'll be one of those cute little old ladies all the old men want to dance with."

She giggled, her nerves forgotten.

From the driver's seat, Jon said, "You two are having way too much fun." Despite his somber tone, his lips twitched.

Camille laid a hand on his shoulder. "We'll be good, Jon."

He chuckled. "Are you guys familiar with the history of Haight Street Community Church?"

They answered in the negative as he merged onto the 101.

"A couple of hippies who converted to Christ started this little church in a storefront, and it grew so much, they bought an old mission building in seventy-five."

Meg gripped the top of the seat in front of her. "How did the anti-gay stuff start?"

"In 2005, they hired a new pastor. Sam Canady." Jon glanced over his shoulder. "It's not that I think pastors shouldn't preach against sin. It's just that the approach this church takes is all wrong."

"They turn people off to Christ."

Jon drummed his fingers on the steering wheel. "The SMERFA people won't know what to make of our signs."

Camille tapped her arm. "Look behind you."

A stack of poster boards filled the space behind the seat. "For God so loved the world," the top one read. "That means you."

"Nice. Did you make those, Camille?"

"With a little help from my friends," Camille singsonged.

She couldn't help laughing when Camille and Jon broke into song, as joyous as grinning puppies. They sang as they neared the Golden Gate Bridge, its red tiara slicing through the periwinkle-blue sky. Beyond them, Alcatraz seemed to float on top of the Bay.

The car merged onto Highway 1, into the Presidio with

its austere white buildings and skinny eucalyptus trees. They zipped by tree-lined Golden Gate Park, where, forty-plus years earlier, anti-war protestors and flower children transformed the place into an anarchy zone during the Summer of Love.

"We're almost there," Jon said. "Camille, did you bring enough sandwiches for all of us?"

"I brought six." Camille pointed a look at Jon's back. "Did you bring the sodas?"

"I did. Meg, we brought fixin's for a picnic afterward."

"That sounds wonderful."

They fell silent as they neared the church. Distant noises suggested the beginnings of a riot, and her joy evaporated. A somber hush filled the car. Meg's heart seized, then accelerated.

After Jon parked, they gathered on the sidewalk. He enfolded Meg's hand in his reassuring grip and began to pray. Camille clasped her other hand, and peace rushed in.

***

Linzee swept aside a crusty plate on her no-frills kitchen table, then hunched over her laptop. An urgent Facebook message from her father awaited her.

What's going on with your phone? Tried to call, found it disconnected. I'm coming to town this week to house hunt. How about a pizza night?

She rubbed her sore knee. A breeze from the window screen fluttered the gingham curtains at her back. *Sure, Dad. Sorry about my phone. I changed my number – long story. Yes, let's do pizza. What night?*

Flying in Wed eve, ETA 730 pm. So, Thursday? Think your mom will want to see me?

She felt her mouth drop, heard a laugh erupt. *I can't speak for her. Why don't you just ask her?*

***

Meg, nerves jangling, sought Jon's eyes, but he kept

watch on the folks in the park across the street. The SMERFA crowd had amped up their intensity to a dangerous level. "God hates Haight Church," they chanted. "Keep your religion off my marriage!"

Security guards roamed the sidewalks and grounds. A man driving by stuck his head out his window and met Meg's eyes. "Go home!"

She held her sign up for him to see. "Jesus, Friend of Sinners," it declared. Another driver directed his venom at Jon. "Get a life!"

Judging by the honks and middle fingers, the people driving by assumed their little clique was connected to Hate Church.

Swathes of whitewash marred the adobe exterior of the ancient church; plywood covered several windows. She wondered what heinous messages the folks inside the graffiti-filled walls were hearing.

"Unbelievable." Jon stepped forward, angling his sign toward the SMERFA gang, and pointed at the words, "Love your enemies—Jesus."

Meg turned to Camille. "Girlfriend, they're not reading our signs."

"No, they're not." Camille's frustration seeped through her clenched teeth. "I have half a mind to scoot over there and shove my sign in their faces."

Meg eyed Camille's sign, which said, "God is Love."

Jon turned to them. "You two stay here. I'm going over there. They need to know what we're about." He nodded toward the church building. "As for those guys, I will probably give them a piece of my mind before the morning's done. In love, of course."

Several news vans pulled to the opposite curb. Meg cringed. "Are we going to be on TV?"

"Looks like it." Jon still watched the commotion across the street.

Camille grimaced. "Say cheese. Smile big for the

camera."

"Love wins! Hate loses!" the crowd on the steps chanted.

Camille clicked her tongue, and Jon stepped off the curb.

Meg wished she could hear the conversation between Jon and the apparent leader of the other group. Jon's passionate gestures, and the young man's red face, merely fed her curiosity. The other man glanced at Jon's sign, and his face gathered in a frown.

"Uh, oh," muttered Camille, her eyes betraying her excitement. "He looks like he's itching for a fight."

Meg sighed. "Why would anyone have a problem with love messages?"

"Maybe because they don't want to love their enemies?"

***

Linzee propped her injured leg on the wicker coffee table and flipped the TV to the musical Les Miz. She closed her eyes, letting the mournful tune about shattered dreams resonate in her spirit, picturing tigers turning Fantine's dreams to shame. Like Eddie had turned her relationship with Nena into a shameful thing.

Sighing, she muted the TV, then picked up her laptop and clicked on the video streaming in from the SMERFA rally. The rally she'd had to miss because of Creeper Eddie's untimely visit. She watched, riveted, as cops and news reporters tried in vain to stem what had turned into a free-for-all.

She was so absorbed in the action, she hardly noticed when Nena opened the front door, laden with grocery bags. "What's up, ruca?"

"Nena, my love, I'm glad you're home. Come look. Zach's showing a video of the rally."

"Give me a sec. Let me put these bags down." Nena headed to the kitchen, then came and stood behind her.

"Look how crazy it's gotten." A small group with signs appeared on an opposite corner, and Linzee leaned in, trying to see what the signs said.

The next image made her jerk back against the sofa cushion. "Well, snap, look at this." She pointed. "This lady looks like my mom, doesn't she?"

***

Bodies filed out of Haight Street Church—grim, stiff-backed figures heading Meg's way.

Others from the park filed across the street, arms outstretched to stop the oncoming traffic. Security guards moved into place, forming human shields.

Meg watched the impending brawl, tight with nerves, and inched closer to Jon, taking shelter behind him. From her vantage point, he looked ten feet high. A line of tension hunched his shoulders, as though he were preparing for launch.

Cries volleyed back and forth across the street. "You're going to Hell!"

"No, *you're* going to Hell."

Someone shoved a guard, who retaliated in like manner. The culprit fell back, and a mass of bodies tumbled to the ground. More horns blared, and drivers yelled four-letter words.

"Keep back!" a guard commanded. "Let the cars get by."

Something whizzed by Meg's head, and she whirled to see a small, jagged rock ping the sidewalk behind her. "Hey, someone threw a rock at us!"

Jon turned and took charge. "Get down, ladies." Her heart raced like a runaway horse as she and Camille crawled behind a newspaper box. Deb, Ray, and Mike huddled half a block further west, well beyond the reach of the rioters.

She and Camille exchanged horrified looks as shouts and objects kept coming at them.

"I think these things are meant for the church people." Camille kept her voice at a near-whisper. "But they think that we're them."

She had to get out of there. As she scanned the area for an escape route, Jon grabbed her and Camille by the elbows and hustled them along the sidewalk to Deb's huddle. En route, something hit her sign, and an egg splattered at her feet.

She gasped and jumped. Sirens sounded in the distance.

"Uh, oh," said Camille. "Cops are coming."

Jon tightened his grip on their elbows. "You guys, we need to book." His urgent tone sounded an alarm. "Leave your signs here. If we stroll casually back to the car, we won't generate any suspicion."

They dropped their signs and meandered away from the gathering crowd, conversing under their breaths, pretending to admire each building they passed. But if any passersby peered too closely at their faces, they were in trouble. A chill crawled up her spine. She almost expected, at any moment, to be grabbed and ordered to halt.

Chapter Sixteen

"**M**eg, sorry you had to go through that." Jon's eyes filled with empathy.

"Girl, you're one tough mama." Camille passed Meg a sandwich and plopped next to her. The six of them lounged on the grass in the shade of a large cedar tree, near the eastern edge of Golden Gate Park, a safe ten blocks away from the danger zone.

Meg looked at her turkey-and-Swiss sandwich. "I keep thinking about Jesus' words, that we are blessed when we're persecuted for Him. It helps me keep it in the right perspective."

"Well, then, we're mighty blessed," Ray said with a hint of sarcasm.

"You know what I really want to do." Jon dropped his voice. "I want to go back to the church and talk to that pastor one-on-one, find out how he justifies his position from the Bible. And maybe engage in a little friendly debate."

"I know you could win him over, Jon," said Deb.

Jon took a bite of sandwich and shook his head. "Not me, Christ," he said around the bite of food. "Who wants to go back there with me?"

She could learn a thing or two about boldness from Jon. She slowly raised her hand when she saw Camille's arm shoot in the air.

"We have a full day ahead," said Ray, regret in his tone.

"But we'll be praying, okay?" said Deb.

"Can I catch a ride back?" Mike turned to Ray. "I can't

stay either."

A young couple sidled by and looked them over with hooded gazes. The young man possessed the lean physique of a skateboarder and held a smoldering cigarette in one hand. The young woman clutched his other hand. Her straw-like dreadlocks hung halfway down her back.

Jon waved. "Hi."

The young man stopped and stared at Jon's shirt. "Jesus, Prince of Peace, huh?" he said.

"Indeed." Jon patted the grass beside him. "Here, come join us. Want a Dr Pepper?"

The man's sneer disappeared, and wariness played over his face. Jon gave him a winsome smile, and the man dropped his cigarette on the sidewalk and ground it out under his Birkenstock.

"What's your name?" Jon asked, his tone as disarming as his expression.

"Uh, Seth," said the young man, exerting caution.

"Jessica." A tentative smile.

Jon patted the grass again. "You can sit down if you want."

Camille grinned at them. "Don't worry. He's harmless."

Seth glanced at Camille without returning her grin. He and Jessica thumped down cross-legged and dropped their backpacks to the grass.

"I wanna know something." Seth peered at Jon's shirt. "Why do Jesus' followers love war so much?" Seth's eyes flashed with righteous anger.

Camille handed them ice-cold cans of Diet Dr Pepper.

"That's an interesting question," said Jon, unfazed. "Especially since we were right in the middle of a riot less than an hour ago."

Seth's eyes lit up. "No joke?" He popped the top of the can. Brown liquid fizzled over.

"No joke." Jon pointed to the east. "Right down the street at Haight Church."

"See, that's what I mean." Seth jerked a finger at Jon. "Those are some haters down there." He tipped the can and poured a river of soda in his mouth.

"But they weren't the ones throwing things at us." Jon remained calm. "The SMERFA guys across the street were."

Seth's chin lifted. "Yeah, well, it's 'cause the Hate Church people make 'em so mad."

"But the Haight Church people weren't throwing anything," Jon repeated. "And neither were we. We were there for peaceful purposes. In fact, none of the Christ-followers threw anything at anybody."

Seth muttered something to Jessica, who giggled.

"Some Christ-followers," Seth smirked.

Camille blurted, "We're all far from perfect."

Seth snorted. "Words can be as powerful of weapons as guns and knives."

Jon nodded. "I agree."

"And religious people wage war with words instead of weapons."

"Sometimes that's true," Jon conceded with a nod. "Know any non-religious people who do that? I do."

"Well, at least they're not hypocrites," Seth bit out. Jessica nodded, her gaze traveling the circle of faces.

"I see." Jon frowned at his half-eaten sandwich, which he seemed to have forgotten about eating. Meg suspected he was praying. She silently asked the Lord to give him the right words to say.

"So, Seth." Jon searched the young man's face. "Let's say you're a Christ-follower."

Seth rolled his eyes. "Okay."

"How would *you* live your life?"

He straightened. Jessica leaned forward, eyes on him. Meg popped the last bite of sandwich in her mouth and watched Seth's face grow smug.

"I'd love everybody, man," Seth grinned at Jessica. "I'd accept everybody. I'd make sure poor people had food, and homeless people had places to live. I definitely wouldn't declare war on other countries."

Jon thrust a thumb into the air. "You seem to have this Christ-following thing figured out."

Pride and embarrassment battled on Seth's face. Pride won.

Jon raised his brows. "So what's stopping you?"

"Stopping me from what?"

"From turning your life over to Christ."

The smug look vanished. "Huh uh, man, I'm not into religion."

"Did I say anything about religion?"

He jerked his head at Jon. "You said turning your life over to Christ."

"But here's the deal. That's not religion."

Seth scrunched his face.

Jessica spoke for the first time. "What is it?"

"It's a relationship." Jon's voice turned gentle. "It's living your life to please Christ, not yourself. It's having a friendship with the God of the universe."

"Them church folks don't live that way."

"It isn't about them church folks."

Seth shook his head, over and over. "Naw. I can't see me ever doing that."

"Doing what?"

"Turning my life over to Christ."

"That disappoints me. You'd make a great Christ-follower."

"It'd be way too hard." A tiny pause ensued while Seth chewed on his words. His face shifted like a kid caught stealing. Meg and Camille shared a grin.

Jon offered a kind smile. "You nailed it. It is way too hard. It's why we're called hypocrites by the world. We church folks screw up a lot."

"Then why do it?"

"Because it's worth it. And because Christ gave his all

for us."

Seth and Jessica had no answer. Jon reached into his pocket and pulled out a booklet. *The Roman Road*. The others ate and listened as he explained the plan of salvation to the couple, who listened without a word.

Ray and Deb stood up and stretched. "We need to go," Deb mouthed. Mike stood as well, waving a half-circle in the air. Meg waved back.

Camille leaned toward Meg. "I'll be right back. I'm going with them to pray."

The two young people sat, riveted to the words in Jon's booklet. Meg stretched her legs and marveled at his fearlessness, wishing she could be as bold about sharing her faith.

"I'm going to have to think on this, man," Seth said when Jon finished with an offer to help them receive Christ.

"Don't wait too long." Jon handed Seth the booklet. "Here, take this with you. My phone number's on the back. Feel free to call me anytime."

The two stood, holding out hands in farewells. "Thanks, man."

"Have a good one." Jessica waved.

Jon watched the two wander away. "You know the saying, 'You plant the seed and let God do the watering?'" He looked at Meg, eyes alight. "If not for that, I'd get discouraged whenever people leave without getting saved."

"I have a good feeling about those two. They really warmed up to you at the end."

He shrugged. "All I can do is pray I'll see them in heaven someday."

Meg smiled, picturing the numerous jewels in Jon's crown that awaited him.

He leaned back on his hands, ankles crossed. "Every now and then, I think about an old Christian song from the eighties. Can't remember the name or the artist, but it was about a guy who dreamed he went to heaven, and all these people came up to him, telling him what he'd done for them while on earth."

"I remember that song."

"You do?"

"I was just a baby Christian back then."

Jon's eyes held a faraway look as if he were gazing into heaven itself. "I sometimes wonder if it'll really be like that."

She folded her legs Indian-style, digging her elbows into her knees. "I know what you mean. I hope when we get there we'll find out we planted some seeds at the rally this morning."

He gazed at the tree branches above him, his face pensive. "If even one person was impacted, it will have been worth it."

A pause fell, and she cast about for something to keep the conversation going. "Did you invite Quincy to our protest?"

Jon's taken-aback look told her he wasn't expecting that question. "Quincy? No. I didn't. Things like protests aren't her cup of tea." He sat up and folded his legs, leaning forward.

Meg fingered a tuft of grass. "Does she have kids?"

"She does." He glanced at a spot beyond her shoulder. "A son. We're—"

"Hey." Meg whirled toward Camille's voice behind her. "How did it go with Seth and Jessica?"

Jon grinned. "They left with my Roman Road booklet and my phone number."

Camille grinned back. "You old seed-planter, you."

He eased himself up, looking pleased. "Sure would be nice to see a few more harvests." He rubbed his hands on his jeans, then stretched. "You two ready to head back to Haight Church now?"

"We are." They gathered up the picnic remains and strolled to Jon's Jeep. But Camille's running chatter prevented Meg from asking Jon what he had been about to say.

***

Jon approached the church from Page Street this time and parked half a block away. The park across from the church appeared deserted.

"Looks like everybody's gone home," he observed as they got out of the Jeep. "Let's hope Pastor Sam Canady is still hanging around."

An innocent stillness draped over the church. An occasional cardboard sign littered the sidewalk, the only trace left of the earlier hostilities. Jon tried a side door, and it opened. She followed him inside, Camille at her heels.

"Can I help you?" A uniformed man built like a brick wall materialized from the dim recesses.

"We're here to see Pastor Canady."

"Do you have an appointment?" The guard's scratchy voice held authority.

"No." As did Jon's. "Is one required?"

"It is."

The guard asserted himself toward them. Meg lurched back, her heel stomping Camille's toe. She heard a grunt of pain. "Sorry," she hissed over her shoulder.

"I suggest you call or email the church to set up a time. He's a very busy man." The guard put his hand on his hip. In the dim light, it could have been a holster.

Even Jon backed off. "We'll do that. Thank you."

They re-emerged into the bright afternoon. "So much for that." Jon glanced up at the bell tower. "But we'll be back."

Chapter Seventeen

Meg pulled to a stop behind Brad's shiny Acura parked in Mom and Dad's circular driveway. She glanced at Richie hunched in the passenger seat. "Got the card?"

"Yep."

They got out and strode toward the front porch of the tan stucco house. There stood her father at the large picture window, waving at them. She waved back and went inside, Richie on her heels. "Happy birthday, Dad." She greeted her father with a hug. "You look great. I hope I look as good as you when I'm seventy." She glanced around. "Where is everybody?"

"Out back." Dad pointed a thumb over his shoulder and beamed at Richie.

"Happy birthday, Grandpa." Richie handed him the musical card she'd bought that played "Celebrate" when opened.

She hugged her mother, relishing her sweet gardenia scent that still evoked long-ago memories of bedtime stories and goodnight kisses. The rest of the family lounged near the pool, including Brad with a new girlfriend. Brad and Linda's divorce two years ago had stunned them all. Now Brad seemed to be stuck reliving his bachelor days. This new girlfriend conformed to his usual pattern: long blond hair, toned and fit body, whiter-than-white teeth—the latest in a long line of Linda clones, none of which had lasted longer than six months.

"Hey, Meg." Brad approached, girlfriend in tow. "This is Heather. Heather, my older sister Meg." Brad pointed to the pool. "Heather's daughter Jennifer is swimming."

Heather's eyes remained blank as she greeted Meg.

"Hi, Heather. So glad to meet you."

"And this is my nephew, Richie."

"Hi, Aunt Meg!" A scream came from behind her. Startled, she spun to see twelve-year-old Ariel in the pool, waving her arms over her head like railroad gates.

"Hi, Ariel!" she shouted back, aping her niece's movements. Ariel charged out of the pool, ran to Meg and gave her a wet hug around the legs, then jumped back into the water.

Laughing, she breathed in the odor of barbecuing meat. Her stomach responded with a rumble, and she made her way to the grill where Dad had resumed his chef duties. "How's it coming along?"

"Almost ready. Is Linzee coming?"

"No, she sent a text that something came up. She sends her love."

"I hear she and that girl are getting married. Is that true?"

Sensing a confrontation coming on, she kept her eyes on the grill. "Unfortunately, yes."

"Sweetheart, I know that goes against your values, but nowadays it's commonplace and accepted, especially around here. It will become easier for you to tolerate in time."

"No, Dad, I don't think so." She made herself breathe in a calming river of air. Dad should know by now she wouldn't abandon her Biblical values, yet he kept hammering away at them.

"When are they getting married?"

She kept her voice smooth, factual. Dad hated emotional displays. "Sometime in September. They're waiting for their minister friend to return from vacation so she can do the ceremony."

"I see." He flipped the pieces of chicken. "You wouldn't

sit out your own daughter's wedding, would you?"

"I'm trying not to think about that yet. I hate being in such a position."

"Lots of parents disapprove of their children's choice of spouse, but they still attend the ceremony."

She stared at the sizzling meat. A plume of steam blasted her face. "This is a little different, Dad."

"No, it isn't."

Dad showed no willingness to understand her point of view. She pressed her lips together. "The point isn't that I disapprove of her choice of spouse. The point is, I don't support same-sex marriage, and I don't want to appear as though I do."

"It will appear as though you don't care about your daughter."

She clicked her tongue. "People can be so judgmental."

He shrugged and glanced at her. "Being scrutinized by others is the way of the world." He frowned at the crackling meat and said, "This looks like it's almost ready. Can you get me the big platter from the kitchen?"

***

Brad, the only decent singer in the bunch, led them in sloppy renditions of Happy Birthday and For He's a Jolly Good Fellow. Cheering, he lifted his can of beer, and Meg lifted her champagne glass. Despite their clashing world views, she enjoyed spending time with her family. Long ago, she'd even shared their world view.

Brad, eyes slightly crossed after three beers, sought Meg's gaze as she relaxed in a lawn chair between Richie and her mother.

"Hey, Meg. I hear Linzee's marrying her girlfriend. True?"

Her heart rate accelerated, signaling the onset of a debate. "True."

"Good for her." Brad's face twisted in a smirk. "She's

taking a stand against the status quo. I salute her."

As usual, Brad knew how to push her buttons.

"What about you, Meg?" Brad continued in dogged tones. "Oh, that's right. Your religion doesn't approve of same-sex marriage, does it?"

She wanted to slap him. "It isn't about me or my religion."

"No?"

"It's about the fact that from day one, in every civilization, marriage has been defined as a union between a man and a woman." A stillness fell over the patio. The children's giggles pierced the silence. "Please tell me why now, after thousands of years, we're suddenly trying to redefine marriage."

Brad's chin jutted, his mouth an upside-down arc. "Because it's taken that long for us to become enlightened."

She tilted her head. "So you're saying, we're finally evolved enough to allow gays to marry?"

Brad nodded, his smug look telling her he'd scored. "That's right."

"So maybe we're evolved and enlightened enough to open marriage up to anyone who wants it. Maybe we don't need restrictions on marriage anymore."

A spasm of doubt crossed his face as if he were suddenly aware of a trap ahead.

"Don't know if I'd go that far." His voice dropped so low, she had to lean forward.

"How far should we go, then? Where do we draw the line?"

Brad's gaze flicked toward Heather, whose smile flashed encouragement. Richie appeared engrossed with his third helping of food. Mom looked at Dad, worry lines sprouting on her forehead.

"If two people love each other, they should be together." Brad punched the air for emphasis. "Especially gays, who can't help being gay. If we tell them they can't get married because they're gay, we're discriminating due to sexual orientation."

"They can't help being gay? You mean they were born that way?"

"Exactly." Brad thumped a palm on his knee. "It's in their brain chemistry."

"Phillippe told me something similar after he left us for that woman. 'Men aren't wired to be monogamous,' is what he claimed."

"That is hardly the same thing as being born gay."

"I'm just saying that we can explain away all kinds of behavior, good or bad, because we are born a certain way."

"Bottom line, Meg, people should be allowed to love whoever they want." Brad and Heather shared triumphant smiles.

She garnered her courage and lifted her chin. "Tell that to the little girl whose father left her mother for another woman."

"That's different," Brad shot back. "Because both parents weren't in agreement."

"What about, people can love whoever they want?"

"I'm not talking about cheating. Gay marriage hurts no one."

"So when you said, people should be allowed to love whoever they want, you didn't really mean it, right?"

Brad shrugged, his expression turning wary. "Sure I did. As long as it isn't hurting anyone else."

"Are you saying that if Phillippe and I had agreed to an open marriage, his loving another woman would have been okay?"

"Not if he did it behind your back."

"But if he did it with my full knowledge and cooperation?"

"Then it wouldn't have been cheating."

"Wow, Brad. How open-minded of you."

Brad cursed, his tight lips betraying his fear that he'd

been played. He refused to look at Meg and instead turned to Heather, her smile saying she was in his corner. Meg wilted in her chair, as drained as if she'd tried to chop down a Sequoia tree with a kitchen knife.

Mom broke the uneasy silence. "The birthday cake is ready."

Everyone jumped up, clearly relieved at the break in tension. Mom had baked a three-layer, round torte cake, white with lemon filling, topped with a fancy *HAPPY BIRTHDAY DEAR.*

Meg approached her mother to offer a hug and an apology. "Mom." Stepping back, she lowered her voice. "I hope Brad and I didn't offend you with our arguing."

Mom searched her face. The worry line between her eyes creased her forehead into two halves. "I'm used to it, sweetie," she replied with a pat on Meg's arm. "The two of you have been going at it for forty years." She gave a light laugh, yet Meg suspected she felt more bothered than she let on.

"Be honest, Mom. What do you honestly think about Linzee marrying her girlfriend? Are you truly okay with it?"

Mom looked at her, a shroud over her eyes. "I only want her to be happy, sweetie. She's my granddaughter, and I love her."

"You don't think it's unnatural?"

Mom hesitated. "I just want her to be happy," she repeated.

Frustrated, she hugged Mom goodbye. Mom had always hidden her true feelings about hot-button issues. But it couldn't hurt anything for her to say what she truly thought.

Brad stood stiff as she hugged him. "Thanks for the rousing debate, brother. I hope you enjoyed it as much as I did. We're old pros, you know." She smiled to let him know there were no hard feelings. He hesitated, returned her grin, and patted her once on the back.

Chapter Eighteen

Meg settled on her queen-sized bed and turned on the TV, hoping she and her friends hadn't made the news. Instead, a still, small voice she recognized prompted her to call Linzee.

When she obeyed, an impatient "Yeah, Mom?" greeted her.

"Hi, Linzee." Plopping down on top of her royal blue comforter, she lowered the TV volume.

"Hey."

"We missed you at Grandpa's birthday."

"Sorry I couldn't make it. I did call him with my well wishes."

"Good. What's new?"

Linzee snapped, "Why do you always ask me that?"

She recoiled as if Linzee had slapped her. "Because I'm a mom. You'll—" She stopped herself from saying, you'll find out for yourself someday.

"Hey, Mom, I was going to call you anyway. I'm curious about something."

"What?"

"Were you at a rally down on Haight Street this morning?" Linzee's tone hurled a challenge.

Her breath caught. Had they made the news already? "Why do you ask?"

"I watched a video feed of the rally, and I saw a lady there who looked just like you."

Cringing, she clutched her hair. Her presence at the rally had floated through cyberspace for anyone to see.

She considered two or three responses, then settled on,

"What was the lady doing?"

"Holding a sign, but I couldn't read it. Was it you, Mom?"

Meg gulped for air. "All right, I admit it. It was me."

"Mom." Linzee sounded horrified. "I can't believe you'd side with a sicko place like Hate Church."

"Wait a minute." She rubbed her forehead. "You're jumping to conclusions."

"Mom, I saw you."

"We weren't siding with Haight Church."

"Don't tell me you're on our side now. I won't believe you."

"We weren't. We were on side C."

Long pause. "Side C?"

"Three groups showed up—SMERFA, Haight Church, and us."

"And who is 'us'?"

"The anti-hate, anti-SMERFA side."

Linzee burst out, "You aren't making any sense."

Meg stared at the wall, picturing Linzee's puzzled face. "A few friends and I went down there with signs to counter the church's hate messages. Our signs said things like, God is Love and Jesus Friend of Sinners."

"Weird."

"You could say we were on Christ's side." She swung her legs off the bed and slid her feet into flip-flops.

"Why would you do that?"

"Because Haight Church is bringing shame to the name of Christ." Her flip-flops slapped the floor as she wandered out the bedroom door and along the hall. Nearing the gallery of family photos, she slowed. "They're fighting fire with fire. We want to fight fire with love."

"Dang, I should've been there. It would've been so bizarre to see you there."

Meg scanned the photo wall and its years of memories. "Why didn't you go?"

"Oh, I hurt my knee this morning. Thought I better stay off it."

"How did you hurt your knee?"

Linzee's silence carried louder than words. Meg's spine prickled. She halted and stared at Linzee's happy baby photo.

"Did something happen?" Her trembling legs carried her into her studio.

"Promise you won't freak?"

Oh, dear Lord –

"What happened, Linzee?"

"Don't freak. First, I found my car with spray paint all over it. Then, while I stood there looking it over, someone tried to attack me."

"Holey socks, Linzee." Meg grabbed the back of the chaise as the room wobbled around her.

"But I fought him off, thanks to those self-defense classes Nena and I took. He ran like his pants were on fire."

Her heart skipping, Meg leaned forward and gripped the chair tighter. "Did you tell the police?"

"Of course, I did. They're going to talk to Blake's parole officer about putting him under surveillance. But I don't think the attacker was Blake. He was too small. But it could be someone he's working with. Probably whoever it is he knows who works for Silicon."

Through a fog, she heard herself say, "What if your harasser isn't Blake?"

"We've been over this." Linzee's longsuffering tone sighed into her ear. "Nobody else has any reason to do this."

Meg shook her head. "But why would Blake Mannson come up with an alias like Edward Levens? We didn't see anything in his profile connecting his name to Eddie's, or him to you."

An idea had been growing in her mind, subtle at first, like the slow-budding daisies outside her window. But now it burst into full, glorious bloom.

"Didn't you tell me Eddie always spells your name right?"

Finally, the question that had been bugging her found its voice. Eddie had to be someone who knew her well enough to know the spelling of her name.

Linzee barely paused. "I think Blake would remember how my name is spelled."

"I don't know, Baby Girl. Most people, other than those closest to you, spell your name the standard way."

She could picture Linzee shrugging at that. "Well, I kind of hope it is him, so we can put him away and move on with our lives."

Her heart gradually eased back toward its normal rhythm. "I understand how you feel, but we don't want to nail the wrong guy."

They chatted a few minutes more, but after she hung up, trembling seized her again. She closed the studio door, sequestering herself in hopes of finding relief from the pounding anxiety. Art offered both a refuge and excellent therapy.

A beam from the setting sun cast pure orange light into the room. She stood before the easel and picked up a charcoal pencil. Holding it to the canvas, she stroked mindlessly, by rote. After a few minutes of fruitlessness, she shook her head. This could prove to be an exercise in futility. Or it could serve to reveal something in her subconscious, something important, a clue. But a clue to what, she couldn't fathom. She only knew something inside her wouldn't rest until she'd spilled her entire heart, her guts, her emotions until there was nothing left.

She eased in a slow breath and tried again. After several minutes of concentration, a face began to form out of the charcoal — an older face with a sinister cast. She stood back. Although the features were blurred, evil intent radiated from them. She grimaced but saw nothing recognizable in the face.

Dabbing at black paint, she lettered a name underneath the face in a calligraphy script. EDWARD LEVENS. A name suitable for a distinguished gentleman with white hair and wise eyes. Not at all in sync with the drawing above the name.

She put a fresh canvas on the easel and began the process over again. She started from the inside and worked her way toward the outer edge, taking her time, deliberating over the details. Before she finished, she ran her thumb along sections of it, leaving smudges. Eventually, a younger face formed out of the jumble of strokes, its features blurred like an old black-and-white photo. Its cocky smile looked pleased with itself. But it didn't look like anyone she knew.

With red acrylic, she dabbed the name ED LEVENS below the face. An apt name for an idealistic college student gazing toward his future. Another mismatch between the drawing and the name.

She sighed. She was wasting her time. She didn't see how this process would get her any closer to identifying the bad guy. Yet the compulsion to keep going made her grab another canvas and set it on the easel. She kept the strokes on this one small, compact. Child-like. Surprised, she stepped back to study the end result. An innocent face looked back at her, looking incapable of inflicting harm on anyone.

EDDIE LEVENS, she painted in bright primary colors. A picture formed in her mind of a ten-year-old standing at bat, his eager stance awaiting the next pitch.

She set the three drawings side by side and looked at her watch, stunned. Almost two hours had elapsed. Puckering her mouth, she squinted at each face and pondered who her daughter's enemy might be.

An older gentleman. A young man. A child. Which of these was the real Edward Levens?

Mr. Ed Levens, CEO–Cyberbullies Inc.

Eddie "The Serpent" Levens.

E. Levens, Villain Extraordinaire.

Wait a minute. E. Levens?

Elevens.

The truth pierced her like a guided missile, sure and true.

But why would a cyber bully have the number eleven in his name? Sheer coincidence? Or was Eddie a James Bond fan?

She clutched the edge of the easel. Something about the number eleven rang a faint bell in her mind. She closed her eyes, but cobwebs filled her head. She tried to shake them away.

Her mind raced backward. A vague picture formed. A car ride. Her laughing son, slapping his knee and saying, "You'd be Kevin Eleven" to his friend in the front seat of her car.

Kevin Eleven.

Dustin Xi. Dustin Eleven.

No. Not a chance. Sweet little Dustin couldn't be involved in anything sordid like gay-bashing.

On the other hand—

Tottering to a chair, she lowered herself to the stable surface while her mind kept spinning.

She remembered Barry, and how she had misjudged him, deeming him incapable of boorish behavior.

She remembered Phillippe, and how she hadn't once suspected he lived a double life.

She remembered how often her optimism, her willingness to believe the best, had steered her wrong.

Shock pushed her to her knees, but despair held her there as she cried out to her Heavenly Father.

Chapter Nineteen

The shock of Meg's discovery lingered into the next day. But when she arrived at FOGY, all felt normal. Mike nodded as she found a seat. Jon's genial smile reminded her goodwill still existed in the world. Quincy perched like a dainty bird between Camille and Deb.

"Tonight our focus is on answered prayer," Jon announced. "So if you have anything to share, don't be afraid to shout it out."

But Meg couldn't speak, much less shout. Her focus kept slipping like a faulty transmission. Her mind and heart couldn't grasp the fact that her son's close friend could be harassing Linzee.

"Meg, do you have any answered prayers to share?"

She looked at Jon, her head filled with cotton where her brain should be. Shaking her head, she recalled all the times she'd seen Richie and Dustin in Richie's room absorbed in the laptop. She had assumed they were having harmless fun. In truth, it may not have been so harmless. Perhaps their immature brains found it amusing to harass Richie's lesbian sister. Neither of them had any obvious reason to be waging a vendetta against her.

"Camille?"

"I do have some thoughts on answered prayer." Camille shifted and swung one Capri-clad leg over the other. "Prayer is like calling a customer service center."

Camille paused, as though waiting for the inevitable question.

Meg obliged. "How is prayer like calling a customer

service center?"

Camille drew out the moment. "Because sometimes all you get is a recording: 'Please hold. Your prayer will be answered in the order received.'"

Laughter and applause erupted. Camille, FOGY's walking, talking laugh-o-meter, grinned and dipped her head.

Outwardly, Meg joined in the merriment. Inwardly, she reminded herself neither boy could know Linzee had changed her phone number. The chasm between brother and sister had never been greater than right now. These days, they behaved as virtual strangers.

She felt like a child on the last day of school—she could hardly wait for it to end.

Resolved, she sought out Mike after the meeting. He stood motionless as she approached as if he'd been waiting for her to fall into step beside him.

"Can we talk?" Guilt at what she was about to ask started to chase away her resolve. She steeled herself against it, reminded herself she was doing it for Linzee.

He nodded and led her to a quiet corner.

"Do you think you could hack into my son's computer for me?"

Not a ripple crossed his face. "I could. When?"

"Does Friday evening work for you?"

"Sure. Meet me at the mall at six. Bring his computer with you."

She glanced over at the refreshment table. Camille leaned against the wall next to Deb and Jon, watching her and Mike. Curiosity twitched all over her friend's face, and she turned away, feeling like a bug under a microscope. Leave it to Camille to turn a simple business-like conversation into the next big romance.

"Thanks, Mike. I'll see you Friday."

As he departed, she took in ten deep breaths, willing herself to appear relaxed, then approached Camille and pasted on a nonchalant smile. "Hey, I've been meaning to ask you if you want to get together for coffee."

"I've been meaning to ask you the same thing, honey." Camille placed a warm hand on her shoulder.

"So much has happened. I'm dying to tell you all about it."

"Well, now I'm dying to hear."

Deb waved goodbye and headed to the exit. Jon, sans Quincy, stepped forward, his mouth open to speak.

Meg glanced around, then back at Jon. "Where's Quincy?"

The quizzical look Jon gave her confused her. "She went home. Why?"

"She was here earlier and—" Meg faltered. How odd that Quincy hadn't ridden with Jon.

Meg shrugged and met Jon's curious gaze. "I apologize for not being with it tonight. I had a lot on my mind. This time, I'm dealing with son drama."

"It never ends, does it?"

"Apparently not."

The curiosity on his face gave way to concern. "You know we're always available to pray with you." His gaze shifted from her to Camille. "Anyway, I wanted to let the two of you know that I emailed Sam Canady to see if he would be willing to chat, and he agreed to meet with me next Saturday afternoon. Do you two want to be there for it?"

Meg bobbed her head. "I wouldn't miss it."

"Count me in." Camille turned to her. "We'll make a day of it. Coffee in the morning, Sam Canady in the afternoon."

She smiled. "What about the evening?"

"I'm sure we'll come up with something," Camille assured her with a wink. "My middle name ain't Trouble for nothing."

She snickered. Jon listened with a bemused smile.

On the drive home, her heart and mind sprinted ahead to the weekend. She prayed for a breakthrough Friday evening. But each time she thought about her planned deception, a finger of guilt prickled up her spine. She had to keep reminding herself who she was doing it for.

When she arrived home, Richie and Dustin lounged in the TV room. "Mom, do you mind if Dustin stays the night?"

She hardly had time to draw a breath and said the first thing that popped into her mind. "Let me think about it."

Puttering to her bedroom, she dropped to her knees and begged God for wisdom, for discernment. Since God didn't seem to be talking to her right now, she returned to the TV room.

"Do you mind pausing that?" She eyed Richie. "I want to talk for a minute."

Richie, his face darkening, waited a beat to punch the remote. Dustin watched her, expressionless.

"What?" snapped Richie.

"Remember I told you about your sister being harassed?"

"Yeah?"

"She got attacked the other morning."

She stole a glance at Dustin, whose face retained its polite detachment. But Richie's eyes lit up. With what, it wasn't clear. "Huh? That is trippy. Is she okay?"

Her son's reaction could be a vicarious thrill some young men feel after hearing of violence. Or something deeper. "She's okay. She's had a lot of self-defense training. Her only injury was a banged-up knee."

She glanced at Dustin. He still appeared unfazed. "Dustin, how well do you know Linzee, my daughter?" She heard challenge in her tone and bit her lip.

Surprise flickered for a split-second on his face. "Not that well, Ma'am. She comes into the coffee shop where I work, but I've never had any personal conversations with her."

"By the way, did you read spy novels as a kid?"

Richie let out a curse. "What's up with these questions, Mom? You're acting really weird."

She glared at him for cursing. "I assume you care about your sister."

"Yeah, I care, okay?" Richie's voice softened. "We'd kind of like to get back to our game now if you don't mind." He raised his brows at Dustin. "Spy novels?"

Spy novels, indeed. Way to raise suspicion, Meg.

Nothing in Dustin's manner, or Richie's, suggested sinister intent. She couldn't refuse to let Dustin stay overnight without arousing even more suspicion.

Until Friday, she'd play it cool. She couldn't have them erasing incriminating evidence from Richie's computer.

She got to her feet, anticipating a long Jacuzzi soak. "Okay, Dustin can stay. But you still have to get to work on time tomorrow."

"I know. Thanks, Mom."

"Thanks, Ma'am."

Chapter Twenty

To: cinnameg9
> *From: Phillippe St. John*
> *Monday 8:58 pm*
> *Hello, Meg, You probably heard I'm being transferred back to the Bay Area. Intel is moving me to headquarters. Things are in an upheaval here in Vancouver. Wondering if you would be open to getting together for a chat once I'm in town. I'll be flying into SFO on Wed, house-hunting rest of week. How about Saturday or Sunday? - Phillippe.*

She sat motionless in her desk chair, face frozen. Dropping her head into her hands, she dug into her scalp hard enough to leave dents.

She reread Phillippe's message, hit reply, and began typing.

"*Dear Monsieur Phillippe Rene Saint Jean, Adultère Extraordinaire,*" she wrote, then bit back a grin and started over.

"*Dear Phillippe not-so-Saint John.*" Scratch that too.

> *To: Phillippe St. John, President — Department of Infidelity*
> *From: Your ex*
> *Phillippe, Is there something on your mind? So many years have passed, so much water under the bridge, I can't imagine what there is to chat about. Things are in a state of upheaval here, too. In fact, they have been ever since 2008 when you emptied half our savings and took off to be with another woman.*
> *But I'll think about it. Next weekend is completely booked. The following weekend might work. Meg.*

Just in time, she stopped herself from hitting Send. Instead, she deleted everything and started over.

Phillippe, what could you possibly want to chat about after all these years? Our kids, perhaps? Sure, let's chat about Linzee and Richie. In case you didn't know, after you abandoned us, Linzee 'came out' as a lesbian. She's now engaged to a woman. She's also being harassed by someone, whom I suspect is our gay-bashing son and his friend.
But I will think about it. Next weekend is completely booked. Meg.

Again, she poised the cursor over Send, then thought better of it.

She tried for a third time.

Phillippe — I'm open to meeting for a chat. We have a lot to catch up on, but next weekend works better for me. Meg.

She reread her message, nodded, and sent it off into cyberspace.

***

"You'll like my dad," Linzee assured Nena as they waited near the front window. "He's pretty cool."

"He ain't a homophobe?"

"Not at all." Lifting the drape, Linzee watched three grade-school boys kicking a soccer ball around, then dropped the drape and thumped down on the sofa. "When I was in eighth grade, he and I had a talk about my sexual orientation."

"I thought he left by then."

"He left us when I was in high school. I was so mad. Took me awhile to get over it and forgive him."

"Don't blame you. What did he say in your big talk?"

She hugged a suede pillow to her chest. "He asked me if

I liked any boys yet. I said no, I didn't really like boys the way other girls did. Then he asked me if I self-identified as gay."

"I bet your mom freaked out."

"Oh, no, I never discussed things like that with her. Neither did he. 'Cause she would've freaked. Whereas my dad never did."

She stood and peered through the window again. A white Ford Taurus cruised slowly through the parking lot. The soccer players jumped out of the way. "I think he's here, Nena." She squinted at the driver. "Silly man." She laughed. "He insisted on picking us up like we were teenagers."

She and Nena stepped to the porch and waved. The driver pulled to a stop, and Linzee rushed to the car.

"Dad."

Her father emerged from the rental car and enfolded her in a smothering hug. She nestled her head in the middle of his broad chest, squeezed his bulging torso, then stepped back to survey him. He sported a head of close-cropped gray hair. Creases laced his rugged face. But his blue eyes danced with love and joy.

When he caught sight of Nena, a wide grin split his face. "Is this little cutie your fiancée?"

Nena beamed. Linzee laughed. "Yeah, Dad, this cutie is my fiancée. Meet Nena. Nena, my dad."

"Call me Phillippe." He grasped Nena's hand. "Congratulations on your engagement, eh?"

"Gracias," muttered Nena, her eyes betraying a rare shyness.

He rattled his keys. "Let's go get pizza, girls."

They piled in, and he drove them to a nearby Round Table.

"Dad, are you getting together with Richie while you're here?"

"I sure am. I'll be seeing him tomorrow for lunch. Probably do the pizza thing again."

"What about Mom?"

His chuckle was abrupt. "She put me off until next weekend."

"Will you still be here then?"

"I sure will. I expect to be here until I find a place to live. Then, it's back to Vancouver to sell that house and move everything down here."

"You must be excited."

Dad grinned, keeping his eyes on the road. "I don't know about excited, but it will be a nice change. Things haven't been going well up there."

"Besides the break-up, you mean?"

"Besides the break-up. My division's sales have dropped off a bit, and Intel's breathing down my neck. They don't want to let me go yet, but they tell me sales have to improve, or I'll be on the chopping block."

She reached over and squeezed his shoulder. "Dad, you can do it. I know you can."

"Thanks, baby. Your faith in me is touching."

She watched the town roll by. Red brick blurred with green trees. Blue clapboard merged with gray pavement. "You know what, Dad? Mom broke up with a man about the same time you and Mary split. Kind of ironic, don't you think?"

Dad turned a smile on her, his teeth gleaming. "Did she now?"

"Don't look at me like that. It doesn't mean she wants you back."

He fell silent, but the grin still played around his lips as he turned into the Round Table lot.

They ordered two large Hawaiian pizzas and a pitcher of Canadian beer while Linzee caught him up on all the recent events.

Dad's face firmed as he stared at her. "Why didn't you tell me earlier about this cyber stalker of yours, eh?"

She shrugged. "I'm telling you now, okay? Besides, I

don't see the messages anymore. And the attack in the parking lot could have been random." She caught a glimpse of Nena rolling her eyes. "Maybe it wasn't related to the harassment at all."

"And your knee?" He took a sip of beer and smacked his lips.

"It's fine, Dad."

"You be sure and tell me if you ever need my help." Dad pinned her with a look. "You know I won't let anyone mess with my little girl."

"I know."

The pizza arrived, and they dug in. The juke box jangled a country tune in the background.

"You're planning to invite your old papa to your wedding, aren't you?"

"Of course, we are."

"When's the big day?" He slid a piece of Canadian bacon into his mouth.

"The second Saturday in September." She speared a piece of pineapple and slurped it onto her tongue. "At our friend Reverend Suzette's house."

"Have you told your mother?"

Nena snorted. "She don't wanna know."

Linzee nodded, her lip curled. "Mom's totally against this, Dad. I think she'd feel totally awkward if she were to go." Her teeth ground into a slice of pizza and wrenched off a bite.

Dad muttered something in French.

"What'd you say?"

He winked at her. "You don't want to know."

Chapter Twenty-One

One of the longest weeks in Meg's recent memory concluded Friday evening at the human melting pot, Town Center Mall.

She hadn't foreseen how hard it would be to feign nonchalance around her son. All week, whenever he and Dustin hung out in Richie's room, she'd drift toward the closed door, straining her ears, but the door must have thickened by a couple of inches. No sound escaped except muffled voices.

According to Linzee, the despicable texts had ceased. "I haven't gotten a text from Eddie for a few days, Mom." Linzee's voice acquired cheery tones. "No emails, either."

"Maybe he's gotten tired of his game and is moving on to someone else." She resisted the urge to whoop and holler. But the urge to tell her daughter her suspicions proved so compelling, she almost took a needle and thread to her lips.

Instead, she'd asked, "How tall do you think your attacker was?"

"Not sure. Definitely not as tall as Blake."

"Taller, or shorter, than you?"

"Maybe around the same?"

Meg didn't know how tall Dustin was, but if it *had* been him standing behind Linzee when she decked him, he might seem to be "around the same."

Thank goodness it was Friday. Since the church always served pizza at youth group, it took a catastrophe for Richie to miss a meeting. No better time to purloin his laptop.

For the third time, Mike waited for her in the food court,

a pile of ridged fries covered in ketchup in front of him. She handed him Richie's laptop, hoping third time was a charm.

He greeted her with a tired nod and set to work. First, he cracked the password—"SHADOW"—then opened a browser.

He glanced at her. "You didn't mention why you wanted to search your son's computer."

"It occurred to me he could be behind all the stuff going on with his sister. He made some derogatory remarks the day Linzee announced her engagement, and not long after, Linzee began getting those messages." She glanced over at a group of teenagers strutting nearby, emitting jungle-like noises. "And I think his friend Dustin is in on it, too."

"Interesting." They eyed Richie's recent searches—game sites, sports, classic cars. "We should look at his email then. What's his address?"

She rattled it off. After some rhythmic clicking, Richie's logon popped up, the username and password already filled in. "Bingo," Mike muttered.

Most of the messages were unread, several of them from Mark, the youth pastor, entitled "Today's Bible Minute." She needed to tell Laura that her husband's emails were being wasted on Richie. Mike pushed the laptop over to her, and she took over the navigation. Scrolling down, she stopped at the name Xi_Dustin. It was dated from June, and she clicked it open.

Bringing Kassidy to game night Saturday, dude? If u do, I'll bring Liane.

Nothing sinister here, merely a plan to double-date. She tried to hear Dustin saying "dude," but couldn't quite make it work.

Mike angled the laptop closer to her. "Let's try Plan B and check if Eddie's email is active on this computer."

When she logged onto Eddie's email site, she half-expected the password to automatically fill in. When it didn't, she threw up her hands and eyed Mike.

"We keep hitting dead ends. If he is Eddie, he's not using this computer to send those emails."

"Either that or he's deleting his browsing history."

Opening a new tab, she pulled up Facebook. Working under the assumption his password stayed consistent, she keyed in SHADOW, and Richie's home page filled the screen.

"He's not too worried about security, is he?"

Since she and Richie were Facebook friends, his home page held no surprises, so she zeroed in on the private messages.

Most of his messages were to and from Kassidy, and most contained the word "hot." Meg's face flamed. She didn't want to know what Richie and Kassidy were doing in their private life.

But she sat upright when she saw a string of messages from Dustin. Skimming through them, she looked for the name Linzee or the word sister. The earliest dated from late May.

Algebra final prep, Dustin wrote. *7:00 my house. Be there or be Squared.*

Ha ha, u funny dude, Richie had replied.

A few weeks later Dustin wrote: *WOW, tonight — Be there or forfeit your quest.*

Richie had replied, *My mom would freak if she knew.*

The imaginary slap across Meg's face made her flinch. Richie was correct. No way would she have knowingly allowed him to dabble in World of Warcraft. Jabbing the down arrow a little too hard, she skimmed the rest of the messages but saw no mentions of Linzee. The letdown feeling surprised her. She ought to be relieved.

She looked at Mike. "There's nothing incriminating here. Let's check Dustin's Facebook page."

She logged off Richie's page, logged back in with Dustin's email. Mike scooted over and utilized the password breaker once again.

Meg chewed her lips and people-watched while the minutes crawled by. "Holy spit," Mike muttered at last. "The password must be in Chinese. In that case, I'm not going to be able to break it."

"All right, never mind. I'll check Richie's phone. They must be using their phones to communicate."

"See if you can grab it when he's in bed."

A flurry of stampeding feet interrupted them, and she glanced up. The gang of youth she'd noticed earlier ran from the entrance of Sears toward the exit behind her, each teen hugging bundles of merchandise.

"Oh no, it's one of those shoplifting gangs." The news these days was filled with stories of aggressive teen gangs invading retail establishments, grabbing whatever they could reach, while the helpless store personnel could only watch, outnumbered and unable to stop them.

"We'd better make a run for it." Mike thrust his laptop under his arm, and she grabbed the laptop and her purse. He clutched her arm and rushed her toward the opposite exit. The pumping adrenaline in her bloodstream shot liquid lightning into her legs, and she took off, seconds before a swarm of crooks roared by, leaping and trampling all over the tables.

***

"Mom, Nena said you needed to talk to me."

"Yes." Meg, enjoying fresh evening air on the back porch, peeked through the window at the kitchen clock. Richie wouldn't be home for another couple of hours. She hunched on the porch steps, enjoying the vista of palm leaves superimposed over the starlit sky. "I cracked the Edward Levens code."

She heard a sharp intake of breath. "What do you mean?"

"E. Levens. I don't know if it's coincidence, but the perp's name has the number eleven in it."

"Mom, you rock. How did you figure it out?"

She smiled. "Because that's how I roll."

Linzee's laugh sputtered out.

Meg's grin faded. "Baby Girl, this might be hard to hear, but I think Richie might have been involved in the harassment."

"Whoa. Serious? How do you figure?"

She pulled in a lungful of cool air. "Richie's friend Dustin's last name is spelled X I, the Roman numeral for eleven."

"Dustin?"

"You know him. He works at Latte Love Shack."

"The nice Asian kid? He's Richie's friend?"

"He is. Because of his last name, I began to wonder if he might be behind all this, which would mean Richie as well." She stood and paced. A long pause stretched.

"Well, snap." Linzee's wobbly voice left Meg wondering if she'd been wrong to share this. "I can't believe I didn't think of that. I am stunned. I am shocked. My own brother? That's crazy-making."

"Maybe I shouldn't have told you. There's no proof. Only a theory. I even had Mike hack into Richie's computer, but we found nothing incriminating."

When Linzee replied, her voice turned husky. "It's a theory which makes sense, though. Richie did make homophobic remarks to me. I did see Dustin looking at me funny a few times. If it *was* them, they hid their tracks well, like Mike said."

Meg noted the use of the past tense. "But you say it's stopped, right?"

"I hope it has. Nena hasn't seen any texts lately."

"The part I don't get is, how did he get your new number?" She stretched her free arm high, as though she were pulling stars from the sky. "You and Richie aren't close."

"Wouldn't he have gotten it from you?"

"He never asked me for it, and how would he have known you changed your number?" She eased back down to the steps.

Linzee's voice was thick. "I don't know."

Meg's eyes stung with unshed tears. "Remember when I asked you how tall your attacker was?"

Linzee sighed. "I wondered why you were asking. It couldn't have been Richie. This person wasn't taller than me, for sure. It's all a blur now. I suppose it could have been Dustin, but he doesn't seem like the type to attack anyone."

"You'd be amazed how many times I've been wrong about people."

"Mom." Linzee's voice broke.

"Mmm?"

"I need a hug." Her daughter burst into sobs.

A dam erupted inside Meg. Doubling over, she wept in sync with her daughter, wishing she could gather Linzee into her arms and rock her side to side, just as though she were little again.

"Baby Girl, consider yourself cyber-hugged."

Linzee's giggles mingled with sobs. She took a long, shuddering breath. "Maybe it's time to change the subject."

Meg waited.

After five seconds, Linzee sighed. "So-o-o-o, guess what?"

"What?"

"Dad's in town, and he took Nena and me out for pizza. We—"

"He emailed me Monday night." She anchored herself against the porch wall.

"Yeah, I understand you two are getting together next weekend."

"I suppose so."

"Way to sound enthusiastic, Mom. After all this time, you two should be able to be friends."

Meg snorted.

"Plus, I got the weirdest feeling he was glad you weren't dating anyone. Almost like he hoped things could be rekindled."

"That's funny." She forced a grin, which likely resembled a grimace.

"Funny? Yeah, I guess it would be a little funny to see my parents get back together."

"Every child wishes their divorced parents would get back together."

"Oh, Mom, I gave up on that idea years ago."

"So did I."

They chatted a few minutes more, and then Meg said goodbye. Her rubbery legs lifted her off the porch and carried her into the house, where waves of emotion assaulted her. Memories of Phillippe—unwelcome, awkward thoughts—tore through her mind.

At the same time, she had to admit the truth of Romans 8:28. She and her daughter were doing some long overdue bonding, mending their fences, thanks to Eddie. And Phillippe. Somehow God was bringing good out of Linzee's ordeal, after all.

Chapter Twenty-Two

Meg's favorite aroma permeated the mall coffee shop next morning. Given the sensory surroundings, last night's craziness seemed a travesty. No doubt the stunned store employees had worked all night to bring order out of chaos. They must have lost thousands of dollars of inventory.

The world has turned into a place where lawlessness reigns.

She caught a glimpse of brassy red at the entrance, and Camille swooped in, dressed in flowered Capris and a white halter top.

"Girlfriend." Camille grinned as they exchanged hugs, and then took their place in line.

"Did you hear what happened here last night?" Meg whispered after she'd ordered her usual latte.

"Oh, the shoplifting gang, you mean?" Camille's eyes lit up as they seated themselves near the mall entrance.

"Yes, they came charging right at Mike and me." She pointed toward Sears. "I haven't moved so fast since Phillippe rushed me to the hospital the day my son was born."

"You and Mike were here?" Camille's eyes grew more animated. "You two dating now?"

"Not at all." She shook her head in an emphatic negative. "He's a kind-hearted friend who's been trying to help me catch my daughter's cyber stalker."

"Okay, whatever you say." A skeptical tilt of the head. "Then what happened?"

"After the kids ran out and the commotion died down, Mike and I were interviewed by mall security."

"Were you on TV?"

"No, we just missed the news crew."

Camille's jaw hardened. "Bejeepers. What is wrong with kids these days?"

"It's why I tell my son not to run in packs."

"They have such a flippity-flip sense of entitlement." Camille's gaze swiveled to the front counter. "Our drinks are ready. I'll get 'em." She returned bearing two foaming cups. "I was a pretty wild kid back in the day. But I don't think it would've occurred to any of us to invade a store and grab as much stuff as we could." She tucked an orange strand of hair behind her ear and winked. "I did do my share of shoplifting on the sly."

Meg tried to visualize a furtive young Camille swiping a candy bar off a shelf and dropping it into her pocket with a casual swish.

"I did a little shoplifting, too, which I regret now." She heard remorse in her tone. "I never got caught, but I should have. It would've taught me a lesson."

"I did a lot of things I regret now, probably way more than you." Camille stirred her drink. "Drugs and alcohol. Making babies way too young. My oldest is thirty-five, can you believe it? I was sixteen when I had her."

"How many kids do you have besides her and Hilary?"

"Two sons, thirty and twenty-eight."

Meg learned each of Camille's three short-lived marriages had produced one of her children, and Hilary's father had been a live-in boyfriend. "One reason I appreciate Bill so much is, he's lasted longer than all the others combined." She beamed, showing a mouthful of perfect teeth. "I'm exaggerating. But it feels like we've been together for twenty years. He's quite the good guy underneath that crusty exterior." She pointed toward the pastry shelf. "In fact, my Bill is like one of those éclairs over there — crusty on the outside, all sweet and creamy on the inside." Camille's deep laugh echoed, drawing attention from nearby customers. "We lived together up until a year ago."

"What happened a year ago?"

"We became Christians," she announced in the inspirational tones of a TV host. "Which, in itself, is a long story. Got some time?"

"I do. Tell me."

"He and I were members of a sailing club, and on one trip we met Jon. I don't know if you know Jon is into sailing."

"I didn't know that."

"We both liked him right away, but we soon found out he was one of those born-again Christians, whereas Bill and I were quite the party animals." Camille's red-lacquered nails tapped out a rapid rhythm as she talked. "As we got to know him, the way he talked about his relationship with God got our attention. We had known religious folks, but they didn't talk the way he did."

"I know exactly what you mean."

"We started asking questions, one thing led to another, and finally one day he led us both in prayers to receive Christ. We started going to church with him." Camille paused for a slurp of cappuccino. "He goes to that big church in Sausalito, the one that broadcasts on TV Sunday mornings. We had no clue churches looked like that. We thought we were going to one of those square little numbers with hard pews and a steeple."

Meg chuckled.

"We've been going ever since. They put us in a small group for baby Christians, as they called us, and as time went on, we realized God wasn't happy with us living together. After Bill moved out, we kept seeing each other, so we figured we might as well get married."

"It must be hard to go from living together back to courting."

"It was, but now we have a marathon love feast to look forward to on our wedding night."

Meg giggled. "TMI, girlfriend, TMI."

Camille's sly grin didn't waver. "Too much info, my foot. We don't take each other for granted anymore."

Meg wrapped her hands around her cup, absorbing its warmth. "I didn't know you knew Jon prior to FOGY."

"He's the reason I started going to the meetings. Prior to that, my daughter's lesbianism bothered me some, but after I met Christ the annoyance really amped up. So Jon brought me to FOGY, and it's helped me learn how to think like Jesus."

"You've lived an eventful life."

"Tell me about it. I wasted most of it. Anyway, I want to hear about you now. Tell me about your exes."

Meg raised a brow. "I haven't had much success in the trust department, starting with my cheating ex-husband. The one who left me for another woman. Which reminds me, he's moving back to the area this week."

"Is that good or bad?"

"I don't know yet. We're getting together next weekend to chat."

"Bleepers."

"And my daughter thinks he has something up his sleeve."

Camille gaped. "Like what?"

She looked down, finding the words difficult to utter. "Like, possible reconciliation."

Camille yelped. "Don't do it, girlie. You need a kind, unselfish, trustworthy Christian man."

"I agree. But I'm not in a big hurry to find one right now."

"Ever done any online dating?"

"No." She wrinkled her nose and laughed. "It feels too much like buying a boyfriend. And lately I've been so consumed with my daughter's issue, I have no emotional energy left for dating."

A frown passed quickly across her friend's face. "We've

been here almost an hour, and we're meeting Jon at two. Do you have time to tell me what's going on with your daughter?"

"Sure." Meg glanced at her flashing phone. "But I need to check this message."

It was from Richie. *Mom, can you pick up me and Dustin at the library?*

"Camille, I need to answer this text real quick."

She keyed a response. *Dude, where's your car?*

The reply came in less than a minute. *We walked here from Dustin's, but it's too far to walk home. And don't call me dude.*

She grinned, picturing Richie's scowl over her attempt at humor.

A thought teased at her like a tendril of smoke. She reread his text. *Can you pick up me and Dustin at the library?*

The library.

A memory from last week rose in her mind. "Welcome to Marin County Library." She tensed and ground her teeth, unable to stop visions of their grinning faces, their fingers composing harassing messages to Linzee.

Swallowing hard, she fumbled over the tiny keyboard. *I can't pick you up. I have a busy day ahead.*

Camille was busy with her own phone, so Meg texted Nena. *Has Linzee gotten any messages from Eddie recently?*

Nena replied right away. *No, btw she told me you think it's her brother.*

She looked up, ready to resume the conversation. "Camille, you know how they say life is stranger than fiction? Well, this bullying story gets stranger all the time."

After Meg had brought her up to date, Camille lifted her perfectly-penciled brows. "In my humble opinion, it sounds like God is doing something in your daughter's life. I learned that from Jon. He says once we start praying, God sometimes answers in ways we don't expect. You know the saying, be careful what you wish for? Jon says, be careful what you pray for."

Meg chewed on her lips. "If it's God, I wish He'd let me in on His scheme."

"Do you ever wonder why those boys came up with Edward for an alias?"

Meg shrugged. "Sure, along with, how did they keep getting her new phone number? She changed it twice."

Camille tapped her fist on the table. "I think I can answer that. The online ordering system at the latte shack, I'm almost positive."

"How do you know?"

"I work at a restaurant; been there for years. Ever heard of the Grapevine Café in Novato?"

"No."

"Now you have. A few months ago, we installed a new system for online ordering. Most restaurants handle their online ordering through a third party, but sometimes a smaller place will hire a consultant to build their own. Is this latte shack a mom-and-pop-type place?"

She shook her head. "No mom, just a pop. The lead singer from that seventies band Poe Boy owns it."

Camille whistled, her steel-rimmed glasses flashing beams of light. "I'm impressed. Anyway, sometimes the order screen will request a contact number in case the restaurant has questions. So I would bet you a grand the coffee shop has the same type of system." Her face grew thoughtful. "Here's what you need to do. Tomorrow morning go online and put in an order. See if it asks you for a contact number. If it does, then when you pick up your order, pretend you're outraged over having to put in your private phone number. They might say something like, 'Oh, it goes to a third party, and we don't see it.' But if they say, 'We keep all contact information in strictest confidence,' you'll know they saw it."

"Why would a customer need to put in a phone number if the restaurant won't see it?"

"So the third-party administrator can send a confirmation message. 'Thank you for your order,'" Camille chirped in a robotic voice. "'Your confirmation number is blah-blah-blah.'"

"Got it. So Dustin could have been lifting Linzee's phone number off her order and passing it along to Richie. Her name is spelled an unusual way. It wouldn't be hard for him to identify her."

"But you won't know until you test it out."

"What a great idea. Thanks, my friend."

"Keep me posted," said Camille, sly smile intact.

Chapter Twenty-Three

Jon's Jeep barreled down the 101 and around a rusty pickup that had come within a foot of side-swiping them. Meg, adrenaline pumping, flew forward and nearly knocked her head against Camille's seat. "Wouldn't it be great if someone invented a driver-to-driver communication system?" she gasped out. "You could record your message to that man, and it would flash it in your window at him."

Jon's eyes sparkled at her in the rear-view mirror. "I like that idea."

Camille tilted her face toward him. "So, Jon, if you had a chance to send a message to that other driver, what would you say?"

He chuckled. "It probably wouldn't be very nice."

"You?" Camille gaped. "You swear at other drivers?"

He chuckled again. "Some of them deserve it." He grew serious. "Then again, sometimes I deserve it."

Rugged brown hills swept by outside the window. Occasionally, they passed a house perched halfway up a rocky incline, looking precarious. Meg sometimes pictured those homes tumbling down the hill, end-over-end, and landing with a splat all over the freeway, sending pieces of houses flying into cars. She cringed at the picture it made but grinned at the absurdity. No doubt those homes were earthquake-proof.

She listened to Camille and Jon banter back and forth for a while, until the topic on her mind grew too loud to ignore.

Inching forward, she waited for a break in the

conversation. "What if Pastor Canady condemns us parents who have gay children?" she blurted. "What if he tells us we raised them wrong?"

The car fell silent for a moment before Jon spoke. "Not to worry, Meg. Whatever claims he makes, I'm going to ask him to back them up with scripture."

"But the Bible says to raise up a child in the way he should go." She gripped the center console, thinking of all she'd learned lately. "I used to be halfway convinced that Linzee *was* born gay. But now, I'm not so sure. In fact, I had a heated argument with my brother about it. He believes homosexuality is innate."

Jon flipped his left-turn blinker and slowed. "Even after all the research that's been done, no one knows for sure what makes someone develop same-sex attractions."

In Linzee's case, Meg was convinced Phillippe's abandonment stood at the heart of it.

"Look at the culture we live in," Camille said. "Gayness is portrayed as cool."

Jon nodded. "There's no pressure on kids these days to deny their urges. Gay characters on TV and movies are presented as sympathetic characters."

Camille swiveled to face her. "Whenever a celebrity comes out of the closet, they're treated as though they did something noble."

Meg nodded. "That is true. They're labeled as brave and given a pat on the back by the media." She folded her hands on the console. "The literature said a lot of gay adults were sexually abused as kids. But as far as I know, Linzee never was."

"Hilary was."

"She was?"

"By a neighbor. A teenage boy who later went to prison for it."

Meg stared straight ahead. Golden Gate Park's wall of trees sprang into view. "That's so tragic, Camille." Tears gathered in her heart. "Think how differently Hilary's life might have turned out if that hadn't happened."

"I try not to think about it. It makes me too angry."

Jon took a hard left. "The enemy is working overtime. Just look around you."

New Age bookstores, signs advertising psychic readings, and cars plastered with rainbow stickers lined both sides of the street.

"Look, guys." Meg pointed. "Here comes the Magic Bus." A tour bus adorned in a psychedelic pattern neared them from the opposite lane. "Have you ever been on it?"

"It's on my bucket list," said Jon.

"I have." Camille turned. "If you want to get in touch with your inner hippie, I highly recommend it."

Meg laughed, and they drove on, past the colorful bus, past equally colorful buildings with baskets of blooms spilling over in an abundance of hues. Meg could only imagine the neighborhood forty-five years earlier—a hotbed of psychedelic clothes, music, and drugs.

Jon pulled up to the old church and parallel-parked. This time, the guard was expecting them, and he led them into the catacombs of the building and down two long halls. A chill permeated the place, and Meg shivered, wishing she'd brought a sweater.

The guard opened a wooden door at the end of the hall and ushered them in. Pastor Sam Canady, a mid-forties, casually-dressed man, looked nothing like a reverend. He gave them each a stiff smile and handshake as Jon made introductions, then gestured to three plush chairs.

"Have a seat." He nodded at the guard, who departed.

Meg chose the end chair, and her finger found a brass tack head and rubbed. She breathed in the various scents in the room: fresh reams of paper, reminiscent of the first day of school. Rich leather, reminding her of a furniture store. Freon, pumping through the air-conditioning unit.

Canady rolled the chair behind his desk. "What can I do

for you folks today?"

Jon leaned forward. "We're hoping to discuss God's Word with you."

Canady's eyes brightened. "My favorite subject."

"Mine, too." Jon smiled while Meg said a silent prayer. "Help us understand something. You preach that God hates gays." Jon's voice gentled as if he hoped to disarm the pastor. "We're wondering which Scriptures support that teaching."

Canady nodded. "Certainly. Have you read my blog?"

"I have."

"I hope, then, you've read the passages that support my position." The pastor swiveled and grasped a Bible from a credenza behind him. "How much time do you have?" Canady opened the Bible. "We'll be here all day if I were to read you every single passage I've studied."

"Just a few is all we need."

Canady pulled a pair of reading glasses onto his nose. "Psalm 97:10 'Ye that love the Lord, hate evil.'" He flipped to a Post-it noted page. "Psalm 101:3 'I will set no wicked thing before mine eyes.'" He turned another section of pages. "Psalm 139:21 'Do I not hate them, O Lord, who hate thee? And am I not grieved with those that rise up against thee?'"

He peered at them over the rim of his glasses. "Any questions so far?"

"Yes." Jon set his jaw. "Remind me of the seven things that the writer of Proverbs says God hates. Proverbs six, I believe." He held out his hand. "May I?"

"Be my guest." Canady handed Jon the Bible. Meg listened to the silence, hearing nothing but breathing and shuffling pages. Unspoken tension vibrated in the air.

"Here it is." Jon fingered the passage. "The list of things God hates. Proverbs 6:16 to 19. 'A proud look, a lying tongue, and hands that shed innocent blood. An heart that deviseth wicked imaginations, feet that be swift in running to mischief. A false witness that speaketh lies, and he that soweth discord among brethren.'"

Jon set the Bible back on Canady's desk and searched the pastor's face. "There you have it. No mention of hating gays."

A muscle twitched in Canady's cheek. "You don't think homosexuals have feet that are swift in running to mischief? Or who stir up discord?"

"Pastor Canady—"

"I prefer Sam."

Jon sat back, ankle on knee. "Sam. Do you remember when you were lost in sin?"

"Can't remember that far back. I accepted Christ as my Savior when I was four."

"Well, according to Psalm 139, you were conceived in sin. Which would mean, from the time you were born, until you were four years old, you were still in your sins."

"Technically, that's true."

"But something brought you to an awareness of your need for Christ. What was it?"

Canady relaxed and leaned forward, his hands folded, tapping lightly as he talked. "My mother explained the gospel to me, and helped me ask Jesus into my heart."

"But what did your mother say exactly which made you realize you needed Jesus in your heart?"

Canady placed his glasses on his head. His green eyes gleamed. "I see where you're going with this. I assure you, she told me what sin was. That it was rebellion against God. As I grew up, I became more aware of how much God hates sin, and how the world seems to be oblivious to the fact that God's condemnation hangs over them."

"They're equally oblivious to God's love. Have you noticed?"

"Telling people God loves them doesn't convict them of sin."

Jon's tone stayed firm. "With all due respect, I beg to

differ. His kindness leads us to repentance. Romans 2:4."

"Which follows the passage condemning homosexual sins." Canady's voice acquired an edge of irritation. "'For the wrath of God is revealed from heaven against all ungodliness and unrighteousness of men, who hold the truth in unrighteousness.' Romans 1:18."

Meg eyed the bookshelf, stacked with Christian non-fiction and theology books. Jon and Sam's 'Battle of the Scriptures' showed no signs of slowing. But sooner or later, one of them would have to cry uncle, or they would be here for hours. She prayed it would be Canady.

By now, the verbal tussle was infused with animosity. Jon's skin was stretched taut across his face. Sam's voice strained in an obvious effort to keep the volume down.

She glanced at her silenced cell phone. The time was nearing four o'clock. Jon's next statement got her attention. "As I mentioned in my email, I'm involved with a support group for parents of gay children. You know what our mission statement is?"

Canady shook his head. Judging by the expression on his face, he didn't want to know.

"'Showing Christ's love, mercy and grace to our gay loved ones.'" Jon rested his hands on Canady's desk. "Many gays, in particular our youth, have been lied to by our culture. They're victims as much as they are sinners. We believe that knocking them over the head with God's condemnation is only going to alienate them further from Christ."

Canady stood, a clear signal he was finished. "Jesus talked about Hell more than any other topic except money."

Jon stood also. "Jesus also told sinners he didn't condemn them, then told them to go and sin no more."

"The problem is, they resent being told to sin no more."

Jon didn't reply this time, but reached out his hand and received Canady's handshake. "Thanks for your time today, Sam. I hope we can talk again sometime."

Within seconds, Canady's long strides carried him to the door. He held it open for them without a word, his face grim. The guard waited to escort them to the street.

"Whew." Meg let go of her breath after she and Camille settled themselves in the Jeep. "I felt a little useless in there. What about you, Camille?"

Camille, seated in back this time, said, "I was there to listen and learn. And pray."

Meg waited until Jon started the engine and merged onto Haight Street. "Do you think we got anywhere with him?"

Camille's head appeared in the space between the seats. "I don't know. He's a stubborn one."

Jon turned. "The seeds have been planted. That's all we can do. How about we have a prayer time on the way home?"

They took turns praying all the way back to San Rafael.

Chapter Twenty-Four

After Camille had left for home, Meg wavered between checking out Latte Love Shack's online ordering, or waiting until morning. The place had closed several hours ago, and wouldn't open again until six a.m. tomorrow.

Practicality battled with curiosity, but eventually, curiosity won out. She carried her laptop from the kitchen to the family room desk and found the site.

The first screen asked her to place an order. The next screen asked only for her name and email. She wondered what would happen if she put in a pretend order. But even after selecting a green tea smoothie, no phone number request popped up. She canceled the order and texted Nena.

You two still up? If so, pls have Linzee call me. Thx.

A minute later her phone rang.

"Hi, Mom." Linzee's voice sounded upbeat.

"Sorry to call so late." Meg leaned an elbow on the desk.

"Not a problem. We always stay up 'til midnight on weekends."

"Is life treating you any better?"

"Much better. It's such a huge load off not getting any more messages from Eddie. I told Officer Klein we had pretty much eliminated Blake as our perp, and he said they were coming to the same conclusion. Apparently not much went on at Blake's house for the undercover cop to see."

"That's because he's not Eddie."

Linzee sighed. "I almost feel sorry for Blake. The cop said he doesn't go out much, just sits in the house all day. Never gets visitors either. They've discontinued the surveillance."

Meg swiveled her chair in a slow rhythm, back and forth. "Like I told you before, your harasser was someone who knows you well enough to use the correct spelling of your name." The chair lurched back as if it were alarmed. "I learned something about online ordering this morning which might be helpful."

She'd barely finished sharing what she'd learned when Linzee interrupted. "I rarely used the online order system. I usually called it in."

"You called it in?"

"Yeah." The silence pulsated. "Wow. It's all so clear now."

"Not to me."

"See, their computer had my phone number linked to my name. Sort of how pizza places work. You know how when you call in your pizza order, they already know who you are and where you're located."

"But that's only for delivery, isn't it?"

"Latte Love Shack has a similar system, but it's more advanced. They don't do deliveries, but it's the same idea. When regular customers call in, the staff can see their name and their favorite menu items. The order's waiting for them when they arrive."

"So after you changed your number, what happened when you called in your order?"

"Since the system didn't recognize my number, the person answering the phone asked me for my name."

"And nobody else has a name like yours." She stood, sending the chair sliding backward. Her feet carried her to the futon, where she dropped.

"And any of the employees could see my name on the order screen."

"Holey socks." Meg folded her legs underneath her and sank into the cushion's softness, her fingers kneading her throbbing temple. "Do you remember if Dustin worked those mornings?"

"I don't remember, Mom. I had no reason to notice. Anyway, I don't call in my orders anymore. Since I'm not using my phone, I go in and use the embedded computers now. It takes longer, but—"

"Good," she cut in. "I hope I spooked those boys when I questioned Richie about it."

"Apparently you did. Way to go, Mom."

The conversation ended with "I love you, I love you back," and a sensation in her chest reminiscent of a furnace warming up a cold room.

Sometime around eleven-thirty, the front door slammed. Richie's lumbering footsteps stomped their way toward the east wing of the house, with a quick detour through the kitchen to the refrigerator.

She didn't call to him lest he see the guilt written all over her. She'd hacked into his Facebook page again and found some revealing messages, but they weren't ones she'd wanted to see.

Kassidy: "Hey hot stuff."

Richie: "No ur hot stuff baby."

Her mouth hung open like a cavern, and a chill swept over her, but she'd kept reading. And unless the exchange happened to be written in some complex, secret code, it appeared Richie and Kassidy had already crossed the line into immorality.

A new heaviness now weighed down her spirit. Richie had seemed to be on track with the Lord as recently as a year ago. But that man-child son of hers had vanished to who knew where. A worldly-minded, wise-cracking young man had snuck in like a midnight thief and taken over Richie's body.

Sometimes she wondered if having kids was worth all the grief. Yet, the wrong choices and failures of their later years couldn't undo all the sweet moments of their childhood. She wouldn't trade in the euphoria of their baby years for anything. The impossibly soft little bodies, the proud baby grins, the tiny wobbling legs when they took their first steps.

Being a parent could send a person to the highest of heights and to the deepest of depths. Right now, she'd sunk pretty near the bottom of the depths.

A sudden craving to feel a man's comforting arms around her almost knocked her clear to the rock-bottom of the abyss.

***

By one a.m., Richie's manly snoring carried from inside his room. Meg, pacing outside his door, eased the door open and crept inside. Her foot brushed a pile of fabric. A tiny red dot twinkled on his computer. The alarm clock glowed. But where was his phone?

She knelt down and groped the fabric pile at her feet, feeling the heavy roughness of cargo cutoffs. She dug around in the pockets and hit pay dirt on the second attempt. Stuffing her guilt, she grasped the phone and crept out of the room, then closed the door ever so softly behind her and slithered back to her own room.

Holding her breath, she touched the messages icon.

Not a single text message appeared in his inbox. How strange, since his thumbs flew at seventy miles per hour over this keyboard every day.

Unless he was one of those kids who deleted his messages at the end of each day. Due to snooping mothers such as herself, no doubt.

A vision of herself dropping the phone and stomping it to bits flit through her mind. She needed to return the phone right now. Breathing hard, she carefully retraced her movements and replaced the phone where she'd found it. Richie's snoring didn't waver. He remained asleep. And clueless.

Chapter Twenty-Five

The boiling August sun had transformed Latte Love Shack's patio tables into hot stovetops. Linzee and Nena sought refuge in the cool interior. The ficus canopy cast green shadows over their clasped hands as Linzee sipped a hazelnut latte.

On the drive over, Nena had frowned when Linzee told her she thought Drucie would be interested to know who they suspected Eddie to be.

"That don't sound too smart to me." Nena glanced over from the driver's seat. "Ain't you afraid she'll spill the beans?"

Linzee had shrugged. "Wish I could see his face if she does. Who would've guessed? Little Dustin, my brother's partner in crime."

"It's like we're in some movie where the villain's the one nobody suspects. What're the chances you would've suspected Dustin if not for your mom?"

"Zilch, maybe?"

Linzee forced her attention back to the present and looked around. "I'm glad he isn't working this morning." She dropped her voice. "I bet he's at my mom's church, along with my brother. Isn't it ironic?"

They laughed, which caught Drucie's attention. "Yo, buds."

Linzee thought she saw Nena roll her eyes.

"Hey, Drucie." Linzee checked Nena's expression. "How's it going?"

"Same old, same old."

"When is your break? I have news."

"Not long. I'll come see you." Drucie trotted away.

Nena pulled her hand away and glared. Linzee cast a pleading look across the table. "C'mon, Nena. She won't bite."

"No, but I might." Nena picked up a napkin and began folding it like an accordion.

Linzee sputtered. "Why do you hate on her so much?"

Nena shrugged. "I ain't hatin' on her. But somethin' about her creeps me out."

Linzee shook her head, took a big swig of sweetened coffee, and changed the subject.

At the appointed time, Drucie dropped to the bench next to Linzee. "I'm all ears, my dude." Drucie was all eyes, as well. She thumped her elbows on the tabletop, her gaze like laser darts.

Linzee grinned as she sipped her second latte, avoiding Nena's glowering gaze. "I discovered an interesting thing this week about your coworker Dustin. How well do you know him?"

Drucie raised her chin and brought it down on her fists. "He's a coworker far as I'm concerned. Why?"

Linzee leaned in, dropping her voice several notches. "My mom thinks he might be Eddie."

Drucie's eyes widened. Her head shot up. "Dude. Why would she think that?"

"For one thing, he's good friends with my brother, who said some homophobic things to me and Nena."

Drucie's mouth elongated.

"My mom thinks they're in on it together, and that Dustin got my new phone numbers from the call-in order system here."

"That is a trip." Drucie gave a short, abrasive laugh. "Goes to show even the sweet innocent ones have something to hide."

"Yeah. But we have no proof of —"

"You still getting those messages?"

"No, they've stopped, thank goodness." Linzee couldn't contain a grin.

"Your mom must be one smart lady."

Linzee nodded. "She is. It was pretty brilliant the way she—"

"I want a refund!" A commotion at the front counter cut off her words. A customer was yelling at the red-faced manager. Matt appeared to be offering soothing words to the customer, but the man didn't back down.

Matt glared and gestured toward their table. Drucie cursed, unbending herself. "I'm being summoned. If you want to talk more, I'll be here Wednesday."

Linzee and Nena decided to depart before the customer's tirade escalated into a free-for-all. They left the shop and drove home, Linzee's heart as light as a helium balloon.

Chapter Twenty-Six

First Baptist's basement room remained blessedly cool after the day's ninety-degree high.

"Has anyone had an opportunity to practice being Jesus this week?" said Jon in a voice of quiet authority. Clad in a royal blue tee and cut-off jeans, he sported a surfer-dude look. Judging by his defined biceps, he'd been hitting the gym.

Meg, recovered from her dark night of the soul, raised her hand. The gloom had loosened its grip on her once she decided she'd talk to the youth pastor about her concerns. She knew Mark would keep their conversation confidential, and would address the subjects of sex and violent online games in youth group. In the meantime, she would pray for the seed to fall on fertile soil in her son's heart.

"Meg?" Jon nodded in her direction.

"What a week." She blew out all the built-up tensions. "I have two praises to share. First, I'm bonding with my daughter again, and second, the harassment has stopped." She caught Camille's eye and grinned. "I see now how God used it to start the healing process. Even though I'm still not okay with Linzee's lifestyle, I'm slowly learning how to put her in God's hands and just love on her."

"That's a real answer to prayer." Jon beamed warmth. "I see a lightness in you I haven't seen for awhile, Meg. I can tell the enemy is backing off, and I suspect God's about to do something."

His words felt like a crackling fireplace on cold feet. Speechless, she smiled back at him. How strange she had never acknowledged to herself what a fine man Jon was. How odd she'd ignored the obvious. If ever a perfect man existed for her, he would be someone like Jon Paulson.

A man after God's own heart.

A vision of a young woman with long shiny hair, seated next to Jon on a green lawn, rose to her mind, and she smothered a sigh. The best men always seemed to be taken. Now if Jon had a clone out there somewhere —

She saw Camille watching her, and returned a nonchalant smile.

With an effort, she wrested her thoughts away from Jon. Neither Quincy nor Mike had shown tonight. She hoped Mike hadn't stayed away on her account. On Friday night, he had once again asked her to join him for Sunday lunch. At her hesitance, he had backed off, palms out. "I was hoping to spend more time with you, but if I'm not your cup of tea, please say so."

She had stammered out, "You're a good man, Mike, and I'm so grateful for all you've done. But I'd rather remain friends for now."

Poor Mike. She felt as guilty as if she'd strolled past a homeless man and refused to give him anything.

After the meeting, Camille and Jon gravitated her way, holding plates. She couldn't stop herself from grinning at Jon. "I found out you and Camille are old friends."

"Uh oh." He chuckled. "She didn't tell you about my sordid past, did she?"

Camille pointed at Jon. "He's joking. This guy is as squeaky clean as a new car." She grinned. "I did tell her about *my* sordid past."

Her heart quickened. "Jon, I can't picture you with a sordid past."

"Only by the grace of God." He bit into a cookie. "Speaking of new cars, are we talking Maserati or Hummer?"

Camille stepped back and appraised him. "Dodge Ram

pickup." She gave a decisive nod.

Meg studied him. "I see you as a BMW."

A smile broke across his face. "I've been called worse."

Camille laughed, then returned to the goodies table. Jon turned a purposeful look on Meg. "Hey, I wanted to tell you, the news you shared tonight made me think of the prayer you prayed your first night here. Do you remember?" He stood with a casual stance; his plate balanced on the tips of his fingers.

Baffled, she shook her head, unable to remember something so specific from four weeks ago.

"You prayed the Lord would do whatever it took to set Linzee free."

"Oh." She jolted at the memory, wondering if she'd been mistaken to pray such a prayer. "I remember now. You have a good memory."

"Not really, it stuck with me because I remember wondering if God would do something you might not be prepared for." He shifted from foot to foot, his plate tilting and threatening to spill the uneaten cookies. "Anyway, God nudged me to pray for you."

"What did He tell you to pray for?"

"Just that if your daughter had to go through a trial, it wouldn't be too traumatic for you."

She regarded him with a sense of wonder. What incredible discernment the man had. A rush of well-being filled her. His words might as well have been gift-wrapped and bedecked with a bright bow.

With a start, she forced her mind to focus on the conversation. "But nothing has changed for her. She and Nena are still together."

He leaned over and set his plate on a chair. "Here's the thing." He rubbed his jaw. "You've established credibility with her. Someday she may realize she wants what you have more than she wants a same-sex relationship."

"That would be a miracle." Despite her upbeat words,

inside she was skeptical that God would actually perform such a feat.

"I know it's a cliché, but God's in the miracle business." He ran his hand through his hair, leaving behind a messy, appealing mop. "Speaking of miracles, did Camille tell you the story of her conversion?"

"Yes, she did, and I understand you were instrumental in it."

"No, it was all God." A light glowed from his eyes. "I just happened to be in the right place at the right time."

"It must have been a dramatic conversion."

"One of the most remarkable I've seen. In spite of my prayers, she and Bill seemed so closed to the gospel. A lot like that couple in the park, Seth and Jessica. I was just about ready to write them off as hopeless cases."

"Good thing you didn't. How long did you pray for them?"

"A good three years or so. God wouldn't let me quit. My point is, don't give up on people."

"Jon, you're such an inspiration."

"I am?" The pleased grin filled his entire face.

"You are. You inspire me to pray with more zeal." She looked into his surprised face. "In fact, I'll bet you're praying for your brother with the same diligence, aren't you?"

"I'm trying to. And I'm clinging to the hope I'll see him in heaven someday." A frown replaced the smile. "He's another hard case. We were raised in a nominally Christian home, went to church a few times a year, and considered ourselves good Christians. Then in college, I went one way, and Curtis went another."

"What happened in college?"

"God became real to me. But Curtis, on the other hand—" He stopped, his face etched with distress. "He was sexually abused by a neighbor as a child. So he walked away from God early on. By the time he got to high school, he was hard core."

Her heart burned inside her as Jon related anecdotes of his brother from childhood, and the day Curtis came out as gay.

"What about Linzee?" His look of interest encouraged her to relate the story of her daughter's coming out.

"I'll always remember the day she told me she was gay." She stared at the blank wall behind Jon as her mind traveled six years into the past. "It was the day of her Winter Formal."

He nodded along.

"She modeled her new yellow dress for me, and I told her she'd probably get mobbed for dances. I'll never forget what she said. She got this funny look on her face and said, 'You don't get it, Mom, do you? I'm not going to get mobbed for dances. At least not by guys. Haven't you figured out I'm gay?'"

"How did you react?"

"I felt like she'd hauled off and slapped me. And then I felt stupid for having missed all the signs."

"What signs?"

"She never seemed interested in boys. She never hung posters of male celebrities in her room. I chalked it up to her being a late bloomer."

Jon stroked his chin, ruminating. The conversation lulled. Most of the others had already left. Only she and Jon, Dean and Esther remained.

He seemed to come to and slapped his forehead. "I've been remiss. Sorry, I lost track of time. I'm supposed to be locking up now." He gestured to her and the Woods to lead the way up the stairs and outside. He tugged on the door, ensured it was locked, and they said their goodbyes. Jon fell into step beside her. "Thanks for listening to my rambling on." He cast her a half-sheepish grin.

"You weren't rambling at all. The things you said encouraged me, more than you know."

They reached her Mustang, and he leaned an elbow on

the roof, hand cradling his head. "I'm going to miss this group." His tone held a hint of wistfulness. Although the darkening sky partially shrouded his face, she could see him regarding her with a decidedly penetrating look.

She wished she knew what he was thinking.

"We'll miss you too. Any ministry would be lucky to have you."

"Well, thank you. As it turns out, a ministry at my church needs volunteers. It involves working with disadvantaged youth." He shifted himself to an upright position, still with the same puzzling expression. "I'm just waiting for the Lord's go-ahead."

Something buzzed nearby, and she realized his phone was going off. She wondered if it was Quincy.

A trace of annoyance crossed his face, and then he nodded to her. "You have a good week, Meg. Thanks for the input tonight." Putting the phone to his ear, he strode to his Jeep.

She lowered her car roof and drove home in a pensive state, unhappy with herself for having such a strong reaction to a man already dating someone. Granted, Jon had bestowed some warm fuzzies on her tonight, but he was like that with everyone. He often thanked Camille for bringing laughter to the group. He rejoiced when any of them evidenced fruits of love.

Without a doubt, God had blessed Jon with the gift of edification.

"God?" She raised the roof of her car to prevent anyone from overhearing. "I'm not ready for this." The mixed feelings in her heart disconcerted her, reminding her of a time her Grandma came to visit but arrived a day early. She'd been excited about Grandma's visit, but when Grandma did arrive, she was caught off guard, unprepared.

Attention from a man like Jon would flatter any woman. But, despite her prayers for a man after God's own heart, she didn't want her heart occupied with someone else's man.

In a few short weeks Jon would move on to a new chapter of his life, and in time, he would be a mere blip in her memory. Perhaps by then, she would be ready for God's special someone.

Chapter Twenty-Seven

Linzee had an hour to kill before she needed to head off to Little Tykes Preschool Wednesday morning. She found an empty table at Latte Love Shack and ordered a hazelnut latte, delivered in minutes by a new barista. She looked around for Dustin, then remembered he'd been working afternoons lately. Considering she'd been looking forward to rattling his cage a little, the twinge of disappointment only deepened her resolve to subtly let him know she knew what he'd been up to.

She removed the lid of her latte and drank deeply as she soaked in the happy hum and bustle, without which her mornings wouldn't be complete. She glimpsed Drucie across the room, but her friend, along with two other baristas, rushed about, threading their way among the mostly-full tables. Matt, the manager, frowned behind the shiny counter.

Drucie passed by once, clutching a tray, but didn't stop to chat, merely swept the air with a wave in her direction. A paper flew off and landed near Linzee's feet. She knelt down to pick it up, then straightened and placed it back on Drucie's tray.

"Thanks, bud." Her friend smiled, then rushed away. Linzee checked the time and logged onto Facebook.

She was nearly finished with her latte when she began to feel sick. Her stomach churned, as though it threatened to eject its contents.

She tried to remember if she'd heard anything about the flu going around, but that only made her head spin. Now she'd have to call in sick. Lorraine would be upset. But right now, she needed to go home and get to bed.

After sending a quick text to her boss, she stood. The room swam around her. She gripped the table and slumped against the awning, suddenly too exhausted to move. The couple at the next table glanced over at her, worry etched on his face, concern seeping from her eyes. "You okay?" the woman asked, but she couldn't muster a reply.

Drucie appeared at her side. "What up with you?" Linzee felt her knees buckle, but Drucie grabbed her before she hit the floor.

"I don't feel good." She moaned. "Got to get to my car."

The room swam faster now, interspersed with pulsating movements, as though a strobe light circled overhead. Drucie muttered something, but the sound faded in and out, and Linzee began to lapse into a dreamscape. She clutched Drucie, only half-aware that her friend was rushing her out the patio exit.

"Dude." Even Drucie's words pulsated. "I'm taking you to your car. Sleep it off, and I'll come check on you on my next break. Don't try to drive home."

As if she could. She moaned again and leaned on her friend as they shuffled out to the parking lot. Just when she started to collapse, a pair of hands caught her and laid her down.

Then blackness descended.

***

While Meg enjoyed a pasta entree and anticipated spending the rest of her evening with her friends Paint and Easel, her phone rang. Nena's name showed on the screen.

How strange. Linzee was supposed to be using her own phone again. "Hello."

"Meg." Nena's voice came through like sandpaper. "Is Linzee there?"

"Hi, Nena. No, I thought you were her. I mean, I

thought she was calling—"

She heard a guttural sound on the other end. "I don't know where she is."

"What?"

"Yeah. She ain't nowhere to be found."

A swoop of air rushed from her lungs as a fist punched her in the chest. "Oh, dear God. Dear God." She was chanting like a robot.

Nena's voice came through in patches, trying to penetrate the roar in her head. "When I got home from work, Linzee wasn't here. Didn't think nothin' of it 'cause she was supposedly working, but she never came home. She didn't answer my texts. I called her a whole bunch of times but she didn't answer them either."

Meg stared at her unfinished pasta, her stomach heaving.

"I called her boss, who said she called in sick. Then I called as many of her friends I could think of, but none of 'em seen her. I drove around to every place I could think of, but her car wasn't anywhere. It ain't like her not to answer my calls." Nena's voice rose to a place close to panic. "She could've been in an accident, or something."

Meg couldn't speak. She feared "or something" more than she feared an accident. She ordered herself not to panic. Linzee was probably stranded somewhere. "Let me check the news for any recent accidents." She grasped the edge of the table and clung there. "Will you please let me know right away if you hear from her?"

"Yep."

Launching herself into the TV room, she fumbled over her laptop and pulled up a local news site. Although she looked at every breaking news headline, she saw no reports of any accidents in the area.

She picked up her phone again, her finger poised over the keyboard. It wouldn't hurt to investigate her suspicion that her son might know something.

Richie answered on the second ring. "Yeah?"

She willed her voice to remain steady. "Richie. Where are you?"

"Kassidy's. Why?"

"Can you come home right away? I need your help with something."

Thick silence. "What kind of help?"

"Please come home and I'll tell you. I don't want to explain it over the phone. C'mon, this is important."

He disconnected without saying goodbye. Precisely nine excruciating minutes later, he bolted through the front door. "Mom, I'm home," he said with his usual burst of energy, folding himself into the recliner. She searched her son's face for the boy he once was, the youth he'd been a few years ago, but saw only a hard masculine edge in his face and eyes.

She took a deep breath and looked at her hands. "I need an honest answer out of you."

Richie tensed. "Is this about sex?"

Her face twisted in an attempt at a smile and she looked her son full in the face. "That's a topic for another time. This time, I want to talk about Linzee."

"'Kay." He seemed to uncoil as his unflinching gaze held hers. Her heart kept up its frightening pace. It took all her feeble strength to keep him from seeing her fear.

"I got a call from Nena. She doesn't know where Linzee is and hasn't been able to reach her."

Richie looked at her for a moment, his expression telling her nothing. He shifted. "Maybe her phone is dead."

"Maybe. But I'm afraid it could be foul play." She heard the beginnings of a quaver in her voice. "You know all the stuff that's been going on with her recently."

"Yeah?"

"Well, I need to know if you and/or Dustin sent her all those harassing text messages."

Richie lowered his brows. "Seriously, Mom?" He shook

his head, over and over. "Why would we do that? Dustin hardly knows her, and actually, neither do I anymore. I barely think about her most of the time."

She scanned his face for the slightest sign of guilt—a shifty gaze, a nervous tic. "It's been on my mind for awhile, and I have reason to believe you and Dustin were behind it."

His brows creased even lower. "No, you don't. We had nothing to do with it. Why would you think that?"

Her voice rose a few notches. "Someone slashed her tires." She sliced the air with an invisible box cutter. "Someone tried to attack her." Her fists thumped the futon. "And today, she's turned up missing. It could be coincidence. Or it could be the latest ploy from the person who kept telling her to kill herself. Someone named Eddie Levens. A name which has the number eleven hidden in it. I bet you didn't know your own mom would figure it out."

Richie shook his head again. "Mom, you're talking crazy. What the heck are you talking about?"

He certainly appeared clueless enough. Unless she had an Oscar-worthy actor for a son, he was innocent.

"I could be wrong." From somewhere deep inside, she conjured up a sincere tone. "But I'm pretty sure Linzee's harasser was someone with a connection to the number eleven. Dustin's last name is the Roman numeral for eleven." She watched Richie's face as comprehension began to dawn. "The only connection between him and Linzee would be you."

Richie uttered a swear word, and she glared at him so hard, he flinched.

"This is ridiculous." His lion's roar of a voice frightened her a little. "For one thing, Dustin would never slash anyone's tires or send them texts to kill themselves. He's one of the most harmless people I've ever known. Secondly, Dustin's on vacation with his family this week, so I know he doesn't have anything to do with her being missing."

He could be lying, of course. He'd done his share of

bare-faced fibbing in his life, even looking her in the eye while he tried to convince her the sky was green.

But if he wasn't lying, then she was making connections where they didn't exist. She had nothing to go on and no idea where to begin.

Linzee could be hurt, or suffering. She could be lost, miles from home. The possible scenarios ranged anywhere from inconvenient to terrifying.

She closed her eyes and breathed in steady breaths. She needed assurance that Linzee was merely stranded somewhere, unable to call anyone. She pleaded with God to watch over Linzee. Yet the stealthy fear she thought had moved on had, in reality, checked back into her heart along with all its family members.

The building panic finally overtook her, and she collapsed on the futon in a crying, shaking heap. Richie yelled out an insincere apology for swearing. Shadow watched her from under beady brows.

"Maybe she's with Dad." Richie's voice blared into her ears and shook her into alertness.

She sat up, hope pulsating inside her. "Call him. Please."

After ten long seconds, she heard, "Hey, Dad, I'm fine. Is Linzee with you?—Oh. Well, Mom says she's missing.—Okay, will do." Richie held out the phone. "Here. He wants to talk to you."

She made a face. "I was hoping I wouldn't have to." She grabbed the phone. "Hi, Phillippe."

"Meg," came Phillippe's mellow voice, overlaid with a faint French accent. She remembered the smooth timber of his voice, how it had always charmed away her ire. That is, until the end. "Linzee's missing?"

"She is, Phillippe. Nobody has seen her or talked to her all day. She called in sick to work."

"Don't jump to conclusions, Meg." He sounded too calm. "She's a big girl. Maybe she and Nena had a fight, and she's hiding out somewhere."

"Phillippe. Did you know she's been stalked recently?" If she could charge through cyberspace and wring his neck, she would. "You know someone vandalized her car twice and tried to assault her?"

"She told me."

"Then how can you think I'm jumping to conclusions?" She heard her own voice rising toward hysteria.

"Calm down, Meg. We need to keep our heads on straight. What's been done so far?"

She took a deep breath and recapped everything she knew. "I plan to file a missing persons report tomorrow." She forced a businesslike tone. "That is, if she hasn't shown up by then. I have to wait at least twenty-four hours."

"It sounds like you're doing all the right things." His voice rang with reassurance. "Do you need me to come over?"

"No, you don't need to do that."

"You sure?"

"I'm sure." Her voice stayed firm.

"Okay, then." He paused. She could sense the wheels whirring in his mind. "Keep me posted."

"I will." She signed off and lay back on the futon, where she huddled through two sitcoms. Richie stared at the screen in silence, broken up by an occasional guffaw.

She wished she could paint right now, or read. At least she could pray some more.

She got up and knelt in the corner, out of Richie's earshot, whispering her heart out. "God, I don't get this." She held back a sob. "My gut tells me Richie and Dustin aren't involved. Please tell me where my Linzee is, God. Did someone take her? Was it Eddie? And God. If Eddie isn't Dustin after all, who on earth is he, anyway?"

A laugh track from the TV assaulted her eardrums. But no voice from the Lord.

Fed up with waiting, she shuffled to her bedroom and

called Nena. "Anything new?" she asked, tugging her hair, nibbling her fingers.

"Nope, still ain't heard from her."

"Do you happen to know if she went to get coffee this morning?"

"I already been to Latte Love Shack, but it was closed. I'mma goin' back tomorrow morning."

She resumed pacing. "Can I go with you? I'm too worried to go to work."

"Um," Nena hedged, her reluctance obvious. "Okay."

"Are you going to call the cop in charge of Linzee's case?"

"I already did, but they don't do nothin' 'til they get a missing persons report."

"Did you and Linzee by chance have a fight?"

"Huh? We didn't have no fight." Nena spit the words. "How come you think that?"

"Her dad suggested Linzee might be hiding somewhere if you two had a fight."

"He's wrong. Didn't happen."

Meg found herself reluctant to disconnect. Staying on the phone with prickly Nena was better than facing her fears alone.

"That all you need?" said Nena after a tense pause.

"Yes. Thanks. See you tomorrow." She signed off.

Although she'd grown accustomed to life without a man in the house, right now she needed a husband's broad shoulder to cry on, his comforting arms around her.

Her desolate spirit cried out for human companionship. Someone besides her silent son.

Camille. The face of her big-hearted friend flashed into her mind. She pulled up the number.

"Camille," she said, her voice crackling like a wounded person's.

"Hey, girl, you don't sound so good." Camille's buoyant voice sounded wonderful right now.

"I hate to ask you this at the last minute, but do you mind coming over for a little while?"

"Yep, I sure can, my friend."

She almost wept at Camille's steady, comforting words.

***

Camille, for once, didn't have a lot to say when Meg poured out the dreadful turn of events, but her friend's mere presence, solid and restful, comforted her. Camille agreed to stay for the night in Linzee's old room. Meg shooed Richie out of the TV room, and he mumbled something about hanging out at Jake's.

"It's like we've been best friends for years, isn't it?" She laughed through her tears. "Like a high school slumber party."

"Can we play Spin the Bottle?" Camille joked.

They laughed some more, then went to the store and stocked up on cookies, chips, ice cream and soda pop, making a quick stop afterwards at Camille's for an overnight bag.

"Here we go, my friend," Camille declared, lining the kitchen counter with goodies. "Nothing like a junk food feast to make you forget your troubles."

They munched snacks, broke out a deck of cards, and played several rounds of gin rummy, which kept her mind occupied.

As the evening wore on, Nena kept sending texts saying she still hadn't heard from Linzee. Camille suggested they hold a prayer vigil. "If it weren't so late," Camille said, "I'd call Jon and ask him to pray. He's quite the prayer warrior. Also, my church has a prayer chain. Do you mind if I ask them to pray?"

"That would be awesome." At last, a tendril of hope wrapped itself around her heart.

Chapter Twenty-Eight

"Did you sleep well?" Meg asked Camille over pancakes the next morning.

"I did. And you?"

"Eventually. All I could do was pray myself to sleep."

"Those prayers are working, girlfriend."

"So is all the laughing we did. It wore me out." She squirted syrup over the pancake stack. "Anyway, I need to meet up with Nena this morning and do some investigating. Do you want to come with?"

"Any opportunity to play hooky, I'll take it."

Meg, her appetite sputtering, forced a bite into her mouth. "My boss told me to take as much time as I need."

"How about I do the driving?"

"You don't have to do that. You've already done so much."

"It's my pleasure, my friend."

She agreed to let Camille drive, and they headed toward the 101 in Camille's little Toyota.

Her phone chimed with a text from Phillippe. *Anything new? P.*

No, she replied. *Still a no-show.*

A four-letter word bleeped on the display. *Anything I can do?*

Nena and I plan to do some searching today.

Check the hospitals. P.

Since that was her plan, she didn't bother to reply.

They arrived at the apartment moments after Nena texted Meg, asking if she was on the way. Meg made introductions, and Nena climbed in the back seat with mumbled directions to Latte Love Shack.

When they arrived, Nena stuck to Meg's side as Meg approached the stern-faced man behind the counter and asked for the manager.

He held out a hand. "That would be me. Matt Anderson. How can I help you?"

Meg received his handshake, then said, "I was wondering if your order records show my daughter coming in yesterday morning. She's missing."

He shrugged. "I can't give you that information unless it comes from the sheriff's office."

Nena's finger traced the knots in the counter. "Lemme talk to the staff who was here yesterday."

"If you want to talk to someone, you'll have to do it on your own. I can't legally release information about our customers."

Meg leaned in. "Is Dustin working today?"

"No, ma'am, he's out this week." Matt's flat tone sent a clear message he was finished answering questions.

Nena nudged Meg. "Look, there's Drucie. She might know if Linzee was here yesterday." Nena made for a table near the patio. Camille, gaping at the wall murals, jumped when Meg grabbed her arm.

"Let's order something while we're here." She pointed to the slab on the table's surface. "Look, Camille, here's the embedded computer I told you about."

They placed their orders and waited for Nena to catch Drucie's attention.

Drucie ambled over to them with their coffees. "Hi, all." She set their cups down and turned to Nena. "It's kind of bizarro seeing you here without Linzee. Is she still sick?"

Meg perked up. "You know about that?" She and Nena spoke almost in unison.

Drucie's eyes widened. "Yeah, didn't she tell you she was here yesterday morning when she got sick? I walked her to her car so she could lie down."

"Uh, Drucie." Nena eyed her. "Linzee never showed yesterday. And she still ain't home."

"Serious?" Drucie's chin dropped about an inch. "I told her not to drive home, but when I went to check on her later, her car was gone. Wowza. I hope she wasn't in an accident."

Meg sought Camille, whose grim face stared back at her, and her heart crumpled. "We hope so too. I'm Meg, Linzee's mom. You may remember me?"

Drucie's eyes lit up in recognition. "Oh, yeah, I thought you looked familiar. In fact, Linzee looks like you."

"Why didn't you call 911?"

"911? For what? She said she didn't feel good and wanted to go to her car. It's not like she was dying, man."

Meg shook her head at the foolishness of youth. For all this woman knew, Linzee may have been seriously ill. It might have been meningitis, making Linzee disoriented as she drove home. She might be passed out in her crashed car, or face-down in a ditch.

"Anyway, I'll keep my fingers crossed." Drucie held up two intertwined fingers, drawing Meg's eye to a tattooed claw peeking from under her shirt sleeve. "Keep me posted, will ya?"

She moved along to the next table. The three of them exchanged looks.

"Linzee could have been in an accident." Meg switched to a hopeful tone. "We need to check the hospitals. Why don't we take these drinks to go?"

***

"Oh, my head." Linzee moaned, her eyes stuck closed. Her whole body screamed with pain and lethargy. Her head pounded like a woodpecker had perched on it. She couldn't remember ever having a headache this intense.

Although the bed proved comfortable, the darkness felt darker than her own room, and a funny odor permeated the air. She put out a hand toward Nena but felt a tug on her wrist. For some reason, her hand had met resistance and wouldn't move any farther.

She moved her leg to where Nena should be, but her bare toe slammed into a wall. She snapped her eyes open. Instead of her room, absolute darkness surrounded her, as dark as though she'd never opened her eyes.

She was far too weary, though, to investigate why a wall had appeared where Nena should be, and she closed her eyes again. She hadn't felt this lousy since her days of parties and hangovers in college.

That was it. She'd partied too much last night and blacked out, and had landed in a strange bed.

Then exhaustion overtook her. Apathy filled her. Her head rolled to the side.

Perhaps this would prove to be a nightmare, and when she awoke, she would find herself safe in her own bed, in her own room.

***

Before hitting the hospitals, Camille drove the three of them to the police station in Mill Valley to check in with Officer Klein.

"He's out patrolling," the receptionist informed them in a voice as hard as her eyes.

Meg stepped forward. "I need to fill out a missing persons report, please."

The heavy-set woman picked up a clipboard and attached a form to it. "Has the person been missing for at least twenty-four hours?"

"Yes. It would have been prior to nine a.m. yesterday morning." She took the clipboard and seated herself on the vinyl chairs provided, then handed the completed form back to the receptionist with a request for Officer Klein to call her.

When they checked in with the two largest area hospitals, Kaiser and Marin Community, they learned that neither emergency room had admitted anyone matching

Linzee's description yesterday or today.

Camille offered her glass-half-full assessment. "Hold your head up, girlfriend. We're not through yet." Meg glanced at Nena, who sneered. Nena had been monosyllabic most of the morning, but Meg couldn't give it any more thought as they moved on to the smaller hospitals.

Still no sign of Linzee.

"How about we take a lunch break." Camille waggled her brows. "Get our minds onto something pleasant like food."

They stopped at a sandwich shop which reminded her of Latte Love Shack. Various murals in a Picasso-type style dominated one wall, with the other walls sponge-painted in tints ranging from hot pink to vivid orange. It almost made her eyes hurt. They approached the counter where a short-haired blond with a nose ring stood behind a register. Meg ordered a roast-beef sandwich, then turned to Nena. "Order whatever you'd like, Nena. I'm buying."

Nena darted a quick glance at her and then looked away, but not before Meg caught a flash of something in her eyes. Gratitude? Surprise?

Nena ordered, "I'll have a BLT."

Camille ordered tuna on rye, and they found an unoccupied table in the corner. At the table nearest theirs, a group of four women, dressed in business casual, worked through mile-high salads and spoke in calm tones. Across the room, a young mother spoon-fed soup to a baby.

The cashier called out their order, and Meg hurried to retrieve the tray. Back at the table, she watched Camille take her first enthusiastic bite. No loss of appetite for that woman. "Camille, I'm beginning to have my doubts about foul play. My heart wants to believe she's stranded somewhere with a dead phone—"

"She'd call." Nena scowled at her. "If she got stranded, she'd find a phone and call. I know it."

"Well, what do you think happened, Nena?"

Nena glared at her sandwich. "You don't wanna know what I think."

"Why? You think it's foul play?"

But Nena wouldn't say anything more. She kept her drawn, sullen face aimed at the table.

"Do you know something we don't know?" Meg kept her tone gentle.

"Maybe. But I don't wanna say anything yet case I'm wrong." She picked up her sandwich and took her first bite, studiously avoiding Meg's eyes. Which only served to pique Meg's curiosity. But judging by the stubborn set of Nena's jaw, trying to get any more out of her would be as futile as a rain dance in Death Valley.

Camille had already gobbled down half her sandwich. "I'll take the rest home." She grabbed a to-go box from the counter, tucked the sandwich inside, and opened her blinding red handbag. Meg caught a glimpse of pill bottles, nail polish, and feathered hair ornaments. "We need to call Jon before we hit the road."

Meg's hands froze on her sandwich. She couldn't face talking to Jon in her frame of mind. But neither could she confess to Camille her newfound feelings for him.

Camille eyed Meg's partially eaten sandwich. "Not hungry?"

"Not really."

"Let's get you a to-go box."

Nena, still absorbed in her BLT, chewed furiously, her gaze on the phone next to her.

Camille returned with the box. "Nena, excuse us for a few. You finish your lunch. We'll be just outside the door."

Camille beckoned to Meg, but she shook her head. "No, go ahead. I'll stay here and keep Nena company."

Nena lifted her head, the despair in her eyes unmistakable. "Go make your call. I don't need company."

Meg, reluctance in every movement, wrapped her sandwich and stepped outside with her friend, who already had her phone to her ear.

"Jon." The boiling sun left beads of sweat on Camille's forehead, which she wiped away with a swipe of the wrist.

"Yeah, I'm good." Camille paced as she talked. "I'm with Meg—

"No, she's having a crisis and could use some mighty prayer, and I mean pounding-the-throne kind of prayer right now—

"Nobody has seen her daughter since yesterday morning—

"Yeah, we did, just got back from the cops, and stopped by most of the hospitals around here. She hasn't been admitted to any of them."

Camille held out the phone to her. "Here. He wants to talk to you."

She knew she should have stayed inside. Heart surging, she took the phone and kept her tone casual. "Hi, Jon."

"Meg." Such concern in his voice. "How are you holding up?"

"Kind of numb, to be honest." She twirled a strand of hair around her finger, willing her voice to remain steady. "We found out Linzee started feeling sick at the coffee shop yesterday morning. Then she went to her car to lie down, and nobody has seen her since. If it weren't for Camille, I don't know what I'd do." A hot wind whipped her sundress around. She grabbed the flying skirt just in time.

"I'm glad she could be there for you. She's a trouper."

"Yes, she is. She stayed with me last night." She met Camille's eyes, and they shared a smile. "I don't think I would have made it otherwise."

He paused, then continued in a somber tone. "We could arrange for a prayer vigil tonight if you'd like. Some folks at my church have them on a regular basis."

"Thanks, Jon. That's so kind of you." She twisted her hair, pulling and tugging it within an inch of its life.

"I'm happy to do it. I'll call you later with the details."

"Great. Here's Camille back."

Camille talked for another minute, said goodbye, then grinned at her. "Bleepers, honey, you got some pink cheeks going on. Did you know you're blushing?"

Meg jumped. "What? No way. You're imagining things."

"Can't blame you for liking Jon," Camille went on, ignoring Meg's denial. "He's the best. I'd go for him myself if I wasn't already involved with Bill. 'Course, that'd make me a cougar, wouldn't it? I mean, he's at least ten years younger than me."

Giggling, Meg moved to a bench in the shade of the eaves. Nena burst out the door without a word, punching away on her phone, then claimed the furthest bench over by the palm tree. "Now, Camille." She gave her friend a stern look, biting her lip to hide a smile. "Don't be getting any ideas."

"You kidding me?" Camille joined her on the bench. "You and Jon would be perfect together. I saw you two talking Monday night like nobody's business, and was thinking what a great couple you two would make."

Her jaw dropped as she stared at her friend. "Camille. He's already dating someone."

"No, he isn't." Camille paused, crinkling her forehead. "Who's he dating?"

"Quincy."

Camille sputtered. "Quincy?" A laugh bubbled up. "You thought they were dating?" She doubled over, laughter snorting out her nose.

Confused, Meg reluctantly joined in with chuckles of her own. "What's so funny?"

"He and Quincy are not dating." Camille threw her head back. "They're first cousins."

"Cousins?" She eyed the nearby manhole, wishing she could crawl inside. "How did I miss that?"

"I don't know. He introduced her as his cousin at the

Woods' potluck." Laughter gave way to snickers. "Must have been before you got there."

"I'm such an idiot."

"Don't worry, girlfriend, I won't tell. Now you know he's up for grabs."

"Camille!"

"You remember the kid playing basketball with Tanner at the potluck?"

She nodded.

"That was Quincy's son. He and Tanner are best buds."

"Why did she come to the FOGY meeting?"

"She's been coming off and on for awhile. Her half-brother is gay. No relation to Jon."

"You mean, everybody but me knew they were cousins? Why didn't you tell me?"

"'Cause this way is much funnier."

She punched Camille's arm. "You're bad. So bad."

Time to change the subject before she further humiliated herself. "Okay, moving on. What do we do now? Got any ideas?"

Camille, still chortling, scratched her head. "Now we wait."

Chapter Twenty-Nine

"What do you think, Camille?" Meg, pacing and fidgeting, had returned home to wait for a call from Officer Klein. "Do you think I got it wrong with the number eleven connection?" She pivoted and resumed her pacing. "My son was adamant that his friend Dustin wouldn't do the things this Eddie person did. And now I'm beginning to have my doubts. At the time, it seemed so clear."

"I don't know, honey. Why don't you pray about it, ask God to make it clear? If you got it wrong, he'll point it out to you."

"I already did ask God. Several times." Her phone chimed, and she lunged for it. Mill Valley Police, said the display. "Hello?"

"This is Officer Klein, calling for Meg St. John."

She gasped. "Speaking."

"I'm calling about the missing persons report you filed on your daughter."

"Yes." Her heart throbbed in her throat.

"I want to clarify some details before we begin our investigation." Officer Klein's smooth voice was like a sedative on her nerves. "It says here her last known location was a coffee shop called Latte Love Shack, and she left because she felt sick."

"Yes."

"Do you know the approximate time she left the coffee shop?"

"She was supposed to be at work by nine a.m., so, sometime prior to that. I forgot to ask the barista the exact time." Her stiff legs paced from one end of the room to the other, like the old wind-up toy soldier from Richie's childhood.

"That's okay. We can find out when we interview her. Do you know the full name of the barista?"

"No, just her first name. Drucie." Her legs lurched to a stop; the toy soldier had wound down. "By the way, we checked with all of the area hospital emergency rooms, but as far as we could find out, she wasn't admitted to any of them."

"We'll be checking again as part of the investigation. Do you have any reason to believe she may have wanted to run away voluntarily?"

"I can't imagine. She was building a life here, has a fiancée, and a full-time job lined up in September."

"We're required to ask. The two previous times I talked to your daughter, she didn't strike me as someone who was unhappy with her life." Paper shuffled on the other end. "Does she have any chronic health issues which might explain her sudden illness?"

"No, I don't think so."

"We'll also find out from the coffee shop if any other customers reported feeling ill."

"Great."

"If we can find her car, we'll be making progress." The officer cleared his throat. "Normally we don't investigate adult disappearances unless we have reason to suspect foul play or endangerment. But since we have a record of two previous assaults against her, we will consider her as possibly endangered."

"Thank you again, Officer. I'll be looking forward to hearing back from you." She disconnected the call and updated Camille, who leaped to her feet.

"I'm going to call Bill, and then I think we should pray."

***

When the doorbell rang that afternoon, Meg half-hoped she'd see Jon's smiling face lighting up her porch.

She opened the door, then jumped back. "Phillippe."

There stood her ex, a bit flabbier, years of living etched on his face, yet with the same coiled energy just below the surface. His worried blue eyes searched her. "Meg."

She stepped back almost by rote, and he trudged through the door.

"Hug?" He tilted his head, surveying her. "In memory of the good times?"

She stood speechless, arms stiff at her side, as Phillippe folded her into his chest, just as he used to. "How are you doing?"

She choked back a sob, her head nestled against his solid, strong chest. "Not good."

He continued to hold her, caressing her back. She felt him lift his head, then he spoke. "I see you have company."

She whirled. Camille, smirking, watched them from the hallway door. Meg managed a quick recovery and made introductions.

"I'll let you two get caught up." Camille sidled to the door and directed a meaningful grin at her. "I'll be back later, my friend. Prayer vigil's at seven tonight."

Meg wanted to grab Camille and insist she stay. But Camille sailed out the door, and Phillippe had already made himself at home on the living room loveseat. Resigning herself to the inevitable, she plopped on the adjacent sofa.

Phillippe seemed to be drinking in the sight of her. "You're as beautiful as ever."

She kept her face expressionless and said nothing.

A veil fell over his face. "Is our son here?"

"No, he's at work."

"How is he dealing with all this?"

"It doesn't seem to have affected him at all. He and Linzee were never close."

"Meg." His tone changed, and she stiffened. He patted

the seat beside him. "Come over here. Let's talk, eh?"

She didn't move. "Phillippe, why are you here?"

A spasm crossed his face. "I'm concerned for my family." His gaze stayed fixed on her. "Linzee's been missing for more than twenty-four hours. That's serious business."

"Why, after seven years, are you suddenly concerned about us?"

He winced and held up his hands. "Guilty as charged. Meg, I don't know how to go back and undo all the mistakes I made. Leaving you and the kids was the worst mistake I ever made."

She flinched at his bleak tone.

"I'm convinced we'd still be a family if I'd stayed. So I suppose I'm here to make amends."

His words punched her in the gut. "Make amends? How?"

"By being here for you. Helping you search for Linzee. I want to be part of your lives again. I want to spend time with my kids, and even you. I think we can maintain an amicable friendship, eh?"

"I'm glad you feel that way, Phillippe, but adultery and abandonment are pretty hard things to simply forgive and forget." She watched his face fall and wondered what had happened to the man she'd shared such intense passion with all those years ago.

Phillippe examined his interlaced fingers. "I don't expect immediate forgiveness." He met her eyes. "But you and I had something special. I realized after Mary left I've never found what I had with you."

"Neither have I, Monsieur." Too bad it took so long for him to realize it.

"I remember when you found God." His gaze roamed the street outside. "You changed. But for the better. And I couldn't go there with you. I wanted to, but couldn't." He paused, then smiled. "I've been thinking about God lately."

"You have?"

"I've been wishing I could have found what you had."

"It's not difficult."

He held up a hand. "I have to go there in my own time and way, Meg."

There's the problem, she wanted to say. In order to find God, you have to go about it on his terms. She opened her mouth to speak, then clamped her lips shut.

"I have to say I admire the job you did with the kids in my absence. They're both exceptional young people."

"Our daughter is gay."

Phillippe shrugged, his eyes flashing caution.

"Doesn't it bother you that Linzee and Nena will never produce biological children?"

Again, he lifted a shoulder. "Many gay couples use In Vitro Fertilization…"

"Then our grandchildren would be raised without a father. Linzee of all people should know how that feels."

"But she wouldn't be happy with a man. If being with a woman makes her happy, then so be it."

As usual, Phillippe considered adult preferences ahead of children's well-being. She shook her head. "It's not natural, Phillippe. I love her dearly, but I'll never be okay with her romantic preference."

"What will you do come September and it's time for her to walk down the aisle?"

"I don't see how I can participate in that."

"You'd miss your own daughter's wedding?" he declared, echoing her father.

"I know, I know." She waved the words away. "It would hurt her deeply if I weren't there." She squeezed her knees. "I'm so torn, Phillippe. How can I celebrate something I don't condone? Yet how can I hurt Linzee?"

"I think it's best you set aside your own beliefs on the subject and be there for your daughter."

She expelled a rush of breath. "What do you think I've

been doing for the last month?"

And I'll keep on doing so — if she's not dead. The thought snuck into her mind before she could snuff it out. She shook her head. Linzee couldn't be dead. She'd feel it in her heart if she were.

"Anyway, it's not a decision I have to make today."

"But when the time comes, I hope you'll make the right one."

They fell silent. Phillippe looked at his watch.

"I need to leave soon. I'm looking at a house at four. But call me if anything comes up. And I'll see you Sunday, eh?"

"All right." She stood, half-wishing he would stay, dreading the hours she'd be alone with her fear.

"Adieu." He stood and pulled her into another hug.

"Adieu," she whispered as he walked out the door. From the window, she watched him fold his imposing physique into a white rental car. She continued watching as the car backed out onto Reno Drive, and disappeared into the depths of the subdivision.

***

"God." Meg groaned. The Jacuzzi water swirled around her, as worked-up as her emotions. "What are you up to, bringing Phillippe back into my life?" She sunk into the depths of the warmth, wanting to stay there until her skin shriveled like the inside of the figs in her refrigerator. "Are you trying to tell me something? Are you telling me my interest in Jon is not of you? That your plan is for Phillippe and me to reconcile?"

She groaned again, and the noise seemed to bounce off the ceiling. "Jon's a far better man, God. So why would you want me back with my cheating ex-husband?"

Hearing nothing, she raised her voice and aimed beyond the ceiling. "Lord, I doubt I could ever completely trust Phillippe again, even with all his talk about God, and wanting to make amends."

She recalled the day after Phillippe moved out when her father gave her a nugget of wisdom. "Once a cheater, always a cheater." But her father didn't know about the redeeming power of God to change the hardest of hearts.

If God did intend for them to reconcile, she wondered if the sparks could be rekindled after all these years. Phillippe, pushing fifty, was still an impressive-looking man, and hadn't lost an ounce of charm.

Resigned, she pushed out the words she knew she needed to say. "God, you have the power to make Phillippe into the man you want him to be." She dropped her voice to a whisper. "Even though it's not my will, if it's yours, please change my heart, too."

Chapter Thirty

Meg climbed into Camille's Toyota at six-thirty p.m. "By prayer vigil, are we talking five people? A hundred?"

Camille aimed the car toward Sausalito. "Probably not a hundred. There are twenty volunteers on the prayer chain, so it depends on how many show up."

A maximum of twenty prayer warriors storming heaven's door? If that didn't get God's attention, she didn't know what would. "Is Bill coming?"

"Nah, I wanted him to, but he's been on the road all week."

"Yeah, relaxing at home must be a rare treat for a long-haul trucker."

"Enough of Bill. I'm dying to know what happened with your ex today."

She related every detail, finishing just as they pulled into the church lot. Camille grunted her displeasure. "*Now* he realizes what a good thing he threw away."

Meg hurried to keep up with her friend as they speed-walked to the main door of the church. Fast-walking Camille led her through long corridors and short ones, down staircases and around corners, until they arrived at the Fireside Room. Jon greeted them, his face a mask of concern. Roughly fifteen other people milled about. A somber hush hung over the room, discouraging conversation.

Jon introduced her and offered a brief explanation, then pointed her to a chair. Feeling conspicuous, she sat. The others gathered around her, laying hands on her head, her shoulders, her back, offering themselves as channels of grace to heaven's throne.

Jon opened the prayer time. "Father God, we come to you on behalf of our sister Meg. We beseech you for answers. We're grateful you know where Linzee is right now, and grateful you are watching over her."

A sob broke from her throat. Hands patted and caressed her.

"We ask for wisdom for the police. Above all, Father God, please give Meg's heart comfort and hope."

Tears ferried down her cheeks. She lowered her face to her knees.

When Jon finished, Camille joined in, her voice a crackling whisper. "God, please be with Meg and watch over Linzee. Thank you for Meg's friendship, God. I've enjoyed getting to know her, and it breaks my heart to see her hurting."

This brought a fresh batch of tears, and she let them flow, let them cleanse away the anguish like a rain shower after a drought. She looked up toward the face of God, desperate for hope, yet trusting he could brush away her troubles as easily as she brushed away the dampness from her face.

***

Jon patted her shoulder as they departed. "God knows where she is, Meg. I'll keep praying, okay? In the meantime, please keep me updated." He handed her a business card. "Here's my cell."

She folded her hand over the card and lifted her mouth in a weak smile. "I will. Thanks again for doing this." Although tears streaked her face, his kind eyes told her it didn't matter in the least.

On the way home, she peeked at Jon's card. "Jon owns Paulson's Boat Repair?"

She marveled she had never made the connection. "I hear his ads on the radio all the time."

"Yeah." Camille sped up. "He's done pretty well with it. Jon is quite the man, isn't he? But you never hear him tooting his own horn."

She had to admit the truth of that.

"You know what?" Camille went on. "I think he's interested in someone."

Her heart dropped as she recalled her tirade in the Jacuzzi. If Jon's interest lay elsewhere, it could mean God's plan for her future included Phillippe. "You do? Why?"

"Whenever he meets someone he's interested in, he always brushes his hair and looks extra spiffy."

She pondered this in wary silence. Prospective dates must be plentiful for a guy like Jon, especially at a five-thousand member megachurch. Some of those young, single women at the prayer vigil tonight—

She jumped when Camille spoke. "Wh—what did you say?"

Camille glanced over. "Maybe it's you."

She sat up, her heart tripping over itself. "It can't be me. Men who are interested in me ask me out—like Mike did. Jon's never given me any special treatment." A sinking sensation accompanied her words. "Besides, I had a talk with God today about my ex-husband."

Camille emitted a strangled sound.

"He must have brought Phillippe back into my life for a reason, right?"

Camille took her eyes off the freeway long enough to launch a grenade in her direction. "Cheatin', adulteratin' Phillippe?"

"Camille, you don't need to rub it in. I'm very aware of what he is. But don't you think God must have a purpose for it?"

"Sure. But I don't necessarily think it's so the two of you can ride off starry-eyed into the sunset together."

Frustration drenched her. "I didn't say that. God simply reminded me that He has the power to soften the toughest of hearts."

"Hmmph."

She needed to steer this conversation elsewhere. "Wasn't that an awesome prayer time? It felt like God was right there in the room."

Camille's tense face relaxed in a smile. "He was, my friend, he was. Jon is right. God knows exactly where Linzee is."

Chapter Thirty-One

When Linzee awoke again, the raging headache had subsided, but her tongue adhered to her mouth. She desperately needed water. And a bathroom.

She lifted one leg and tried to set it on the floor. But something yanked on it, and it wouldn't budge. She tried moving the other one, but it met with the same resistance.

Cursing, she tried swinging both legs at the same time, and this time, it worked. Her feet landed, accompanied by clattering. And the floor seemed unusually high.

She tried to hoist herself up with her arms but again met with some sort of resistance. Something felt wrong with her arms. They wouldn't move.

Rolling sideways, she tried to lift herself off the bed. Head spinning, breathing hard, she finally worked herself upright, and waited for the swaying to stop.

Now for some light. She shuffled over to where she thought a light switch should be but instead rammed into something hard.

"Ouch. Snap!"

Since she couldn't get her arms to work, she couldn't grope for the switch.

Stomping her foot, she heard a clanging noise again.

A loud clanging noise—

Her heart lurched. That better not be what it sounded like.

Her bare foot explored the floor around her. Something hard and cold slithered under her toes, like metal. Like a chain.

Metal — chain — loud clanging noise —

Shackles. Someone had put her in shackles. She was in prison. A dungeon prison. Or else she was blind. She blinked her eyes several times to make sure they were open, but she still saw pure nothingness. Nothing but a black abyss.

Her breaths came hard and fast as she tried to stem her panic. She couldn't think what she could've done to land herself in prison. Unless she'd driven drunk and gotten pulled over. And if she were blind, she didn't see how she could bear an entire lifetime of sightlessness. Of helplessness.

"Hello?" Her voice came out as weak and quavery as if she were ninety years old.

It was so frustrating to not remember how she got here. Anything could have happened. Perhaps this wasn't a prison cell. Perhaps some kinky pervert who was into bondage had lured her to this strange room.

She attempted to move her hands again. But the shackles on her wrists clanged in protest.

The reality of her predicament struck her like a grenade. She was imprisoned in a pitch-black room somewhere, God only knew where, with shackles on her arms and legs. With no bathroom. No food. No water.

Panic exploded inside her, and she screamed.

***

Meg sipped coffee in her breakfast nook and gazed at the warm morning outside, wishing it could warm up her frozen heart.

"Sweet Baby Girl, where are you?" Her heart had been crying for hours. "Your mommy misses you."

Her phone dinged, and she saw a text from Laura.

Meg, we're still praying for Lindsey. Have you heard anything?

No, not so far. The cops are looking for her car.

Do you need company right now?

That would be nice.

Be right over.

When Laura arrived, Meg folded her in a big hug, rendered somewhat awkward by Laura's baby bump. "I'm so glad you're here."

"I would hate to be alone too if I were in your shoes."

"Come sit down. I have so much to tell you."

They settled on the sofa. She pulled the matching ottoman over and lifted Laura's feet onto it.

"Oh, thanks." Laura winced. "I'm told the discomfort is only going to get worse."

"True, but it's temporary." Meg tucked a pillow behind Laura's back. "And the payoff is incredible. Once that baby's born, you won't remember any of this." She crossed her legs Indian-style and leaned toward her friend. Laura's beautiful face looked puffier than usual, a possible symptom of toxemia.

She laid a hand on Laura's arm. "How are your checkups? Are you doing okay physically? Blood pressure normal, all that?"

Laura shifted. "My blood pressure is a little elevated, but not to a dangerous point. The baby's heartbeat is in the one-fifty, one-sixty range, so I suspect it's a girl. Of course, Mark wants a son, but I would love a little girl. I want to name her Violet, my favorite color." Laura's sweet laugh reminded Meg of wind chimes. "Violet Grace Flynn."

"Beautiful name. I hope you get your Violet Grace this time. And that Mark gets his son in round two."

"Round two?" Laura grimaced. "I'm not even finished with round one."

"If it's any consolation, it gets easier each time."

Her phone beeped. It was a text from Jon, asking if she had any news.

"Laura." She set her phone on the table. "I've got to thank you for telling me about FOGY. It is such a great ministry."

She told her friend about her experiences with FOGY, with SMERFA, with Haight Church. The morning flew by.

Her phone rang as lunchtime neared. Mill Valley Police. She yelped, then jammed the phone to her ear. "Hello?"

"This is Officer Klein calling for Meg St. John."

"Speaking."

"Good news, we found your daughter's car."

Oh, thank the Lord. She thrust her index finger in the air.

"We found it abandoned this morning at McNears Beach. Someone reported it as having been sitting there for two days, and it turned out to be a match with the plate and description for your daughter's car."

"McNears Beach? That's several miles east of here." She tugged a strand of hair, swirling it around her fingers.

"Yes, we don't know how it got there or what happened to her once it got there. Needless to say, she wasn't in the car."

The room swam around her. Thumping down on the sofa, she sucked in a deep breath. "Now what?"

"We did find her laptop and handbag under the seat. You can come down to the station and pick them up. We dusted those items and the whole car for fingerprints. We're working to see if we can get a match in our database."

"And if you can't?"

"We'll keep investigating. Yesterday we interviewed the staff at Latte Love Shack. Drucie Ward confirmed what you told me. She remembers it was around eight-thirty a.m. when she helped Linzee to her car, and the phone log records confirmed Linzee called in at seven fifty-five to place her order."

She shot to her feet again, unable to stop pacing.

"We also interviewed the manager, who said none of the staff took any extended time away from work after your daughter left. So it doesn't appear, at this point, that any of them were involved. On the surface, it would appear that she either tried to drive away and then abandoned the car, or someone stole the car while she was in it."

No. She couldn't go there. "All right then, I'll come down to the station soon."

Laura's face exerted curiosity after Meg said goodbye.

"The good news is, they found Linzee's car with her stuff inside." Meg reached for her purse. "The bad news is, they didn't find Linzee. I need to go to the police station to pick up her stuff. Want to come with?"

Laura agreed, and they piled into Meg's car. "Meg," Laura began, her mouth opening, then shutting.

"Hmm?" She ground the gear into reverse.

"Is it possible that Linzee and her girlfriend cooked up a scheme to make it look like Linzee got kidnapped?"

Her jaw dropped as she backed onto Reno Drive. Hearing a shout, she slammed on the brakes barely in time to miss a skateboarder whizzing by. "The possibility never even crossed my mind." She backed out to the middle of the street, then stopped, eyeing Laura as if her friend had suddenly sprouted green hair. "Why would they do such a thing?"

Laura's face turned pink. "I don't know why. But people do these things all the time."

"Not Linzee. Not a chance." She shook her head. "My Linzee is the most guileless person you'd ever want to meet. If they did do it, Nena would've been the brains behind it." She shifted into first and rolled down the street.

Laura kept her head averted. "I heard of a man who was being pressured to take over the family business. He didn't want to, so instead, he and his wife came up with an elaborate plan to fake his death. They pulled it off, then took off with the insurance money and moved to Hawaii. Of course, the truth finally caught up with them."

Meg swerved around a bicyclist. "Linzee has no motive for faking her own death. Or kidnapping."

"That you know of. But wouldn't it be better than her

being in danger?"

"I suppose it would. But if I ever find out this was all a big ruse, I'm going to wring her little neck for scaring us so."

***

By seven a.m. Friday, Nena knew what she had to do. Ever since Linzee disappeared, a sneaking suspicion had gnawed at her mind like a persistent termite.

Since she didn't have to be at work until eight, she stopped by Latte Love Shack, claimed a table for two by the window, then punched in her order for a straight-up sixteen-ounce black coffee. Drucie flitted from table to table. She knew Drucie's regular shift spanned from six until two, Wednesday through Sunday. Matt, the manager, oversaw the front counter and worked nearly every day. Today, Bryce manned the phones, and a new barista named Brianna prepared the drinks.

Moments later, Drucie approached with her coffee.

"Hiya." She sloshed the cup down next to Nena. "Still no Linzee?"

Nena's jaw sagged, and she shook her head. "Still missing."

"That sucks. The cops came in yesterday and interviewed us. It was intense." Drucie barked out a laugh. "Especially for me, since I practically carried her to her car."

"What was the matter with her?"

"I'm not sure. I saw her leaning against the table like she was having a dizzy spell, so I booked it right over. I thought it might be low blood sugar, you know."

"Naw. I never known her to have low blood sugar."

"Hope there wasn't something wrong with her drink."

Nena took a sip of steaming coffee, puckering her lips at the kick of hot caffeine. "I heard Dustin ain't here this week."

"Correctomundo. He's on vacation."

"Linzee thought he was her cyber stalker."

"Pfft. That kid wouldn't hurt a flea. Unless he has a hidden side we don't know about."

"He's friends with Linzee's bro, the hard-core homophobe." Nena twisted her mouth. "You know what Bro said to us when he found out we were engaged? He goes, 'Gross,' and stuck his finger down his mouth."

Drucie clucked. "Yeah, Linzee told me."

Nena shook her head. "I wonder about him. Like, he's this big, tough-lookin' *hombre*, the type who might harass someone."

"Never met the dude. I wouldn't know. Hey, I need to make my rounds, but why dontcha come in again tomorrow, talk some more?"

Drucie waved and moved on, while Nena sat, mental wheels spinning.

Chapter Thirty-Two

Linzee's high wails echoed off the prison walls like a police siren. Waves of panic crashed over her, then subsided, only to build again to an even greater intensity.

A door she hadn't known was there flew open, and a head poked in.

"Hey, cool it with the racket, dude," a familiar hoarse voice demanded. Blessed light split the darkness, but Linzee could only stare at the person who had brought it in, unable to believe her eyes.

An overhead light switched on, and Drucie entered the room, trailed by an unfamiliar woman pointing a gun. Drucie approached with a hardness in her eyes Linzee hadn't seen since high school.

"I'm gonna take the shackles off your arms now." Drucie clutched a small metal key. "But if you try any funny business, you're dead meat. Allison's a good shot. By the way, this is Allison, my girlfriend. Allison, meet Linzee." She made the introductions as if this were an ordinary day at the coffee shop. Allison made the briefest of nods in Linzee's direction.

This had to be a dream.

Once free of the shackles, her arms felt nearly numb. She started to shake them out, but Allison waved the gun around as if to warn her again about *funny business*.

"Drucie, *what* is going on?" She hoped her demanding tone covered up the high-octane fear underneath. "Are you Edward Levens?"

In reply, Drucie chuckled and dropped to the mattress

Linzee had vacated.

"So, you need anything? Food? Water?" Drucie's calm manner only served to accelerate Linzee's pulse rate. "A bathroom?"

"Yes. All of the above." She clenched her jaw to keep the panic at bay. "Bathroom first."

"The bathroom's right there." Drucie pointed toward the other room. "Allison, go with her and make sure she stays there."

The outer room had the look of a basement rec room, containing old couches and a scratched-up ping-pong table in the middle. Sinister-looking posters of obscure rock bands covered the walls. Death metal, no doubt.

Linzee limped into the little bathroom to the right, where Allison allowed her to use the toilet at gunpoint. From the corner of her eye, Allison loomed huge and threatening, and Linzee felt the other woman's stony gaze on her. Silently, she begged the universe to wake her up and get her out of this nightmare.

Upon her return to the prison-like room, she checked out her surroundings. The little room must have been a pantry in a former life. A windowless, concrete pantry. The perfect prison cell. Empty shelves jutted from the walls. The mattress she'd been lying on filled one corner. Linzee sniffed again. The funny smell must be a mixture of old food odors and ancient cigarette smoke.

Drucie pointed to a stack of bottles in the corner. "There's water for you." Allison sat cross-legged on the floor, keeping the weapon aimed at Linzee. "We'll bring you a sandwich in a few."

Linzee grabbed a water bottle, gulped down half of it, and eased to the floor, stretching her legs out as far as possible. "So are you going to tell me what's going on?"

"Yeah. Karma."

"Karma?"

"Karma. Just want to see you get what's coming to

you."

"Get what's coming to me?" She might as well be Echo the Oread.

Drucie wheezed out a laugh. "You don't get it, do you?"

"No, Drucie, I don't." She raised her voice again. "Why don't you enlighten me?"

"You don't remember senior year?"

"You're talking in riddles." A revelation hit her. "Does this have to do with my breaking up with you?"

Drucie gaped at Allison. "The girl's a genius."

"You mean you've harbored a grudge against me all these years because I broke up with you?"

Drucie heaved a mock-patient sigh. "Guess I have to explain in short sentences, dude. First of all, you broke up with me on my birthday. Remember?"

"Well, now I do."

"November eleventh. Double eleven, my lucky day."

Double eleven. Linzee opened her mouth to speak, but Drucie cut her off.

"Then you go and turn it into an unlucky day." Her voice was taut as a whip and lashed Linzee with each word. "You messed with karma. Which is why my entire senior year sucked."

"But why does it matter now, five years later?"

"Why does it matter?" Drucie echoed, in the manner of someone talking to a slow child. "One day, last month, out of the blue, here comes Linzee St. John struttin' into my coffee shop, all happy and glowing, man. She tells me, 'I just graduated from UCLA.' I think to myself, now, how is that fair? This is the girl who ruined my future. She doesn't deserve to be happy."

Linzee's breath caught in her throat. She swallowed hard. "How did I ruin your future?"

"You don't remember the big plans we made for after graduation?"

"Sure I remember." She rubbed her numb ankles. "We

planned to attend UCLA. You were going to apply to their film school."

"And you were going to help me get my grades high enough to get accepted."

Linzee squirmed. "You mean, do your homework for you."

"Correctomundo. We were in solidarity, man. But, I didn't get accepted. All because you decided you were too good for me."

"I did not think that."

"I got stuck here going to junior college. You went off to follow your dreams without me. And then you rubbed my face in it. You shouldn't have done that, you know."

"Drucie, I am so sorry." She made a desperate attempt at sincerity. "I didn't realize—"

"Too late for sorry." Drucie snarled. "At least I kept you from winning Homecoming."

"You?" Linzee gaped. "How did you do that?"

"Wasn't hard. I was Senior Class secretary, remember? I helped count the votes." Cupping her hand around her mouth, Drucie lowered her voice to a mock whisper. "I changed a bunch of votes from you to Natasha."

A swear word flew out of Linzee's mouth. She hadn't once entertained the idea that someone's sabotage had brought about her loss.

"Drucie, you can still follow your dreams," she protested. "It's not too late. Don't let *me* stop you."

"Wrong. UCLA film school would've been my ticket to the big time." Drucie's voice rose, grating with bitterness. "I could've been famous by now. And rich. But they declined my application. My grades weren't good enough."

"It was wrong of you to expect me to do your homework for you."

"Whatev." Drucie shrugged. "I'm done talking. Gonna put the shackles back on you."

"No. Why?"

"'Cause. You're gonna stay put 'til I'm done with you."

The ominous words brought fresh trembles to her limbs. "Wh-what do you mean by that?" She hated the quaking fear in her voice.

"Wouldn't you like to know." Drucie's harsh laugh sent chills up her spine. With the gun in her face, she could only watch as Drucie stepped behind her and clamped the chains around her hands. She bit back sobs, but tears still dribbled down her cheeks.

"Later, dude." Her former friend flicked the light off as she and Allison left the room, plunging Linzee back into utter darkness, alone with her terror.

***

Friday evening, Meg opened her front door to a welcome sight. Camille and Bill's smiles greeted her like a rainbow after a hailstorm. She opened the door wide, and they stepped inside.

"Honey, how are you doing?" said Camille.

"Well, you know how it is when your kid goes missing." Her feeble smile must look pathetic. "You can't think about anything else. I haven't done any housework for two days. I can't even practice art therapy on myself. I haven't been able to focus during devotions. I won't go on social media because Linzee's photo is all over it."

"Seriously?" Camille's usual curved-up mouth drooped. "Here, maybe a hug will help." She wrapped her arms around Meg's shoulders and squeezed.

Meg sniffed and pulled out of Camille's embrace. "Thanks." She rubbed her face vigorously. "And how was your day at work?"

"Well, no headache this time, but I did get a bad case of foot ache, which means I hopped around like a bunny rabbit all day."

Bill placed a hand on Camille's shoulder. "And when she got home, she got a nice foot rub, courtesy of yours truly."

A vision of Camille literally hopping from table to table brought a smile to her face. Bless Camille's jolly heart. She could light candles in the darkest of circumstances.

"We're going for a bite to eat at Denny's." Camille reached for her hand. "Why don't you come along? You need to eat, my friend."

A decidedly better alternative than sitting around like a broken-down automaton. She thought back over her wretched day — a day spent updating friends and family for hours at a time. Phillippe had even come over for a short while, and she'd found herself crying on his broad, powerful shoulder.

"We want to help you get your mind off your troubles tonight." Camille pulled her into the balmy evening. "I know it's hard to wait, but they'll call you right away if there's any news."

"You're right."

Camille commiserated with her throughout the short drive to Denny's. They found a corner booth, the kind with vinyl seats which stuck to her thighs whenever she wore shorts, such as tonight.

She picked up the menu and studied it. Most likely a Cobb salad was about all she could handle as far as food was concerned. These days, steak and salad tasted identical — both had the flavor and consistency of cardboard.

"Hey, I had an idea." Camille set her menu down. "After all this is over, and your daughter has been found, it would be fun to go out dancing sometime."

A frown creased her face. "There isn't much reason to dance right now."

"I know, my friend, I know."

"What kind of dancing did you have in mind?"

"Bill and I love line dancing. We go to that country western place called Hank's. You'd love it."

"I haven't been out dancing since two boyfriends ago."

Camille raised her brows. "Your dear Dr. Dwork never took you out dancing?"

"Dear Dr. Dwork would have considered country line dancing as beneath him."

"Well, pfft."

"Hmmph." To Meg's astonishment, a giggle percolated out of her mouth.

***

After further discussion, Camille agreed to stay overnight at Meg's again.

"Another girls night, eh?" Bill moaned.

"Yeah, we had a grand old time the other night, Bill, my love. It was like high school all over again."

The evening with Camille and Bill proved cathartic. Back at her house, she and Camille dug out the junk food and some comedies. It nearly made her forget the chilling reality awaiting her when all the fun was over.

Chapter Thirty-Three

Five minutes felt like an hour in Linzee's prison cell. After an indeterminate span of time, her jailers returned with three In-n-Out Burger bags. Drucie tossed one on the mattress, along with a water bottle, and once again loosed the shackles around Linzee's wrists.

Drucie reminded her not to try anything. The steel weapon pointing at Linzee emphasized the warning in a most unmistakable way. "Your punch packs a wallop, ya' know. You practically broke my nose when you elbowed me that morning."

Linzee whimpered as she fumbled in the bag. "I had no clue it was you." She wanted to say, "Then you shouldn't have messed with me." But she didn't see a happy ending in that scenario.

She felt Drucie's glare. "Aren't you going to thank me for the food? I didn't have to bring it. I could've let you go hungry."

"Thanks," she whispered, unable to look at her captor. Drucie had her right where she wanted her. And enjoyed it, too. "How long are you going to keep me here?" She gulped as large a bite of burger as she could manage.

Drucie cleared her throat and looked at Allison. "Till Monday."

"What's today?"

"Friday."

"Why Monday? Are you going to let me go home?"

"Monday we're blowing this town. We haven't decided what we're going to do with you. It's still under discussion."

A spasm quaked through Linzee's gut.

"We might let you off somewhere in the boonies, let you find your own way home. Then again, we might decide to put you out of your misery before then." Drucie shrugged, as though the two alternatives held equal merit. "Allison and I will be out of the country, so it won't really matter." She looked at Allison and laughed, then back at Linzee. "You'll be interested to know your little fiancée came in for coffee today and kept talking about Dustin and your brother. She seems to think they done the dirty deeds." Drucie aimed an imaginary mike at her mouth and intoned a tuneless chant about dirty deeds, done dirt cheap. Allison's deep chuckle made for a ghoulish duet.

Linzee shuddered. Nena would be of no help to her. The cops would be focusing on the wrong suspects. Her fate appeared sealed. Drucie could decide to leave her here to rot. A surge of adrenaline punched through her at the thought, and she entertained a brief vision of herself flying off the bed, knocking Allison and her hideous gun to the floor.

But that would only get her shot.

Still, she would almost prefer to be put out of her misery than to end up like the Poe character Fortunato, whose enemy buried him alive in a crypt.

Buried alive. Could Drucie truly be that unfeeling, so cruel?

Nobody knew where she was. Mom must be as frantic as she was, not to mention Nena. She gulped down some water and wondered if Nena or her mom had filed a missing persons report, and if the police were looking for her.

She chewed, then swallowed around a lump in her throat. "I don't even understand how I got here. Can you explain?"

Allison sneered. As did Drucie. "Yeah. Ever heard of a roofie?"

Linzee's eyes popped open wide. "You gave me a

roofie? The date-rape drug?"

"Don't have a cow, man. I'm not interested in date rape."

"Then why?" She examined her burger, hoping it wasn't laced with anything, but too hungry to care.

Drucie snorted. "Didn't we already have this conversation? You put out bad karma, man."

"Well, I don't believe in karma, *man*." She swallowed another bite of burger and stuffed a wad of fries in her mouth.

"What do you believe in then?" Drucie's tone mocked her. "God?"

The question gave Linzee pause. Did she believe in God?

Memories from her childhood bobbed around in her mind like lifejackets tossed to a drowning man.

Her mind swirled with snippets of Bible stories, assurances from her mother that God loved her, a sense of wonder at nature around her, and a certainty that it reflected the hand of God.

She remembered learning Jesus Christ had died on the cross for all her sins.

When had she stopped caring about Him, God—her Heavenly Father?

The swirling memories slowed to a stop, forming into a rich tapestry, and firmly planted itself in Linzee's mind and heart.

When she replied, her voice rang with assurance. "Yes. I do believe in God."

Her captor twisted her mouth. "Psssh. You can have your fairy tales."

"And you can have yours, Drucie."

Drucie responded with a snort and refastened the manacles, then she and Allison grabbed their bags of food, switched off the light and left her again in utter blackness. But this time, the darkness didn't feel quite so dark. A sudden peace wrapped around her like soft mist, a sense of peace she hadn't felt since childhood. In truth, her father's arms had felt the same way when he used to tuck her into bed at night.

Chapter Thirty-Four

Nena rolled into Latte Love Shack Saturday morning on a mission. She wasn't leaving until she got Drucie to talk.

She'd honed her people-radar to an incredible precision throughout her twenty-two years. When she'd started picking up a creepy vibe from Drucie, she'd paid attention.

Linzee wasn't as shrewd a judge of human nature. She possessed a beautiful soul and assumed the world had her best interests at heart. But Nena knew that for most people, their own interests trumped others' every time.

"Hey." She waved at Drucie, found a table, and placed her order. Within minutes, Drucie delivered a raspberry cappuccino.

Nena sipped the sweet concoction and grimaced. "When's your break?"

"Not long. Need to talk?"

"Yeah. Life sucks right now." She managed a tight-lipped frown.

"No doubt, dude. I'll come over."

When Drucie approached a few minutes later, Nena plastered a *mejor amiga* expression on her face. "*Hola.*" She made herself look Drucie in the eye as if they truly were best friends.

"What up?"

"I'm wishin' the cops would go talk to Linzee's bro."

Drucie sprawled on the opposite bench. "Why haven't they?"

"He ain't a suspect."

Drucie grunted. "You ought to find out what the bro

was doing that morning."

"Yeah, I will. Meg will know." She took another sugary gulp and waited two seconds. "Maybe Dustin ain't really on vacation."

Drucie's brows rose. "Why wouldn't he be?"

"Ain't it convenient he's supposedly gone this week? He and Bro could've hijacked Linzee's car."

"Huh. You have a point." Drucie's face scrunched. "He'll be back next week. The cops will probably come back and question him."

Nena thought for a moment, then tried another piece of bait. "They found Linzee's car at McNears Beach. But not Linzee."

Drucie let out a whistle. "That's a ways from here. I hope they find her soon." Abruptly, she stood. "Gotsta get back. My break's over. Ten minute's way too short." She ended her proclamation with a curse and sauntered away, leaving Nena staring at the wall, wanting to pound her head against it over another dead end.

She grasped her half-full cappuccino and made for the exit. Por Dios, she would get to the bottom of this, or die trying.

***

Linzee opened her eyes and wondered what day it was.

The blackness nearly drowned her, yet her prison cell no longer felt like deep space. The silence had filled with an intangible something which hadn't been there before.

At once she knew, as certain as she knew her own name, her mother and countless others were praying for her.

"God?" She aimed a whisper at the ceiling. "Are you there?"

She heard nothing, but she lay there, basking in the unexpected, peaceful, and comforting sensation. Then, at last, she poured her heart out to the God she'd ignored for too many years.

"God." She gasped for breath. "Please don't let Drucie get away with this. Please don't let Dustin and Richie get into trouble for something they didn't do. And please, Lord, send someone to get me out of here."

A tune as squeaky as a rusty instrument burst from her throat then smoothed out and soared toward heaven.

"Jesus loves me, this I know,
For the Bible tells me so —"

***

Meg lay tense and huddled on the couch. Outside the window, a trio of teens strolled along the sidewalk in carefree abandon, their struts announcing all was well in their world.

Her phone chimed, displaying Jon's number. "Hello?"

"Hi, Meg." Her heart leaped at the sound of his voice. "How are you doing?"

She unclenched herself. "Hi, Jon. Feeling like I'm in a nightmare I can't wake up from." She puckered her mouth to quell its trembling. "How are you?"

"I'm fine, but I'm more concerned about you." The compassion in his voice nearly made her weep. "I remember my mother used to tell us her kid radar was always on. She seemed to sense what we were up to, especially if it was bad. Is your kid radar telling you anything?"

"I don't know what it's telling me." She sniffed. "For a while, I was afraid my son and his friend were harassing her. But I can't imagine Richie harming or kidnapping his own sister."

"You thought it was your son doing all that?"

"Yeah, it seems crazy now. But I could tell this Eddie person was someone who knew her well."

"I see." Jon paused. "It's possible that wherever she is now is unrelated to the harassment."

Skepticism soured her spirit, although she knew Jon was only trying to look on the bright side.

"Anyway, I called to tell you my church prayer team meets every Sunday morning. I hope you can drop by tomorrow at nine-thirty."

"Jon, it's so sweet of you to think of me. I'm starting to feel like I'm losing hope."

"Don't lose hope. We'll keep seeking the throne of heaven for you."

"I can't express how grateful I am." Her voice sounded weak and childlike to her ears. "I wish I could make it up to you in some way."

"You don't have to make it up to me," he said with a trace of amusement. "That's what the body of Christ is for. Talk to Camille about a ride. She said she and Bill could pick you up."

If only she could ride with him.

He went on, his upbeat voice easing her anxiety. "They usually attend the ten-thirty service. I hope you can stay for it."

"I know it would do me a world of good." Her heart stirred. "I could use an uplifting worship service right now."

"It will be, I promise. I think you'll like tomorrow's sermon. He's preaching on James 1."

"You'll save us a seat, won't you?"

He paused. *Way to be obvious, Meg.*

"Well, I would." Was that regret in his voice? "But I promised my good buddy the youth pastor I'd help with his worship service."

"Oh. Do you help with the music?" She flipped onto her back and examined the ceiling, seeing his crinkle-eyed smile superimposed over it.

"When I'm needed. He sometimes asks me to fill in on guitar and vocals when one of the regulars can't make it."

"That's great. I didn't know you had a gift for music." *Not to mention his many other gifts.*

"The gift came from my parents. They gave me a guitar for my fifth birthday, roughly thirty-six years ago.

Hopefully, I've mastered it by now," he said in his usual wry, offhand way.

An uncertain pause followed. She dared not ask the question uppermost in her mind: *Would you sing for me sometime?*

"I'll bet you're being modest." She heard a smile in her voice and hoped he heard it, too. "You're probably quite good, aren't you?"

She could sense him processing this. "Thanks for the vote of confidence." He chuckled. "I'm not Elton John, but the kids don't seem to mind."

Her smile widened.

Speaking of Elton John, he'd recently tied the knot. With a man.

"Jon?" She forced out a bright tone. "There's something I've been meaning to ask you."

"Sure. Ask away."

"Let's assume my daughter is going to be found, safe and sound."

"Glad you're thinking positive."

"Well, her wedding ceremony will be held in September." She shifted onto her side, cradling the phone as if it were Jon himself. "I'm so undecided as to whether I should attend. On one hand, if I go, it will look like I support same-sex marriage. But if I don't go, Linzee would be so hurt, not to mention the flak I'd get for it."

"Gotcha."

"I'd love your take on this. What should I do?"

"Hmm. That's a tough position to be in."

"No kidding."

"The good news is, you're not the first parent to wrestle with that question."

"What's the bad news?"

"The bad news is, there's no right answer."

"There's not?"

"Here's the thing. The Bible doesn't mention gay

marriage. It just defines marriage as a union between a man and a woman. In Jesus' day, people in the Jewish culture didn't come out of the closet. Gays didn't marry. Back then, the punishment for homosexual activity was stoning."

"Ugh."

"Yeah. We live in a much kinder world. Anyway, when the Bible is silent on a decision I need to make, I use the verse in First Corinthians that says, 'Whatsoever ye do, do all to the glory of God.'"

She pondered this. "So I simply need to decide, does taking a stand against same-sex marriage glorify God more than showing love and support for my daughter? Or vice versa?"

"Not a simple decision at all. My suggestion is, fast and pray about this. You have two months. And if you sense God telling you to be there, He'll give you the change of heart you'll need to bear it."

She would need it.

"And if He says, 'Stay home Meg,' He'll give you the words to say to Linzee and anyone else who objects."

"It sounds like a win-win."

"Doing God's will is always a win-win."

Another smile tugged the corners of her mouth. "Thank you for your words of wisdom. Your level of faith is amazing."

"I don't know about that. I struggle with faith myself."

"I mean, your confidence that God will come through at just the right time is so reassuring."

"Well, God had to bonk me on my thick skull umpteen times before I finally got it."

She chuckled. "My skull's pretty thick too."

They shared a laugh, then Jon said, "I'll add your dilemma to my prayer list. See you tomorrow?"

"You will, Lord willing."

She hung up with the first genuine smile she'd had all day, and bounced to her feet.

But before long she was thinking about Linzee again. A frown tossed aside the smile, bringing with it a jaw clenched so tight her brain ached, and pacing so frantic her carpet must be crying out. Granted, tragedy visited nearly everyone at some point in life, but this trial felt so different than previous ones. She remembered the months after Phillippe had left when the aftermath was like a dark room with barely a glimmer of light under the door.

This time, however, reminded her of a cave in Colorado she'd visited. During the tour, the guide had demonstrated the absolute blackness of a cave by remotely switching off the lights for a full minute. She would never forget his grave, disembodied tone when he told them, "Without any light at all, after a couple of days your mind will start to hallucinate." He'd let them absorb this for a moment before he switched the lights back on.

Although she didn't think she would start hallucinating if Linzee were never found, she didn't see how she could ever feel joy again. The absence of joy, not to mention hope, would be as absolute as the darkness of that cave.

Chapter Thirty-Five

Nena, clutching her smartphone and iPad, timed her arrival at Latte Love Shack Sunday morning to coincide with Drucie's break. She found an empty table and placed her order, arranging her face with the proper mournful expression. Not a difficult task considering her state of mind. A new sensation had taken root in her. When she had glanced in the mirror this morning, she was startled to see wide eyes and a frozen face staring back at her.

"Heya." Drucie approached with Nena's coffee. "You don't look so hot."

"I don't feel so hot." She could hear her plaintive tone. So far, pretending she suspected Dustin and Richie of masterminding Linzee's disappearance hadn't gotten her anywhere. She needed something solid to link Drucie to Linzee's harasser, something she could take to the cops.

She crossed her fingers this time. "I'mma missin' Linzee. Them cops ain't doin' nothin'. I keep thinkin' she's lying dead in a ditch somewhere." She watched Drucie without a flinch. The other woman's face stayed smooth, but Nena caught a split-second flicker of emotion in her eyes.

"I sure hope not. Do you want to chat? My break's in five minutes."

"Yeah, come out to the patio."

She gathered up her things and proceeded to a patio table. Soon Drucie appeared.

"So." Drucie plopped down beside her, set a knee on the bench, and turned to face her. "Any leads?"

"Nada. Zilch." Nena sipped her coffee and mustered a

confiding expression. "I'mma wanna know what *you* think happened to her."

"Me?" Drucie's puckered mouth made craters in her cheeks. "I have no clue."

"Her dad thought she ran away. But she ain't the type. At least, not since I've known her. You've known her awhile, right?"

Drucie leaned her elbow on the table and gave a half-snort of laughter. "Since high school. We even had a fling."

"Serious?" Nena said, her poker face hiding her shock. "She never said nothin'."

Drucie shrugged, but the corners of her mouth tightened. "It was no big deal."

Nena recoiled at the thought of lovely Linzee with this freak. A rush of jealousy took her by surprise. She and Linzee had always been open with each other about previous relationships.

Yet, Linzee hadn't told her about Drucie.

She wanted to shake more information out of the other woman. "Did you end it, or did she?"

Drucie shrugged again. "It was kind of mutual."

Nena fastened her gaze on Drucie's eyes and saw a brittle spark there. A tiny tic of the eyelid. Details she would have missed if she hadn't been closely watching.

Drucie yawned as though the subject bored her, and, grasping an elbow, pulled her right arm across her body and stretched it. The ugly scorpion was practically in Nena's face. Tiny letters encircling a claw caught her attention. "What's your tat say?"

Drucie released her arm. "What?"

Nena pointed. "Your scorpion tattoo. I never noticed them letters on it before."

"Oh. It says Scorpio. My zodiac sign."

Scorpio. November's sign.

An idea honed in on her. "You was born in November."

"Yep. On the eleventh."

The leap of her heart nearly sent her charging for the door, but she willed it to slow down, almost missing Drucie's next words.

"Eleven eleven. My lucky day."

Nena feigned interest while her red flag detector went off at high frequency.

A breakup. A possible motive for revenge. The number eleven.

She eyed Drucie, convinced she was eying the face of Eddie, aka E. Levens.

All she needed was some proof. Another link to the name Edward Levens.

Speaking of names—a memory nagged at her. A conversation she'd had about a weird name. She cast her mind back, straining to remember. Back to last week. Linzee sitting at the computer with Blake Mannson's profile on the screen.

Then a light bulb flipped on. *"You'll never guess what her full name is,"* Linzee had said with a laugh. *"Drucilla—"* something, something.

But she couldn't remember. Because she hadn't been paying attention.

She squinted down at her iPad. "I'mma check Facebook, see what they're saying about Linzee now." She hoped Drucie would take the hint and leave.

Drucie did. She waved and trotted away. Nena tapped the Facebook icon, found Linzee's profile, and pulled up her friends list. "D-R-U-C-I-E," Nena keyed into the search box.

The requested profile popped up, and her eyes widened. The proof she needed stared her right in the face.

Keeping her movements smooth and unhurried, she gathered her things and strode to the exit. She needed to get out of here and over to the cop shop before Drucie saw the smoke coming out of her ears.

***

Meg sat beside Camille in the vast sanctuary of Victory Church, tuned in to the sermon on James 1.

"My brethren, count it all joy when ye fall into diverse temptations—"

Her phone vibrated in her skirt pocket, but she ignored it.

"—knowing this, that the trying of your faith worketh patience."

The phone buzzed again, and her leg jittered. It might be important. It might be the cops summoning her with good news.

She slipped the phone into the palm of her hand and saw a text from Nena. *Call me. Got news.*

She nudged Camille and jabbed at the phone. Camille squinted, her mouth in an O.

Meg raised her eyebrows as if to ask, what do we do now? Camille raised hers in reply. Meg sat, undecided and getting antsier by the minute.

Another text buzzed her phone, vibrating through her hand. *It's about Linzee.*

She absolutely had to get out of here. Grabbing a piece of paper off the rack in front of her, she wrote a note to Camille.

"Can we can sneak out?"

Camille nodded and whispered. "Just do it." She turned to Bill and whispered again.

They stood and slipped past the other folks. Meg grimaced apologies as she nearly tread on toes and slammed into knees. She tilted her face toward the floor and hid behind her veil of hair. Folks must be wondering why she was hustling out of the service as if she were on fire.

Once outside, she and Camille plopped on a bench. Her hands shook so hard she could barely manage the phone.

"Nena?" She stared at the majestic view of the Bay spread out before them, the city skyline beyond peeking out of the haze like fuzzy Lego structures.

"Hey," came Nena's froggy voice, laced with an edge of hope. "I got good news."

"What?"

"I'm at the cop shop. Can you meet me here?"

"I'm with Camille. I don't have my car. What are you doing at the police station?"

"Seein' if they can get a search warrant for Drucie's house. I think Linzee's there."

"Drucie? Holey socks. Why do you suspect Drucie?" Her gaze slid sideways to Camille, who listened intently.

"I had my suspicions, and I been tryin' to get her to talk. Today she said something that sounded incriminating. Now I can prove she's Eddie."

"I'm floored." She stood and paced along the cobblestoned patio. "Let me see what I can do. I'll call you right back."

After she had updated Camille, her friend responded with a high-five. "Drucie? The little gal with nuts and bolts all over her face? She's the prime suspect now?"

"Uh huh. Nena's been doing some detective work." She smiled for the first time all morning.

"Well, let's get over there, then. I'll drop you off, come back and get Bill, and meet back up with you."

En route, she called Phillippe and asked him to meet them at the police station. When they arrived, they rushed inside to find Nena talking to the officer on duty, the whites of her eyes betraying her emotions.

"Time for some mega-prayers." Camille hugged Meg and departed for Sausalito.

Phillippe arrived shortly after, his face taut with fear and hope. This time, she received his hug with no hesitation.

From there, events snowballed. After hearing Nena's recap of the morning's conversation and seeing the evidence, the officer proceeded to obtain a search warrant for Drucie's house. Camille, panting, arrived with Bill and Jon. Meg jumped in her chair, her head swiveling back and forth between Jon and her ex-husband.

Phillippe sat two chairs over, leaning toward her just as he did when they were married. Jon and Bill sized him up in obvious curiosity.

She took a deep breath and made introductions. Camille tossed her an "oops" look as if to say, "Sorry, honey, if I made things awkward for you by bringing Jon."

The four of them engaged in stilted conversation while they waited for the cops to finish the search warrant paperwork. Nena emerged from the interview room and joined them, scrutinizing Jon and Bill. Meg made further introductions.

"Nena deserves a big attagirl for her efforts." She smiled at Nena, who responded by wrinkling her nose. A grin twitched at her lips. The three men each shook her hand, and Bill high-fived her.

The two officers in charge of the search appeared to be polar opposites. The young, burly cop seemed the cheerier of the two. The older, grim cop's jowls and shoulders drooped, as though he carried the world on his shoulders. He gave permission for them to follow, instructing them to remain in their cars while they searched the house.

"How do they know where Drucie lives?" Meg turned to Nena as they followed the cops out to the parking lot.

"They got the employees' addresses when they interrogated 'em."

"What if Linzee's not there?"

Nena's face scrunched. "I think she's there, unless—" She let her words die away, unwilling to voice the alternative. Meg didn't want to even entertain any other alternatives.

Phillippe strolled beside her. "Want to ride with me?"

She didn't, as she preferred to ride with Jon. "Thanks, Phillippe, but I think Nena would rather I stick with her."

"I'll follow you, then."

She nodded and piled onto the bench seat in Bill's

pickup, squeezed between Jon and Nena. Jon's knees made dents in the back of Camille's seat.

"Meg." Jon turned to face her. "Is that a smile I see?" His dark eyes searched her face as if he were watching the sun chase away clouds.

She relished his gaze that left her breathless. "It sure would be nice to have a reason to smile again."

"I was intrigued when Camille ran up to me and said God's about to answer our prayers."

Flustered at his nearness, she wiped damp palms on her denim skirt. Camille shifted, facing her. "That was premature of me, wasn't it?"

"You can't help being the world's biggest optimist, Camille. The world could use a few more of you."

Camille's good cheer was contagious. Already a glimmer of anticipation sparkled in the distance. Dare she hope they'd find Linzee alive?

But what if they didn't?

No, she couldn't go there. They were so close, she could almost hear heaven's angels rejoicing already.

She gripped the hand Camille offered, desperate to absorb even a fraction of her friend's radiant faith. Jon took her other hand, and they bowed their heads in prayer.

Chapter Thirty-Six

Linzee sighed, itching with boredom. Even worse, the metal cutting into her wrists generated non-stop pain, like an infected tooth. She longed to just yank them off, but that was an impossible feat. Yet in the midst of her black despair, she found herself reminiscing about happier times. Singing upbeat songs. Talking to God.

She wished she had a Bible here, and light by which to read. She craved the familiar stories she learned in Sunday school.

This must be what being "born again" was all about. The term got tossed around at church all the time, but the term had become linked, in her mind, to the wild-eyed fanatics who protested outside abortion clinics, who shook their fingers at any sexual expression they didn't approve of.

Perhaps the term held a deeper meaning. Maybe the fanatics weren't just expressing personal opinions. Like Mom, and her opposition to Linzee's sexual preference that she and Nena had chalked up to homophobia.

Now, a memory from long ago demanded her attention. A youth group study on Romans 1. God's opinion on same-sex relationships. At the time, she hadn't cared about God's standards. She had pursued the gay lifestyle anyway.

Yesterday, at least it seemed like yesterday, she experienced God's personal Father-love for her. Today she did care what He thought, which forced her to face the dilemma she could no longer ignore: Once she got out of here, *if* she got out of here, she didn't see how she could go back to her life with Nena as though nothing were different.

On the other hand, she didn't know how she could leave Nena, who hadn't done anything to deserve it.

"God, I need help knowing what to do about Nena." Her voice was a mere whisper. But somehow she knew God heard her whispers as well as her shouts. "And I need strength to endure this awfulness."

She didn't hold out much hope that anyone would deduce her whereabouts before Monday, as long as Nena assumed Dustin and Richie were the instigators.

At least Drucie and Allison weren't being completely inhumane. They turned the light on at regular intervals, brought her food, allowed her to shower and groom, and gave her old shorts and tee-shirts to wear. But always with the gun pointed at her and death-metal music blaring in the background, grating on Linzee's nerves like a broken muffler.

How could she have missed Drucie's true nature? The tremendous shock that ripped through her the moment she realized her "friend" had turned into her worst enemy beat the 2009 Inglewood earthquake hands down.

She recalled Senior Award night when Drucie had won the "Most Likely to Star in a Horror Movie" award. She had been a fine actress back then, and she had lost none of her talent for role-playing. Despite that, Linzee hadn't once detected Drucie's interest in her harassment as anything but genuine.

She should have remembered the date of Drucie's birthday. She should have known who E. Levens was. How like Drucie, the spy-movie lover, to use aliases and secret codes.

The details of their breakup clarified in her memory, as though it had happened yesterday.

For Drucie's birthday, Linzee had offered to treat her to dinner at a steak-and-seafood restaurant. Once they'd settled into a booth, Drucie held out her smartphone.

"Listen to this, Linz. 'If you were born today, you are

driven and passionate. You are a mystic with deep creative powers. You shun superficial relationships, preferring deep, intense connections with those you love and—'"

"Do you mind if we not talk about your superstitions for one night?" Linzee said, fed up with the constant references to karma, horoscopes, and hidden meanings.

"Yeah, I mind." Drucie had glared at her. "It's my birthday so we should talk about what I want."

"You know I think it's all a load of hogwash."

An argument had erupted. Drucie had sworn at her and called her names, and Linzee had thrown down her fork and jumped to her feet. "This isn't working for me anymore. I'm done." She'd tossed her own curses at Drucie and walked out.

Later in the evening, Drucie had sent her an apologetic text asking for another chance, but Linzee had told her no, they should be just friends. Eventually, they had begun speaking again. She had never suspected that behind Drucie's droll, low-key façade, a raging forest fire hid. She couldn't have imagined that Drucie could or would stoop to kidnapping.

When Linzee had first walked into Latte Love Shack earlier this summer and had seen a familiar face from high school, it had taken her a minute to recognize Drucie. With the piercings on her face and stripes in her hair, her old friend had lost any soft edges she may have once had. Drucie had greeted her in such a friendly manner and had seemed so pleased to see her, five years ago had felt like ancient history.

***

A faraway pounding jolted Linzee up to a sitting position.

It couldn't be Drucie and Allison. They never pounded. They just blasted music whenever they arrived.

The pounding continued, and she heard yelling—deep,

masculine voices demanding something. But she couldn't make out what they were saying.

Soon she heard stomping overhead, as though the voices had morphed into feet. She didn't know whether to be frightened or hopeful. If these were burglars, up to no good, what were the chances they would find her in this obscure corner of the basement?

The footsteps were getting closer.

And then she heard the most beautiful sound in the world.

"This is the police," someone yelled. "Anybody here?"

She screeched and screamed as loud as she'd ever screamed in her life.

"In here," she shouted. "I'm in here." She rolled off the bed and hopped toward the door, kicking and yelling, putting out the loudest racket she could.

The door flew open, and beautiful light streamed in. Surprised faces peered in at her. Strong yet gentle arms lifted her from her dungeon and carried her to safety.

Overcome with joy and relief, Linzee wept. "Thank you, God."

***

Meg and Phillippe paced the sidewalk across the street from Drucie's childhood home. The other four waited in Bill's truck. At the opposite curb, an ambulance pulled up, and two paramedics jumped out.

"An ambulance?" Fear clutched her heart as she visualized her daughter still and lifeless. "Why do they need an ambulance?"

"I think it's just standard practice." Phillippe's calm tone belied the serious nature of the sight. "If they find her, they'll want to take her to the hospital first thing."

If they find her? Nena had seemed so certain.

"Hey." Phillippe's voice penetrated her reverie. "Are you dating that man?"

She lurched at the sudden change of subject.

"The one with glasses?" he went on.

"How can you ask such a question at a time like this?" she retorted. "No, we're not dating. He's a good friend."

"He seems a little more concerned than a mere friend ought to be."

She glanced at the pickup's open windows. "Shhh. They can probably hear you." She strode several paces beyond the truck, then whirled to face him, dropping her voice to a fierce whisper. "That's the kind of person Jon is. He's been arranging prayer vigils and whatnot for Linzee, simply because he has a caring heart."

Phillippe ground to a halt. He stared at her for a moment.

"What?" She tilted her head at him.

"I see the way it is now." He nodded. "There's something going on there, eh?" His head still bobbed, and he cast her a half-smirk. "I must say, you've always had great taste in men."

"Phillippe." She back-handed him, but he only chuckled harder. "I told you I'm not dating him."

A shout resounded from the open window of the truck. Her head shot up, and her gaze made a beeline for the little brown house across the street.

The taller cop had just exited. He lugged a bundle in his arms.

Linzee.

Meg's face crumpled like a piece of tinfoil, and she burst into sobs. "Is she alive?" Frozen, she watched the tall policeman hand Linzee over to the paramedics, who laid her on the stretcher and bent over her. The older policeman escorted a chunky young woman in handcuffs out of the house and stuffed her into the back of the patrol car.

Curtains in nearby windows moved ever so slightly, betraying curious onlookers. Neighbors streamed out their doors, craning their necks and gaping.

Meg unfroze herself and rushed across the street. The younger deputy gestured at the house as he approached Meg. "As you can see, we found her." Metal glittered impressively on his chest and belt. "We arrested the roommate and radioed for one of our partners to get over to the coffee shop and apprehend Miss Ward before her shift ends at two." Compassion softened his eyes. "Your daughter has been shackled and held prisoner in their basement for four days, so we're taking her to the hospital to get her checked out."

She gasped, understanding now why Linzee had been carried out. "I can't thank you enough." Sobs choked her words.

Phillippe materialized at her side and grasped the officer's hand, pumping it over and over.

The policeman nodded. "All in a day's work."

"I want to see her." She ran to the stretcher, feasting on the sight of her daughter's alert eyes.

The paramedic paused in her examination of Linzee's hands and looked up. "Are you the mother?"

"Yes."

The woman stepped aside, and Meg grasped her daughter's hand, flinching at the ugly welts around her wrist. "Linzee, baby?"

Linzee offered a wan grin. "Mom," she managed, then turned her head. "Dad."

Meg turned to the woman. "Is she okay?"

A reassuring nod. "She's alert and in one piece. We'll give her a more thorough examination on the way to the hospital." The woman moved to the head of the stretcher while the other paramedic, his balding head shiny under the afternoon sun, grasped the end. "We're going to load her in now, and you can meet up with her at the hospital."

Meg watched them move her daughter into the cavernous vehicle, then hurried back across the street to her ecstatic friends. "She's alive!"

Jon smiled from one end of his face to the other. "Praise God, thank you, God," he said over and over. Nena's eyes glinted, and she blinked. A tiny smile betrayed her relief. Camille yelped and hollered.

Laughing, Meg hopped into the truck and tucked herself between Jon and Nena. Bill peeled out behind the ambulance.

Camille chimed in from the passenger seat. "You should've seen your face when the cop brought her out."

"Hey, what about me?" muttered Nena.

"Of course, Nena." Meg softened her tone. "You know, we're all eager to know what proof you found."

Nena recapped her conversations with Drucie as they followed the ambulance to Marin General Hospital. When Nena mentioned Drucie's birthday, Meg's jaw dropped. Camille swiveled and patted her knee. "There you go, honeybun. Your eleven connection." But Meg's glee evaporated once she realized she had incriminated two innocent young men, even if only in her mind.

She turned to Nena. "But was it enough for the police?"

"Hey. I ain't finished. You know how you figgered out E. Levens."

"Yes?"

"Well, I got to thinkin', how come she choose a name like Edward? What's up with that? Started wonderin' if it was her last name. Then I be like, hey, Linzee once told me Drucie's full name, but I forgot it." Nena stopped and turned to Meg, her eyes snapping like shooting stars.

"I looked her up on Facebook. Her last name is—"

"Ward," said Meg and Nena in unison.

A two-second pause filled the cab.

"Drucilla P. Ward." Nena punched the seat. "D. Ward."

"Holey socks." Meg gasped out a laugh.

Camille whooped.

Jon laughed. "Nena and Meg crack the case. You know what they say. Great minds think alike."

Meg couldn't stop grinning. "Nena, we'd make a great detective duo."

Camille clapped a hand on Meg's knee and squeezed. "Drucie hid her alias in two boxes, one inside the other. You unpacked the first one—"

"And Nena unpacked the second one." Bill grinned at her in the rearview mirror.

"Here's to Meg and Nena." Camille whooped again, banging out a percussion of pats on Meg's knee.

They celebrated all the way to the hospital.

***

Bill's truck rolled into the hospital's emergency parking lot less than a minute behind the ambulance. Jon hopped out first and offered Meg a helping hand. He steadied her as she jumped down, then patted her shoulder. "Don't worry about coming to the meeting tomorrow night. Stay with your daughter and I'll check in with you later to see how she's doing."

Camille embraced Meg with a swaying, ten-second hug, then returned to the truck and hopped in. Bill roared off.

Meg, Phillippe, and Nena settled in at Linzee's bedside. Plenty of tears, hugs, and kisses passed back and forth. Meg basked in the sight of Linzee wearing a brave grin. Even Nena's open displays of affection toward Linzee couldn't dampen Meg's joy.

But her daughter's face, pale as a cadaver's, frightened her. The doctor in charge, Dr. DeGraff, told them Linzee was slightly dehydrated and likely a few pounds thinner. It might take some time for her arms to feel normal again. But she was a strong, healthy young woman. She would recover. The hospital would keep her overnight, and she should be ready to go home the next morning.

The TV news reports kept flashing Drucie's mug shot for all to see. The reporter launched into an update, his face grave. "The police arrested Miss Ward fifteen minutes before her shift ended. It took several officers to subdue her."

Nena snorted when Drucie's scowling face popped up on the screen, and launched into the details of her role in the rescue. Linzee and Nena laughed and high-fived, then Linzee shared her story. Phillippe clutched his daughter's hand as though she might run away.

After Phillippe had left for his hotel, a nurse brought in an extra cot for Nena. Meg curled up in an uncomfortable recliner, the smile still intact, sending up praises to God. Despite her physical discomfort, for the first time in days she enjoyed deep and peaceful slumber.

Chapter Thirty-Seven

Linzee massaged her gimpy arm, pain contorting her face, and scooted to a prone position on the sofa. Nena lounged in the easy chair. The TV blared in the background.

A Pepsi commercial began, and the sound suddenly vanished. "Hey. Linzee."

Nena rarely addressed her as "Linzee." Not only that, Nena's peevish mood had mystified Linzee ever since they'd left the hospital this morning. Nena ought to be relieved, glad, celebrating Linzee's homecoming. Instead, she spoke only in business-like tones. The rest of the time, she stared at the TV with a scowl on her face.

Judging by Nena's tone, she was finally ready to level with Linzee. And Linzee had a feeling it wasn't good.

She turned her head. Nena held the remote aloft. Her dark, glittering gaze nailed Linzee.

"You never said nothin' 'bout you and Drucie's fling in high school." An alarming tone vibrated in Nena's words. "She told me it weren't a big deal. But I could tell by her face that it was."

Linzee's heart lurched. "She suggested I keep it zipped."

Nena chortled. "'She suggested.' Hah. How come you be takin' orders from her?"

Linzee had no reply. Nena continued her tongue-lashing.

"It was a shockeroo, amiga. How come you be with that freak?"

"Well, obviously, she wasn't a freak then."

"I bet she was, but you don't ever pick up on stuff. Would've been nice if I'd a known. Wish you told me."

"I'm sorry."

"You made me out to be a fool that I didn't know. Got any other secrets I ought to know about?"

"I said I'm sorry." Linzee felt as petulant as a five-year-old.

Nena turned away and jabbed the remote. They watched a CSI rerun in edgy silence for awhile.

Once her heart finished thudding, Linzee broached the subject which had been on her mind since Friday.

"Nena, can we talk?"

"When the show's over." Nena kept her eyes on the screen.

Five minutes later Nena snapped off the TV and turned to Linzee. "Yeah?"

Linzee floundered to explain. "Something strange happened to me in that basement."

Nena listened with raised brows.

"Like an epiphany."

"An epiphany? What'cha talkin' about?"

"Like God was in there with me."

Nena rolled her eyes. "Oh, c'mon. You was havin' a foxhole moment."

"A what?"

"You know. When them soldiers are in battle, hidin' in a foxhole thinkin' they gonna die any minute, they always run cryin' to God to save 'em. Then they go home and forget all about it. Like the sayin' says, there ain't no atheists in foxholes."

Linzee looked at her hands. "No, it was more than that. It's like he's still here. What I'm trying to say is, I feel like I need to go stay with my mom for awhile. Being trapped in that basement for four days traumatized me, and I need my mom."

"You gotta be kiddin' me."

"Nena, it's nothing against you. It's totally me. It's what I need to do right now. I've got to sort things out."

Nena looked at her with steel in her eyes, and a chilly silence yawned between them. Linzee felt tears begin somewhere in her heart.

In truth, she'd purposely omitted one small detail, one she couldn't share with Nena. When the cop had lifted her in his arms and carried her up the stairs, she had opened her eyes to see a most piercing set of blue eyes looking down at her. The lightning bolt which flashed for a split second between her and her rescuer had boggled her mind. She couldn't get it out of her head.

She knew how modern psychology would explain it away. Many modern psychologists believed sexual orientation was carved in stone, therefore, the little zing she'd felt resulted from an overwrought emotional state. They would say she was Titania in A Midsummer Night's Dream, who, while under Puck's spell, had fallen madly in love with a donkey head the moment she laid eyes on it.

She felt pretty sure that sweet young policeman was no donkey head.

Linzee eased her way off the sofa and into the bedroom, retrieving a bag from under the bed. She sobbed and trembled as she packed.

***

Meg heard the front door open and shut again. When her daughter peeked in the room, her heart leaped. "Linzee, baby. I was about to call you."

Linzee said nothing, merely wrapped her arms around Meg's shoulders and hung there. Meg patted her over and over, holding her like she was a child again.

"Mom, can we talk?"

"Of course. Come sit down."

"Can I stay here for awhile?"

Meg took a step back, hardly believing what she was

hearing. "You left Nena?"

"Well, sort of. I need to explain. Can I stay tonight?"

"Absolutely."

"Let me go get my overnight bag."

"You came prepared. You knew your mom wouldn't turn you away, didn't you?"

Linzee grinned. "That's what I love about you, Mom." She turned and hobbled back to her car, and returned clutching a goldenrod duffel bag trimmed in black.

When they had settled themselves on the couch like two best friends, Linzee began. "Mom, I think I found God while I was at Drucie's."

Meg gaped again. With all this gaping she'd been doing, her mouth might freeze in a permanently open position. "You found God?"

"Yeah. It was weird. There was this glow in my heart."

Meg raised her brows.

***

Linzee knew her next words might send Mom hurtling off the sofa. She grinned, anticipating a reaction. "And then when the cop carried me up the stairs, something else strange happened."

When she finished telling Mom of the connection she'd felt with the cop, Mom leaned forward, her smile as white as a rose across her face. "It sounds like God is starting to change your heart, Baby Girl. Maybe you ought to drop by the police station tomorrow and thank the man. See if you get the same reaction."

"Great idea." One week ago, she wouldn't have dreamed she'd ever look forward to visiting a man. But today, she couldn't wait to see the tall young cop again. He'd been so gentle when he removed the shackles. She'd enjoyed the firm way he rubbed her ankles to get the blood circulating again. She wanted to tell him how grateful she was — face to face.

With this new truth dawning on her, she had to say it aloud in order to believe it. "It's like I don't feel right about being with Nena anymore."

"Praise the Good Lord," Mom said.

Chapter Thirty-Eight

The aroma of grilling chicken brought a clenching hunger to Meg's stomach. Linzee stood at the stove, flipping and stirring in preparation for her father's visit.

"What's on the menu?" Meg peered into the pan.

"Cashew chicken on rice." Linzee tossed the diced vegetables into the skillet. "Dad's favorite entrée." Steam rose like a volcano.

"When is he supposed to be here?"

"Any minute." The doorbell clamored, and Linzee dropped the spatula. "Here, Mom, take over. I'll let him in."

Meg inhaled the sizzling steam and felt a pulsating sensation near her hip, like a muscle spasm. She rubbed at the spot, but something hard impeded her fingers.

She looked down. She had forgotten about her cell phone. It vibrated in her jeans pocket. She pulled it out as Phillippe and a beaming Richie sauntered in. Shadow tailed them, whoofing.

"Hello?"

Phillippe waved. "Do I smell my favorite dinner?" His voice rumbled across the room.

"Hello?" she said again into the phone.

A pause followed. Then Jon spoke. "Meg? Did I catch you at a bad time?"

Air whooshed out her lungs. "Oh, Jon, hi. No, this is fine."

Phillippe's laugh thundered. She rolled her eyes to the ceiling, hunger pangs forgotten.

Jon spoke again. "It sounds like you have company."

"Hold on a minute." She gestured to Linzee to take over the cooking, then hurried to her bedroom. She plopped face-up on top of her comforter and sank into the depths of the mattress.

"Sorry, Jon. I got distracted for a minute. Linzee's father dropped by. She's cooking him dinner." She chuckled, then wished she could wrest the words back.

"I see," he said, drawing out the words as though confused. "Are you at Linzee's?"

"No, she's here at my house." Her voice dropped while her spirits soared. "God is working on her, Jon. She's staying here while she figures things out. We had a fantastic conversation last night." She felt an uncontrollable grin stretch across her face as she shared the news.

"She found God?" His voice rose. "That is unbelievable. I told you God is in the miracle business."

She laughed. "You certainly did."

"Does Linzee spend much time with her father?"

"No, he's been out of her life until a couple of weeks ago. Now he's in the process of moving back here from Canada." Her spirits nose-dived at the thought. More words poured out before she could stop them. "I don't understand why God would bring my ex-husband back into my life. Especially since—" She slid to a stop before she said something she would regret. Something like, *especially since I'm really interested in you.*

"Here's the thing," Jon said. "I find the timing interesting."

"What do you mean?"

"What if God brought him back to town because now is the time Linzee needs him most?"

She stared at the ceiling, pondering this. Waving tree shadows played on the walls, and the neighbor's dog barked nearby.

She would never get over Jon's unfathomable insight.

"You just answered a question I've been wondering for

days." Her voice tightened. "And now I feel humbled. Here I was, thinking God's purpose in it was all about me."

"Don't kick yourself. We've all done it."

She gathered a handful of comforter. "Your answer makes so much sense. Linzee does need her father. Yet he's not a believer."

"He may be a future believer."

"Maybe. It's one more thing to pray about."

"We'll never run out of things to pray about, will we?"

A soft knock sounded at the door. She bounced off the bed, phone clamped to her ear. Linzee stood there, looking cute in a red gingham apron.

"Dinner's ready," she mouthed.

Meg gave her a thumbs-up and nodded. "Jon, I need to go. But thank you so much for calling. I needed your words of wisdom tonight."

"Not a problem. Thank you for sharing your good news. I'll see you Monday night, then? It'll be my last meeting as a FOGY leader."

"Already? I will definitely be there."

"Great. See you then."

"Bye." She clamped down on a grin as she joined her daughter, son, and ex at the dining room table.

"Phillippe." She looked him straight in the eye. "I want you to know how much I appreciated you being here for us."

Linzee looked up. "Yeah, Dad. You rocked."

Meg let loose the smile she'd been holding. "Shall we thank the Lord?"

***

Dusk had fallen. Golden patches hung in the sky as Phillippe and Richie left with full stomachs. Linzee and Meg collapsed on the living room sofas. Shadow snored at her feet, his light whiffs rising and falling, his body expanding and contracting with each breath.

Linzee's face sagged. "Mom, I feel terrible about Nena." She plucked lint off a couch pillow. "She doesn't understand why I left. Especially since she played such a huge role in my rescue. I mean, if it hadn't been for her and her smarts, God only knows where I'd be right now, and Drucie would be AWOL."

"I understand." Meg's heart swelled with love for her courageous daughter. "When God first grabbed hold of me, I found I sometimes had to do hard things. You might not believe this but, I had to stop hanging out with certain friends. My family didn't understand what had happened to me and kept slapping the 'religious' label on me."

"Yeah, that's what Nena said today when I went over there to get the rest of my stuff. 'Oh, you got religion.' Even though I thanked her over and over, she is so upset."

"God's been speaking to me about Nena." Meg leaned over, her elbow propped on the cushion. "I think He's telling me to reach out to her."

Linzee leaned her elbows on her thighs. "If I thought it was possible for her and me to remain friends, I would. But, I don't think it would work."

"There's a verse in Second Corinthians I like. 'For the love of Christ compels us.'" She paused, remembering both joys and sorrows from her early days as a Christian. "It's not easy to leave such a close relationship when you know the other person didn't do anything to deserve it."

"You're right. But I feel like the Lord is pleased with me." Linzee tossed the pillow down and picked up another one, hugging it close to herself. "Guess what. I went by the cop shop today to talk to that cop." Her face lit up with a shy grin, an expression Meg hadn't seen on her face for years.

"Was he there?"

"He was, and he acted so nice and polite when I told him I came in to thank him. He smiled and said, 'No thanks needed, just doing my job.' But he grinned real big. I think I made his day."

Meg laughed. "Did he still look good to you?"

Hugging the pillow, Linzee let another grin escape. "Let's put it this way – if he'd asked me out for dinner, I would've said yes."

Meg felt her own grin press into her cheeks. "Well, well."

"Speaking of which, Mom—" Linzee pierced her with a look. "When the cops carried me into the hospital, I thought I saw you saying goodbye to some guy."

"You must mean my friend Jon." Her bare toe caressed Shadow's back. "He wanted to be there since he arranged a couple of prayer vigils for you."

"Serious? Are you sure he's just a friend?"

She chuckled. "I'm sure. He likes to be an encouragement to people. I wish you could meet him. He would be a great person for you to ask questions of regarding your walk with God."

Linzee smirked. "He looked nice from far away. How about up close? Any chance he could become more than a friend?"

Warmth crept over her face. "Well, to be honest, it's what I want, but I don't expect to see him much after this. He's leaving the Monday night prayer group I go to." She averted her face and concentrated on the sensation of Shadow's bristly fur on her bare foot, knowing Linzee would see in her eyes how she felt about Jon.

But, like a hummingbird, Linzee darted to a new topic. "You know what? I've been thinking about Drucie a lot. Like, what's going through her head now while she's sitting in jail." Linzee squeezed the pillow with her fists as if she wished it were Drucie's face. "I hope she's getting a little taste of what I went through."

"Did you ever have any clue she might pull such a thing?"

"Not really. Most quirky, edgy people I've known are perfectly harmless. Then again, I'm a terrible judge of character, as Nena is quick to remind me—was." Her head fell forward, and a stream of golden hair draped the pillow in her lap.

Meg nodded. "You got that from me, I'm sorry to say. I'm too ready to see the good in everyone."

Linzee swung one leg underneath the other. "Innocent until proven guilty. Guess that's why I've always been drawn to shrewd people like Nena. It's like they balance me out."

"Speaking of Drucie, when we pulled up to her house, I wondered if it was the same house she lived in during high school."

Linzee nodded. "It was, but I didn't realize it until I saw it from the cop car window. The basement didn't look familiar to me, but then I remembered we never went down there. Back then, it was used for storage."

"Do her parents live somewhere else now?"

Linzee shook her head. "They're both dead. Drucie inherited their house."

"How did they die?" Meg waited, her elbow on the sofa's arm, resting her head in her hand.

"Some kind of accident, but..."

"But what?"

Linzee's eyes narrowed as she kneaded the pillow. "Drucie was really evasive about the details."

Meg's spine prickled as she imagined a dozen scenarios. Linzee shivered, which spooked a shiver out of Meg.

"Are you thinking what I'm thinking?" she whispered.

Linzee's wide gaze met hers. "That it wasn't really an accident?"

Meg nodded, shivering again, and thankful beyond words Drucie hadn't arranged an *accident* for Linzee.

"Did you ever find out what happened in the hours between the roofie and the end of Drucie's shift?"

Linzee's face blanched. "She chloroformed me. Can you believe it? She had each detail planned to the minute, the witch."

Meg's breathing quickened, feeling her daughter's outrage. "Holey socks."

Linzee's eyes shone with emotion. "When I went to see the cop today he gave me an update on Allison's confession. Allison posed as a customer that day. She's the one who drove my car away. There's no way Drucie could have pulled off such a thing by herself. Her girlfriend was in on it from the get-go." Linzee's head tilted toward the window as Richie's car pulled into the drive. "You know, Mom, I keep thinking about the time I almost told Drucie you found the eleven in Eddie's name, but then a commotion happened, and she had to go." Her shimmering eyes widened. "I almost spilled the beans. If I had, Drucie would never have told Nena her birthday."

"It must have been one of those God things, Baby Girl. He brought about the interruption. He already had everything under control."

The front door whipped open, and Richie burst into the room, along with Dustin, Jake, and Kassidy. Shadow jumped up and yelped, wagging his tail furiously.

"Hi, all." Meg waved.

"Hey," said Richie.

"Hi, Ma'am." Dustin looked at Linzee with a flash of recognition and his trademark faint smile.

Kassidy gave a shy wave. Shadow barked.

"Richie." Linzee cocked her finger and waved him over. "C'mere."

Richie hesitated. "What?"

"Just you. Not the others."

"Guys, wait for me in there." Richie pointed. "Be right with ya."

His friends meandered down the hall. Linzee patted the seat next to her. Richie sat facing her, his back to Meg.

"I want to apologize for labeling you a homophobe." Linzee looked at her brother from under lowered lids, then at Meg. "And to you too, Mom."

Richie didn't move. "Okay—"

Linzee reached over and grabbed him around the shoulders. "I love you, bro."

Meg couldn't see her son's face, but she would bet it was lit up bright as Christmas.

"Love you back," he mumbled, sounding ten years old again.

Her heart stirred. God was reminding her of something she needed to do. She moved over next to her son and laid a hand on his shoulder. Richie turned his head and met her eyes.

"I also owe you an apology," she said. "And Dustin, too. There are some things I need to explain to both of you. Can you go get him, please?"

He nodded and made his way to the room where his friends waited, returning with Dustin. Shadow sat on his haunches, his expectant look matching Dustin's and Richie's. His tail swished back and forth as he watched them silently. Linzee stayed equally still.

Dustin and Richie settled on nearby chairs. She pressed her hands into her thighs and decided to start with a safe topic. "How was your vacation, Dustin?"

"Good. We stopped by Death Valley and Scotty's Castle on our way to Vegas."

"Nice." She smiled. "When you got back, were you shocked to find out Drucie had been arrested for kidnapping Linzee?"

The knowing expression on his face told her he already knew they'd been suspects in her eyes. But he merely nodded. "Yes, ma'am. I was. My boss told me what happened."

She slid her hands to her knees. "I want to apologize for suspecting you of being Linzee's harasser. But I want to explain why I jumped to that conclusion."

After a pause, Linzee said, "I need to apologize for that,

too."

Dustin looked at Linzee, then back at her. "Richie told me about it. The number eleven thing."

Richie raised his brows at her and shrugged. She squeezed her knees. "I'm so sorry. It turns out I was right about it, but wrong about who it was."

"That's alright, Ma'am. No harm done. Drucie was hung up on the number eleven." Dustin's wide-eyed face came as close to animated as she would probably ever see. "I was in Latte Love Shack one day ordering tea, and she saw my name on the computer. She told me, 'Dude, your last name is eleven.' Then she brought me a form and said, 'Here, fill out this application. You definitely belong here.' I thought she was strange, but I filled in the application and got hired."

Meg's mind churned with a million thoughts. "So it was due to Drucie's influence that I got so sidetracked, thinking you were E. Levens." She dropped her head to her hands, her fingers digging into her hair. "I feel awful."

Richie spoke his next words in a voice as gentle as Shadow's listening breaths. "Mom. Linzee. It's okay. It's all good." The words ran lightly across her heart and snapped her final thread of self-control.

Through a veil of tears, she stood and managed to stretch her arms around all three in a group hug. Then, unable to speak without choking, she sniffed and made her way to her studio, turning around once to smile at them. All three stared back at her, open-mouthed.

Shadow's nails clicked across the floor as he trotted after her. She turned, her hand out. "C'mere, boy." He neared her and licked her hand. "Let's go paint."

***

Soft fluorescent light illuminated Meg's studio. She rested her tongue in the corner of her mouth and plied watercolors on the canvas. Shadow, lying nearby, snored in oblivion.

A rainbow descended from roiling clouds. A mass of figures gathered at the bottom. On the other side, a translucent beam flowed from the clouds to the ground. Linzee's red-booted legs knelt inside the God-light.

Standing back to appraise, Meg nodded. This would be her own special painting, not to be sold at shows. This one she deemed worthy to be framed and placed in a prominent position on her bedroom wall. And someday, she would show it to Linzee.

Spent, she collapsed on the futon, fingers scratching Shadow's head, and poured out her thanksgiving to her Heavenly Father.

Chapter Thirty-Nine

The start time for FOGY fast approached, but Meg and Camille stood in a checkout line, laden with treats for Jon's last meeting. Meg clutched paper plates, plastic utensils, and cups. Camille balanced a large round chocolate cake on her palm, two liters of soda pop teetering under her arms.

"Think we got too much?" Meg said.

Camille shrugged. "Better too much than too little."

"We ought to have everyone tell what Jon has meant to them."

"Great idea, but he would hate it."

Meg stifled a sigh. "I can't believe he's leaving."

Camille showed her trademark smirk. "He could still ask you out, you know."

"Don't you think he would have by now if he'd wanted to?"

"You'd think, but with Jon, you never can tell. Don't give up on him yet, my friend."

The line crept forward, and they set their wares on the conveyor belt. "Welcome to Safeway," said the cashier, a pleasant-faced older woman. "Paper or plastic?"

"Plastic," said Camille, turning to her. "Bill and I could arrange a double date."

"Camille, please don't try to run interference for me." She hadn't intended to sound quite so pleading. "If he doesn't want to spend time with me, finagling a double date won't do any good. He'd just feel pressured."

They fumbled in their wallets, paid for the goodies, and reemerged into the warm August evening.

Although they arrived ten minutes late, the group members applauded when they saw the contents of the grocery bags. Camille smiled and bowed, and they set out the goodies and a card saying, "Goodbye From All of Us."

Most of the regulars had shown tonight, including Quincy, looking frail in a white sundress, and Mike, who bestowed his usual nod on her. She smiled in return. Jon wore a navy blue tee shirt with "John 3:16" printed on it. Meg tried not to stare at his muscular legs, clad in royal blue athletic shorts and flip-flops. Instead, she settled next to Camille in a chair across from him and averted her eyes.

Jon called the meeting to order. "This is a bittersweet night for me. You all have meant so much to me. Words can't express the way God has blessed me through all of you." Meg thought she detected a sheen to his eyes. He seemed to be scrutinizing the wall behind Camille. "As for my future ministry, God's confirmed for me what He wants me to do next, and I look forward to going wherever He leads.

"I'm turning the reins over to Dean now." He turned to Dean, two chairs over, and extended his hand. Passed the baton. "I have full confidence in him. I do plan to stay in touch, and please feel free to call or message me anytime. This isn't the end of our friendships by any means. I'll only be a phone call away." He bent forward, elbows on knees. "And you're all invited on my next sailboat trip which will be sometime in the next few weeks." His eyes met Meg's, and he smiled.

After that, she didn't hear much until Dean called on her. "I understand there's been a miraculous turn of events in Meg's life," Dean announced. "Do you want to share, Meg?"

She nodded, blinking back tears. "Someone told me recently that God is in the miracle business." She exchanged a smile with Jon and hoped he remembered. Then she shared Linzee's story, and tears flowed all around.

During refreshment time, she and Camille served cake and directed everyone to sign the good-bye card. A cluster of folks surrounded Jon to hug him and pump his hand.

At last, he turned and headed toward her and Camille just as she thrust a bite of cake in her mouth.

"Jon, there's a card for you." Camille pointed. "Everyone signed it. Go on, take it."

He hesitated near the table, casting a half-smile at the card covered in well-wishes and signatures. "Well, this was nice of everyone."

Meg hoped he'd like what she wrote: "Jon—To a great man of God—Thank you for your friendship, your prayers, and your wisdom. Your care and concern during Linzee's ordeal meant a lot to me. God bless you to the max. Meg."

Jon tucked the card under his right arm with an appreciative smile. "This will make for good bedtime reading." He grabbed a chair and straddled it, leaning his left forearm on the chair back, his gaze on the wall clock.

Camille cleared her throat. "About that boat ride, Jon?"

He slid his gaze to Camille. "What about it?"

"When exactly is it?"

"Unless something comes up, I'm thinking the third or fourth weekend in September."

"Okay." Camille turned to her. "We'll want to keep that weekend free, won't we, Meg?"

She wanted to zip Camille's mouth shut. She stole a look at Jon, who gazed back at her.

"Meg, if you come sailing with us, why don't you bring Linzee? Think she'd like that?"

Her heart gave an unaccountable dive. "She'd love it."

"Some of the best ministry opportunities happen on my boat." He glanced at the clock again. "Look what time it is." He stood and slid the chair back to its home. "We need to get out of here before the cleaning crew catches us."

Camille laughed. "They may attack us with their mops."

He chuckled. "No, but they might tell the church board,

who wouldn't be happy we overstayed our welcome."

"Here, Jon." Camille handed him the remaining cake. "This is yours. Enjoy." She and Meg made a quick cleanup, then headed outside.

Darkness had begun its descent but lingering golden rays still lit up the western horizon. Jon, partial cake in hand, escorted them to Camille's car. Meg, nearly in tears, received Jon's one-armed shoulder hug, keeping her head down so he wouldn't see her sorrow.

"It's been quite a ride, hasn't it?" He kept his arm around her and patted her shoulder. She wasn't sure if he was speaking to both of them, or only to her. "It's been great having you in the group, Meg," he said, sounding half-choked. He patted her again, high-fived Camille, then turned and strolled, head down, to his car.

She and Camille stayed silent as they rode toward Camille's house where Meg had left her car. Unshed tears tickled her eyes.

"Don't be upset." Camille glanced over. "Maybe he needs more time to figure out what a great catch you are."

"Or maybe he has some other great catch he's pursuing." She sniffed. "This feels exactly like the night Barry broke up with me."

"You got it bad." Camille clucked. "I'll pray real hard, my friend."

***

Nena lay under her car watching motor oil drip into a pan when her phone rang. She scooted herself upright and checked the display.

Megaphobe. She bared her teeth.

Might as well see what she wanted. Maybe Linzee had come to her senses.

"Yeah?" She didn't even try to soften her tone. Megaphobe and her religious brainwashing was to blame for Linzee leaving one week ago yesterday. Eight long days ago.

"Nena?"

What a deceptively sweet voice.

"Are you okay?"

"Yep." She wanted to punch the off button in the woman's face. "What do you want?"

"Just wanted to check in, see how you're doing. I never really thanked you for all you did to help find Linzee."

Nena said nothing, merely paced in circles around her car. The silence drew out, pulsing uncomfortably.

She pushed as much bitterness as she could into her next words. "Guess it was all for nuthin', huh? Didn't think she'd reward me with a breakup."

Appalled, she felt a lump form in her throat. Then Megaphobe went and made it worse by saying, "Nena, I know you're hurting—"

"You don't know nuthin' from nuthin'."

"And I want you to know I'm praying for you."

She snorted. "Prayin' I'll turn into a religious nut like you and your daughter?"

Megaphobe—Meg—sucked in a breath. "I'm praying God will wrap His arms around you and give you a hug."

She singsonged her reply. "Aw, how sweet."

"And I'm praying you'll find joy."

She paced some more, having run out of words.

Meg continued, but her sugar-sweet tones felt slightly less annoying. "If you ever need to talk, please give me a call. I'll always be here for you."

A guttural noise flew from Nena's throat, and she hit the off button. Her throat ached with unshed tears. She ordered her feet back to her apartment where she lay on the couch and swallowed sobs.

She didn't know what to think, how to feel, about Meg anymore. The woman had changed so much in just a few short weeks. And when Linzee went missing, they'd managed to put aside their differences and develop a camaraderie of sorts.

Then there was that whole SMERFA vs. Hate Church scenario. Linzee said Meg and her friends had demonstrated against both sides. They weren't pro-gay. Neither were they pro-hate. The issue had always seemed black-and-white to her. Either you're for us, or you're against us. But Linzee said they were "pro-Christ." Meg, and that *loco* red-haired woman, and the tall dude Meg was so gaga over—she'd picked up that vibe from the get-go—hadn't said a word about gay issues the entire time she hung with them. They hadn't once made her feel unwelcome. In fact, she couldn't remember the last time she smiled so much. She couldn't remember a time she'd hung with religious freaks and actually enjoyed herself.

No wonder Linzee defected to the other side. But now, what would she do without her best friend, confidante, and soul mate? Por Dios, Linzee didn't even think they should remain friends.

With tears flowing, she picked up the phone and squinted through the dampness. *Sorry I hung up on u,* she typed. *Thx 4 calling.* Then she hit Send.

Chapter Forty

A rare overcast day greeted Meg Saturday morning, yet the temperature remained a balmy seventy-five degrees as she drove to Latte Love Shack to meet Jon. Their first date. Or non-date. She couldn't decide if meeting for coffee qualified as a date. Jeremy Camp's song Overcome blasted on the CD player, but she hardly heard it with her mind so busy replaying her Wednesday evening phone conversation with Jon.

Earlier that day, she'd felt ready to chalk up her friendship with Jon as a wonderful but temporary blessing from the Lord. Then he'd called that very evening, wondering if she'd meet him for coffee, leaving her shocked and breathless.

He'd told her he'd been praying about something and wanted to share it with her, which only served to spin the wheels of speculation in her mind. Something he'd been praying about, and wanted to share with her. It didn't sound like he had romance on his mind.

She'd asked Camille, but her friend hadn't a clue what Jon was up to. Meg wondered if it had to do with Linzee. Or perhaps he had an idea for his upcoming sailboat excursion for which he needed a woman's input. Perhaps it had to do with his new ministry.

She recalled his words from Monday night. "I look forward to going wherever God leads."

Going wherever God leads. People usually said that when they knew it was likely they'd be relocating in the near future.

He *had* seemed a little choked up that night.

Her mind switched into analysis mode. "Unless something comes up," he'd qualified in regards to his boat trip. "I'll only be a phone call away," he told the group.

The more she thought about it, the more certain she felt. He was planning to sell his business and pull up roots, and he wanted to say his final goodbyes.

Which would make this coffee get-together a non-date.

Her clammy hands trembled on the steering wheel as she poured out her distress to God. She couldn't forget what had happened the last time she drove halfway to meet a man for coffee. Barry had helped her remove her bullet-proof vest, and then shot her through the heart. Would she leave today with her heart re-shattered?

At the off-ramp, Meg braked and took a quick glance at herself in her visor mirror. She'd taken a little extra care to look and smell good this morning. She wore a flowery skirt and pink blouse, along with a whiff of lavender in her hair. But if Jon planned to tell her goodbye, her efforts were wasted.

Turning into the parking lot of Latte Love Shack, she told her thudding heart to calm down. She parked, swung her feet onto the pavement, and conjured up a breezy manner.

Jon, with his gleaming grill of a smile, lounged at the entry. He stood up and squeezed her across the shoulders. "Hi, Meg."

"Hi."

He gestured toward the interior. "There's an empty table by the window."

She followed him, heart twittering, to a booth, where they put in their orders. She looked around, half expecting the place to look or feel different. But the walls, the tables, the vibe, all looked and felt exactly the same.

"Good to see you again, Meg."

"Likewise, Jon." Today he wore a simple black polo

shirt, and she found her attention captured by his broad shoulders, the stray chest hairs peeking from the top of his shirt, his firm biceps stretching the fabric of his shirt sleeves.

Her face glowing, she hoped he didn't think she looked like an idiot.

His gaze rested on her face. "You look nice today," he said with man-like simplicity.

"Thanks." She forced herself to keep talking. She had to delay the moment of reckoning as long as possible. "I have to admit I was surprised to hear from you. But I'm glad you called. This is a real treat."

"Remember the first time we met here?"

"I do remember. This feels like déjà vu."

A new barista approached the table with their drinks. Meg offered her a kind smile. The girl's movements appeared unpolished and hesitant, unlike Drucie's effortless precision.

"Thank you." She picked up the nutmeg and cinnamon shakers, then looked at Jon and chuckled. "You know, Linzee never wants to set foot in this place again."

Instead of replying, Jon sipped his mocha and watched her flip the shakers upside down, as she tapped first one, then the other. Spices sprayed into her cup.

She set the shakers down and met his twinkling eyes. Goose bumps crawled up her arms, and she smiled at him with a tilt of the head.

"What?"

"Oh." Jon's intent gaze set her heart to pounding. "I like the way you doctored your drink. Anyway, thanks for agreeing to meet me."

"Thanks for inviting me." She exhaled and grappled for a safe topic. "How was your week?"

His face returned to its usual easygoing expression. "Really hectic. End of summer is always extra busy at the shop."

"I hear your ads on the radio all the time. They're quite

entertaining."

"Oh, you mean this one?" His eyes glinted. He set down his cup and cleared his throat. "Arrr," he growled in a deep pirate voice. "Ahoy me mateys, ye best be bringin' yer ship to Paulson's. Me n th' crew'll keep it shipshape fer ye. Arrr.'" He winked.

She laughed. "That was you on the radio?"

"It was."

"You're a man of many talents."

"Like they say, don't quit your day job." He grinned. "The boat shop has been a good venture, plus puts food on the table. Keeps a roof over my head." He inclined his head toward her and picked up his cup. "Speaking of jobs, yours sounds pretty impressive. How long have you been at that fancy-schmancy store?"

"Ten years, if you can believe it. But my office is quite plain Jane—nothing fancy-schmancy about it."

He appraised her for a moment, then nodded. "I can see you fitting in at a place like Noelle's. Personally, I do most of my shopping at Wal Marche," he added with a straight face. But his eyes exerted amusement.

She laughed again. "To be honest, so do I." They grinned at each other.

She looked down at her latte, overcome with a spasm of dread. When she looked up, his expression had turned quizzical.

Flustered, she blurted, "Will you be seeing your son this weekend?"

"Not 'til tomorrow." He took a long sip. "Remember I mentioned in one of the meetings I planned to appeal the court's decision to award custody to his mother? Well, the judge turned it down despite the fact that Tanner's being raised by two women." He shook his head as though dumbfounded. "Basically, the judge was saying my son doesn't need his father."

"Oh Jon, I'm so sorry."

"At least I have visitation rights on weekends. I'm still praying God will move in this situation so I can raise him again."

"God is in the miracle business, you know." They shared a wry smile.

"Yes, He is. What a miracle He did for your daughter."

"And it seemed to happen so fast. So many other parents have been praying for years and haven't seen results."

"God's timing is completely out of our hands." Jon's fingers drummed a rhythm on his cup. "Sometimes, He answers almost immediately, like He did with Linzee. But I have a feeling you had already been praying for her for years. Am I right?"

"Oh. Yes, you're right, I have been."

"To those of us who haven't known you long, it might seem like you got quick results. But most likely this has been in the works for a long time. I know some parents who prayed thirty years for their wayward children."

She watched, fascinated, as various expressions flit across his face, and found herself wishing she could render all those expressions on canvas. Her very own keepsakes of Jon.

"My ex-wife left me five years ago." He leaned his arms on the table, his face somber. "And I've been praying for her and my two sons ever since. So far only Tanner has shown any interest in things of the Lord. My older son stopped going to church the same time his mother did."

"It must be so hard for you. What is he up to these days?"

Jon tilted his cup to his mouth and tapped the bottom, urging out the last drop. "Connor is eighteen and is starting his freshman year at Berkeley. Majoring in political science."

"He's into political activism, then?"

"If he isn't now, he will be after four years at Berzerkly," he said in his deadpan way.

She grinned. "Connor and Tanner. I like those names. They go well together."

He said nothing, merely folded his hands around his cup, his glasses reflecting soft daylight from the window behind her. He studied her for a moment, as intent as if he were studying a piece of art. Her heart rate lurched into overdrive as though she'd guzzled three shots of espresso.

At last, he spoke. "You're probably wondering why I invited you here."

She stirred her drink and watched the turbulence swirl in her cup. "You said you'd been praying about something you wanted to share with me."

"Yes."

She met his gaze and tried for a steady tone. "Is it about your new ministry?"

The bronze flecks in his eyes sparkled. "No. This concerns you, Meg."

"It does?"

"And me."

Her eyebrows leaped. "What are you saying?"

He held her gaze, gentle yet determined. "I'm saying, I've enjoyed getting to know you this summer, and I don't want it to end."

She felt her mouth drop open. "You prayed about you and me?"

"I did." He gripped his empty cup, leaving creases. "I think we connected, don't you? But I wasn't free to pursue a relationship with you until my leadership position with FOGY ended. Well, now I'm free."

His eyes held entreaty, his mouth a hopeful half-smile.

"You mean, you're not moving?"

He laughed. "Moving? Where did you get that idea?"

"You said some things Monday night, and then you said you'd been praying about something, and—" She broke off when she saw the look on his face. Amusement, mingled with consternation, mingled with—

"Meg." His voice held resolve. "I've been praying that God would keep the doors open for you and me to spend more time together. Get to know each other." His cup crumpled in his hands. "I'm hoping it's what you want, too."

Her heart felt ready to explode, and she grabbed for a breath. "I do want that. You're a terrific guy, Jon."

His smile broke loose, and he reached for her hands. "In that case," he nodded toward the empty seat beside her, "may I join you over there?"

"You sure may," she said, relishing the feel of her hands wrapped inside his.

He kept his grasp on her hands as he moved around and squeezed in beside her, while his eyes carried her to a new place. Then his arms enfolded her and nestled her head against his heart.

Right where she belonged.

THE END

AUTHOR AFTERWORD

Dear Readers:

When I began writing this book three years ago, gay marriage was not yet legal in the US. At the time, I approached this story as if it were a likely future scenario. Two years later, it was no longer a "what if." It became reality when, in June 2015, the US Supreme Court affirmed the right of same-sex couples to marry. Unfortunately, it's an issue which has polarized our nation, and even our churches. So I pray Meg's story offers you a message of hope during these tumultuous times.

If you are a Christian parent grieving over a gay son or daughter, my heart goes out to you. I want you to know, I've seen God accomplish miracles in response to believers' prayers. I believe in the power of prayer! And although I can't promise that God will work in your life the same way He worked in Meg's and Linzee's, I do believe He heeds our cries for our wayward children. Your son or daughter may never "go straight." But, like Jesus, like Meg and her friends, love them anyway and never stop praying.

You may be wondering why I would tackle such a controversial topic as gay marriage. Very few Christian fiction books contain gay characters, yet fiction is a great medium for imparting life lessons. I don't claim to have all the answers. My goal was not to push an agenda. I simply wanted to tell the story of one Christian mom, and how she chose to live out Christ's law of love.

The organization Families Of Gay Youth is purely fictional, and I wish I could claim that similar organizations exist. While researching this book, I found one support-type group similar to the fictitious FOGY: Spatula Ministries. But it apparently no longer exists. I am not aware of any other, but would welcome reader input. If you know of a real-life FOGY-type ministry, please email me at dawn@dawnvcahill.com, and I will be sure to get the word out on my website.

The late author Barbara Johnson founded Spatula Ministries after her own son came out of the closet. You might enjoy her book, *Where Does A Mother Go to Resign?* (see Resources).

As I mentioned, few Christian novels include homosexual characters. One that comes to mind is Gayle Roper's novel Spring Rain, a heart-tugging story of a young gay man with AIDS. I highly recommend it for the author's compassionate, Biblical approach to the AIDS issue. I hope that more Christian authors will be courageous enough to tackle this and related issues in the future. After all, this is the not-so-brave new world in which we live. And we Christians need to be prepared to deal with it.

RESOURCES

This book required a daunting amount of research. I consulted so many websites — scientific, religious, psychological — that it would take several pages to list them all. But despite my hours spent on Google and other resources, I found very few conclusive answers. Only lots of disagreements on questions such as, Does a gay gene exist? What causes someone to be gay? So if you're looking for answers to those questions, I encourage you to do your own internet research, as well as consult some of the following resources.

Ministries and Organizations:
Focus on the Family (www.focusonthefamily.com), a ministry that advocates for traditional, Biblical family values.

National Association for Research and Therapies for Homosexuality (NARTH) (www.narth.com), a non-religious organization that refers those struggling with unwanted same-sex attraction to qualified therapists.

A New Creation Ministry (http://www.anewcreation ministry.org/) exists to help those struggling with sexual identity confusion find freedom and change in a relationship with Christ.

His Way Out Ministries (http://hiswayout.com/) helps the Body of Christ minister effectively to those enslaved to same-sex attractions and other forms of sexual brokenness.

Books:
Where Does A Mother Go to Resign? (Bethany House Publishers, Bloomington, MN, 1979) by Barbara Johnson

Making Gay Okay – How Rationalizing Homosexual Behavior is Changing Everything (Ignatius Press, San Francisco, 2014) by Robert R. Reilly

A Queer Thing Happened to America (EqualTime Books, Concord NC, 2011) by Michael L. Brown

Spring Rain – *Seaside Seasons, Book One* (Multnomah Publishers, Sisters OR, 2001) by Gayle Roper

ACKNOWLEDGEMENTS

This novel wouldn't have been possible without assistance from some wonderful folks offering their expertise.

Thanks to Steve Mathisen, Odd Sock Proofreading and Copyediting. You deserve a lot of credit for helping make this a stronger manuscript. To Dineen Miller, cover designer. You rock!

To Jane Thompson and Marsha Bernabe, beta readers, for your helpful feedback. Thank you for your honesty in pointing out what worked, and what didn't.

To critique partners Gail, Wendy, Alice and Carlin – many thanks for your patient attention to detail.

Many other fellow authors from American Christian Fiction Writers (ACFW) and Christian Indie Authors lent their assistance in various ways.

Thank you all for your roles in this exciting project.

www.ingramcontent.com/pod-product-compliance
Lightning Source LLC
Chambersburg PA
CBHW030243200626
46816CB00002BA/480